# *Becoming*

## FOUAD AZIM

PAGE PUBLISHING, INC.
New York, NY

First originally published by Page Publishing, Inc. 2017

Certain liberties have been taken when describing the school system, for the sake of a coherent and consistent story line and to make it easier for those readers not familiar with local schools in Pakistan.

This is a fictional work and any similarities with actual persons or events is purely coincidental.

ISBN 978-1-68409-431-8 (Paperback)
ISBN 978-1-68409-492-9 (Hardcover)
ISBN 978-1-68409-432-5 (Digital)

Printed in the United States of America

For Ammi jaan, mother and friend,
who loved unconditionally.
And for Shafee and for Zaki.

# Praise for Becoming

*1) By Ella Vincent; Pacific Book Review*

Author Fouad Azim has written *Becoming*, an emotionally gripping novel about young love in the 1990's Pakistan which will enthrall readers. This book is a unique coming-of-age novel about young love in a land far away...

Junaid's sensitivity and devotion to Nyla is admirable and makes him a relatable protagonist. Nyla is a strong character that isn't just a passive love interest for Junaid. She's a self-sufficient young woman that is brave throughout *Becoming* as she fights the cultural traditions that try to keep her from Junaid. Jahal is the perfect antagonist as the psychologically disturbed villain of the novel....Azim's writing doesn't limit him to a one-dimensional monster. Jahal is more of a wounded soul than a soulless anti-hero.

Azim's writing is evocative and poignant. The hills and caves of Pakistan are described so vividly that readers can imagine they are in the rugged terrain of the South Asian countryside. He also easily captures the complicated social lives of teenagers and how fraught young relationships can be in *Becoming's* dialogue.

Azim also expertly handles sweet romance and dangerous drama throughout the novel. This story has exciting and suspenseful moments which will leave readers wanting more.

*Becoming* would be best for fans of the Kite Runner and Khaled Hosseini. The novels both have similar stories about friendships in South Asian countries and both authors write masterfully about love.

Perfect for readers of all ages… Fouad Azim's novel shows how love can conquer hate, making *Becoming* an unforgettable novel which all readers will love.

------------------------------------------------------------------------

*2) By D. Donovan, Senior Reviewer, Midwest Book Review*

Nyla and Junaid are classmates attending a small school in the mountains of Pakistan in the 1990s. Their friendship, which evolves into love, and their coming of age is one story; but the real heart of the evolutionary process documented in *Becoming* lies in its wider-reaching story of how young people in a different culture share experiences common to the rest of the world's emerging young adults.

From kindly matron teachers and their educational challenges in reaching very different students to how the golden rule is imparted to struggling kids barely passing not only in class but in their relationships to the world around them, *Becoming* charts individual courses that intersect, collide, merge, or are changed by circumstance and psychology.

The first difference to note in this coming-of-age romance is the strength of the female character, Nyla, who at times fights both her own heart and cultural traditions. Unlike the characters of many women who become helpless in the face of love and its circumstances, Nyla is an empowered, complete individual in her own right, seeking more from life than love and commitment.

Junaid's love for this independent, feisty young woman may defy some of his own cultural traditions, but he too has spunk and determination; and when they confront an emotionally unstable but creative young peer who views their blossoming relationship as a negative force in his life, the three find themselves entwined in a complicated series of encounters that test not only their experiences, but their different backgrounds.

The world of Pakistan's hill country comes to life as the story evolves. All three characters grow and change from their encounters, and readers are treated to in-depth realizations woven into a story line which comes from different viewpoints.

This brings us to the second notable difference in this coming of age romance: the author's ability to create full-faceted characters from the intersection of different personalities from peers to adults: "As she passed back the graded essays to the students before the closing bell, she said she would ask for the two best essays to be read aloud by the respective authors. It amazed her to see a glint of hope in the eyes of Junaid, and she looked away wondering what he imagined was the worth of his miserable effort."

From differences between friendship and love and the process of growing one from the other to handling peer jealousies, attractions, and interactions gone awry, the psychology is deftly and nicely done, fully exploring different characters' feelings and their sources: "He did feel left out and more than a little jealous that another man, a good-looking man, knew Nyla well enough to keep her occupied with interesting memories. Nor was it lost on him that he himself had been introduced as her "friend" and not her boyfriend."

The result is a lovely story recommended for mature teens and new adult audiences alike; especially those who want their characters complex, their cultural and social encounters well-developed, and their evolving love to include the influence and realistic angst of peers and adults alike.

Readers of coming of age stories set in other countries will relish the struggles of Nyla, Junaid, and others who strive to evolve in many ways, and will find *Becoming* a lovely read packed with atmosphere, depth, and detail.

# *Foreword*

This is a story of blooming love and betrayal, about children coming of age, of conscience and the sociopaths who lack it; it is a story about trust and how true love empowers and heals us. In the end, it is a story about humanity and the eternal struggle between good and evil.

Nyla and Junaid are classmates learning about the world around them and in the process discovering themselves. They must endure and survive a path fraught with confusion and peril if they hope to emerge victorious, though not necessarily unscathed. They will learn of innocence and its loss, about how budding love can be snuffed out if not cared for and its formidable power when nurtured and protected. They will become closely acquainted with evil, with its insidious presence in plain sight and how it mangles and corrupts those it touches. They will have to confront and defeat it if they can. If you think you recognize some of the characters described herein, it is only because the human experience around the world and in the different cultures is not unique, and we all share some of the same burdens and the joys of similar emotions and trials as we go about learning to find ourselves.

The setting is the foothills of the Margalla Mountain range, a part of the lesser Himalayas, north of Islamabad in Pakistan, during the 1990s. For the sake of a coherent and consistent story line and to make it easier for those readers not familiar with local schools in Pakistan, certain liberties have been taken when describing the school system. This is a fictional work and any similarities with actual persons or events is purely coincidental.

# Chapter 1

"I don't wanna go to school!" said Junaid with a pout and an underlying tremble in his pleading voice, "Teacher's mean to me!" The ten-year-old's mother Zaynub knew he was going to school just as well as he did himself. This was his weekday morning routine to get his adoring mom to say the sweet things she always said and to pack him off to school with all the affection he could tolerate.

Junaid's teacher, Miss Zarina Begum, was a kindly and portly middle-aged lady who was about at the end of her rope when dealing with the special challenge that he presented. There were twenty-five students in her fifth grade class, and she was liked if not loved by most of them. She enjoyed teaching and was used to dealing with all manner of ability in her students. She had yet to figure out young Junaid however. That she was flustered by this young boy was known to just one other teacher and only vaguely understood by the other children in her class. It was not that he was rude or noisy or talkative or that he was disturbing the class, it was just that he presented a remarkable challenge for her to educate him as she felt he needed to be educated. He had his own mind and lived at his own pace and rhythm that was resolutely impervious to any attempts to mold him to the norm as she understood it to be.

In the ten months that she had known him as her student, there was one aspect of his character that she was most perplexed and at the same time secretly impressed by. He was blatantly and utterly honest, to a fault, under all circumstances and openly without regard to any consequence. While she believed in and taught her charges to be honest and reminded them of the ultimate goodness of this golden rule, she was nonetheless confounded by the practice of this same quality in routine life by this child who was barely passing her class.

This morning, two weeks before the Eid Holidays, she sat at her desk watching the children as they came with their backpacks and lunch boxes and placed those on hooks and shelves along the side of the classroom before taking their usual places. She looked at them with some pride and satisfaction, knowing each child well and automatically associating the correct parent with each of her pupils. She knew the strengths and weaknesses of each and was a master of nudging them in a certain way to produce the best of their ability. It was no wonder that she had been named Teacher of the Year for the past two years.

Her glance lingered for a moment on young Junaid as he occupied his place directly behind one of her most gifted students, Nyla. He always sat there, without fail. Zarina Begum wondered if Junaid, by some miracle, had actually brought in a complete homework today. If he had, it would be a first and if she was a betting woman she would have bet against that a hundred times out of a hundred. He met her glance momentarily and looked down instinctively fidgeting uncomfortably. In his hands, he clutched the single page homework essay on nature.

He had spent a lot of time thinking about the essay since leaving school yesterday. He had gone home, snacked, and then changed into his clothes and shoes he wore to go hiking in the woods behind their home. He loved the outdoors and was at home amongst the trees and bushes, the birds, and the small animals. Junaid knew which berries were edible and which made a great sling shot ammo. He made his own slingshot cutting a perfect Y from the branch of a birch tree and using two long rubber strips sliced off from the rubber inner tubing of his bike's old tire. He got a piece of leather from the shoemaker and trimmed it into a rectangular shape with holes on each end to pass the rubber strips through. Junaid, even as a young boy, had an uncanny talent using his slingshot and could routinely hit barely visible scorpions and hornets with ease. He now used it only for target practice and for peace of mind while hiking in case of an encounter with snakes that were apt to sun themselves on hiking paths and trails. He learned to swim and fish in the cold mountain streams that rushed down and through the woods that he called his own. He would astound his friends by catching fish with his bare hands and climbing trees with ease and agility. Junaid would sit motionless in a tree or in a bush and watch the birds and rabbits and jackals and so many more come and go. At the end of the day with the sun setting he would go back home, shower, eat, and sleep like a log after spending a few minutes at a homework that he should have finished hours earlier.

He loved nature and wondered what he could write in an essay that would convey what he felt.

In the end, he wrote a little something and slept dreaming of the blackberry tree that he had found that afternoon.

Miss Zarina walked collecting homework assignments from each student. Some had written several pages and some had written a few, but only one of her students had just a few lines scribbled on part of a single page. She reached down to take the paper from his hands and looked at Junaid's brown eyes framed by long eyelashes and for a fleeting moment thought she saw confidence and hope, but it was quickly replaced by uncertainty. The five pages of neatly handwritten even lines on Nyla's essay delighted her, and she smiled and patted her star student's back as Junaid minutely examined the cuticles on his fingers.

Later in the day as the students did their daily assignments, Miss Zarina read and graded the essays. She could tell the effort some had put into their homework and could detect from the words and phrases that the parents of several had large input in the final product. Nyla had written her essay in an organized, meticulous manner, using words that showed the research and work that must have gone into it. It was an easy A, a well-deserved one, and one that pleased Miss Zarina once again. Parveen, another one of her talented students had done a remarkable job of paraphrasing and rewording some of the books she had quoted as reference and was deserving of an A- for the effort alone, if not for the originality.

After reading these essays, Miss Zarina looked at the piece of paper with the name Junaid Kafrooni written near the bottom. There was not much to read here, just a few lines and she read those hastily.

*"Nature is a blackberry tree with a cardinal on one branch and a blue jay on another. Nature is a snapping turtle waiting for the minnow to pass close enough. It is also a squirrel hiding dry seeds in an empty woodpecker nest for winter. Nature is autumn when the leaves turn golden and red and make a carpet for the woods. Nature is all of this and many other beautiful things that happen even when no one is looking."*

She read this once again and was struck by the directness and clarity but disappointed by what she felt was a very short and thoughtlessly written essay. What else could she expect from him but this? The lack of apparent effort frustrated her. She automatically gave these lines a C- and moved on to the next essay.

As she passed back the graded essays to the students before the closing bell, she said she would ask for the two best essays to be read aloud by the respective authors. It amazed her to see a glint of hope in the eyes of Junaid, and she looked away wondering what he imagined was the worth of his miserable effort. Junaid did not get to read his five sentences in front of Zarina Begum's class. He listened to Nyla's essay as she read it slowly, and by the time Parveen was reading hers, his mind was back in the woods where he wanted to check to see if the dove nest in the oak tree had any eggs in it yet.

Later that night, Miss Zarina, just before her mind was engulfed in sleep, almost subconsciously reflected upon her disappointment with Junaid's essay on nature, and she wondered sleepily whether the disappointment was due to the poor perceived effort or due to the fact that there were not more of those lines for her to read...

# Chapter 2

"TGIF," said Junaid to himself as he placed his lunch box under his backpack and went over to sit in his seat. He was looking forward to the weekend and was hoping Miss Zarina would not pick on him to answer any questions she may fancy asking the students about the sun and the moon. That entire week she had focused on the solar system and the class had learned all about the different planets and their moons and the star that was the Sun. Junaid had read the class textbook about the planets, but he had learned most of what he knew of the heavens from reading various books from the school library on his own. He loved the woods and the birds and the animals but astronomy intrigued him. He had a hard time understanding the distances involved and the sizes of the different stars, planets, and the Milky Way itself. His father, a thoughtful and quiet man of few words, was a good resource and explained to Junaid concepts that were amazing to him. He was fascinated by the distances between stars and the number of stars in the Milky Way and the untold number of galaxies like the Milky Way.

Zarina Begum had given the children a quiz at the end of every day of the week, and today she was going to ask them to come to the blackboard one at a time and draw what they thought they imagined the solar system to look like in space.

Jahal, a twelve-year-old burly boy who was almost three inches taller than Junaid, went up to the board first and drew a ball in the middle with eight circles around it to represent the planets around the sun. Parveen drew Saturn with its rings with the sun in the distance and Nyla drew the moon with the planet Earth visible as a half moon does in the dark sky. Next up was Junaid, who was painfully shy of standing in front of the class and the giggling and joking from some of them did not make him feel any more confident. He stood with a piece of chalk in his right hand next to the blackboard for what he felt was too long and could not decide how to show what he felt the solar system looked like in the vastness of space. As he hesitated, Miss Zarina encouraged him to not waste any more time. He reached up with a trembling hand but pulled back again, visibly perspiring and nervously biting his lower lip. As some of the students started to tease him, he finally moved forward and put a single dot in the middle of the blackboard and stepped down and back to his seat. There was a moment of silence and then the class erupted in laughter.

Zarina Begum had spent a week teaching her students all about the wonders of the heavens, and she felt anger and mostly bafflement as to what she perceived amounted to a personal insult. She felt the laughter of the students as much directed at herself as it did toward Junaid, now sheepishly looking down at his hands and blushing furiously with shame.

He knew it was coming, and it did.

"Junaid!" said Zarina Begum her voice brimming with annoyance and frustration.

"Yes, Miss?" replied a meek, barely audible voice.

"Is this what I have taught you all this week?" said Miss Zarina sounding very cross, as she stood with her arms tense by her side.

"No, Miss," replied Junaid softly, not looking up.

The class was deathly quiet, a few were amused at Junaid's expense, others felt pity.

"Is this what you think of what I have spent days and nights preparing for all of you?"

"No, Miss," said a little trembling voice.

"Go stand in the corner until recess, Junaid!"

"Yes, Miss," said Junaid as he hurriedly got up off his seat and walked to the back of the class.

A partially suppressed bout of giggles rippled through the class.

"Junaid is a dummy!" said a high-pitched voice and another wave of giggles almost felt like a physical shove to the slim boy staring at the corner.

"Don't call him a dummy, Parveen!" said an angry voice.

Junaid was facing the wall and turned around to see Nyla glaring angrily at Parveen. The class was suddenly quiet again as the surprised students looked at the two girls staring at each other.

The tension was broken when Miss Zarina told the class to all face forward and open their textbooks.

During recess, his classmates went out to sit and have lunch on the benches around the playground but Junaid decided to stay and eat at his seat. He ate the sandwich his mom had made for him and drank the still cold apple juice, but today he did not touch the juicy red apple he always had after his lunch.

The remainder of the school day was relatively quiet. Junaid kept to himself and counted the minutes until the school bell rang at the end of the day.

As he walked back home, he was happy and relieved. The smile on his face faded for some reason when he saw Nyla and Jahal walking home together, Jahal carrying her heavy backpack.

The uneasiness left him however when he took a turn toward his home around a corner and his thoughts drifted to all he would do in the woods that weekend.

Arriving in front of her home, Nyla thanked a smiling Jahal who had insisted on carrying her books for her. Later that evening when she opened her backpack to start on her assignments, she found a shiny red apple and a note with the words "Thank you." She was surprised and wondered who could have put these in her backpack. She smiled as she recalled Jahal carrying her backpack home and how happy he was to have done so. He was the tallest boy in the class and was always smiling and wanting to do things for her. She knew Parveen did not like him to talk to her at all.

As Junaid sleepily closed his eyes that night, he wondered if Nyla had found the apple and the thank you note and if she was happy. A smile crossed his lips as sleep overtook him.

# *Chapter 3*

"Thanks, it was delicious," whispered Nyla. The class was about to start and Miss Zarina was writing the daily message on the blackboard. Nyla was sitting behind Jahal's seat, and Junaid was sitting behind her, with Parveen sitting to Jahal's right. Jahal, facing forward as he was, did not respond to the whisper that was heard by Junaid and Parveen as well.

"I mean the apple, thanks," said Nyla, leaning slightly forward. Jahal looked back at her with a quizzical expression, and as he did so, he heard Junaid whisper, "You are welcome, Nyla."

Nyla's eyes were suddenly wide open, and she froze just as Jahal's eyebrows went up and Parveen looked quickly back at Junaid and Nyla.

Junaid could not see Nyla's startled expression as she sat back straight in her seat and rolled her eyes upward. She knew now what she had wondered about last night. Junaid had a faint smile on his lips despite the poisonous look he got from Jahal and Parveen. Had he been able to see Nyla's expression, he may have felt differently.

Junaid, feeling pleased and with Miss Zarina facing the chalkboard, leaned back in his chair with a joyous smile on his face. The case was quite different for the other three, each feeling uncomfortable in their own right. Nyla was frustrated that she had guessed wrong and in doing so had likely made Jahal upset with her and Junaid. She had seen the look Jahal had given Junaid sitting behind her. Parveen remembered her comment yesterday about Junaid and how that had made Nyla so angry. Now this bit of news about the apple had her thinking. Jahal was surprised that another boy had given a gift to a girl he liked so much. He had told his mother about Nyla and was hoping to ask her to come and do homework with him after school. He felt that Nyla liked him too since she had let him carry her backpack for her and thanked him so sweetly for it. He was relieved and happy however that Nyla had seemed surprised when she had heard Junaid's whisper. In fact he was positive that he had seen her roll her eyes and look quite unhappy. Nor had he seen her turn around to face Junaid or say anything to him. So he was certain she did not care for Junaid and that Junaid should know better than to make a move on his girl. He needed to be taught a lesson.

Junaid did not concern himself with how Parveen and especially Jahal had looked at him.

He was glad that Nyla had spoken up for him and had now thanked him for the little gesture of gratitude he had shown her. As far as he was concerned, that is all there was to this matter.

After school ended that day, Junaid picked up his backpack and lunch box and started his usual walk toward his home. As he walked beyond the bushes that bordered the playground he was grabbed from behind and pushed roughly down to the ground.

He landed on his back and his head hit the ground hard. Jahal was looking down angrily at him, eyes flashing fire and lips drawn back in anger as he held the smaller Junaid down with hands on his throat. "Stay away from Nyla, you little wimp!" he growled.

Junaid's left hand had twisted behind him as he had fallen, and it was hurting. He was shocked and could not say a word. He felt no fear but was bewildered by the way he had been attacked and the words he had heard. Just as quickly, Jahal got off him and stood above him glaring. He kicked Junaid's lunch box away and picking up his own backpack walked off with a smirk on his face.

Junaid did not get up right away and sat on the ground with his arms around his drawn up knees. His eyes were closed and he was thinking, trying to make sense of what had just happened. In his young and simple mind there was confusion. As he was about to get up off the ground, he saw Nyla walk toward him. She saw him sitting on the ground with grass, dirt, and leaves on his clothes and the back of his head, his lunch box a good ten feet from him. Surprised, she stopped and stood next to him. Junaid looked up at her and then brushing the hair off his face, he swallowed and looked away. She asked him why he was sitting on the ground with dirt on his clothes. "I fell," he said after a few moments, refusing to look at her and not wanting to tell her any more than that. Getting up to his feet, he picked up his backpack and then the lunch box, both in his right hand. Without saying another word, he walked away from her toward his home. Nyla stared after him and then turned to go home.

As she arrived at her home, she saw Jahal outside waiting for her. He smiled and came over to her.

"Hey, Nyla!" he said brightly.

"Hi," she replied quietly, still thinking about seeing Junaid sitting on the ground.

"Listen, I was wondering if you could help me with the math homework, I do not understand it," he asked excitedly, coming to stand close to her, looking at her face expectantly.

"Well, what don't you understand?" she inquired, taking a small step backward.

"None of it really," replied Jahal, inching toward her again.

"When do you want me to help you? It is due tomorrow!" she reminded him with a fleeting and forced smile.

"I know, I was thinking you could come over now and we could have a snack and then study?" He appealed, leaning in.

She hesitated and he pleaded again.

"Well, OK, but I can only stay for a few minutes, and I have to tell my mom where I am going," she said with a half-hearted shrug of her shoulders.

He lived only a few houses away, and their parents knew each other.

She told her mother she would be back in half an hour and came back out with the math book in her hands. Walking with a swagger by her side, he smugly said, "And you don't have to worry about that dummy Junaid bothering you again!"

She stopped and looked at him. "What do you mean?"

"Well, I saw how he was bothering you at school today, how upset he made you, so I took care of it." He beamed with pride.

"You took care of what, Jahal?" she asked him, looking puzzled.

"Well, after school today I told him not to bug you again, the little rat," he said with contempt.

"You saw him after school today?" she asked with a little understanding awakening inside her.

"Yeah, I saw him after school. He would not listen, so I had to throw him to the ground." He smirked.

"You what!" she stared at him incredulously, holding the book tightly against her chest.

"Yeah, he was acting tough, so I roughed him up a bit and told him to stay away from you!" he gloated, expecting her gratitude.

She knew Junaid was not the most responsible kid in the class, but she also knew he was a gentle and kind boy who would have a difficult time picking a fight with anyone much less a much bigger boy like Jahal. She had spoken up for Junaid in class because she felt it was the right thing to do. She was taken by surprise to learn that Junaid and not Jahal had given her the apple and the thank you note, but her expression of surprise was not one of disgust but rather a sign of acknowledgement of her own mistaken assumption and the awkward way in which three people including herself had learned of it.

If she did not want to see Parveen insult Junaid with words, she hated to see Jahal hurt him physically. She remembered now how she had seen Junaid on the ground, covered with dirt, and how he had left hurriedly without saying anything about what had really happened. She wondered if Junaid thought she felt the same as Jahal did. The thought made her uneasy. What if Junaid thought she was mad at him for giving her the thank you note? What if Junaid felt the words that came out of Jahal's mouth represented her feelings too!

All these thoughts troubled her greatly. She felt guilty without having done anything to deserve the feeling. "I need to go home now. I don't want you to ever touch Junaid or say anything to hurt his feelings for my sake again. Do you understand, Jahal?"

"But I only did it to help you, Nyla!" He looked puzzled, unable to comprehend why she would be upset with him.

"You do not need to protect me from Junaid or anyone else, ever!" she said, looking at him angrily and then turned and left him standing, staring at her go.

There was turmoil within her and she was somewhat surprised at what she wanted to do as soon as possible. She wanted the evening and night to be over quickly so she could see Junaid and somehow explain to him that what happened to him had nothing to do with her own feelings about him. She did not feel anything special for Junaid other than the fact that she did not want to see him get hurt or for anyone to hurt him in any way. She did not know what that feeling was or how to put it into words.

It was a long night for Nyla. It was also a long night for Junaid.

There was one difference in their thoughts that night.

Nyla could not wait to get back to school the next day, for reasons other than her usual love for school. Junaid, on the other hand, did not want to go to school the next day for reasons other than his usual dislike for school.

# Chapter 4

She was one of the first students to get to school that day. Sitting at her desk she saw her classmates trickle in and occupy their seats. Eventually, Miss Zarina came in and sat down waiting for everyone to settle in. Nyla waited impatiently as Junaid had still not arrived. Finally, Miss Zarina took the roll call and marked him absent just as he walked in. He put the lunch box and backpack on the side and for the first time ever he sat in a different seat, three places to the right and behind Nyla. She had noticed when he was putting up his backpack on the hook that he used only his right hand to lift it up with some difficulty. His sitting anywhere but behind her for the first time made her uneasy and confirmed what Jahal had told her yesterday. She tilted her head to look at him and saw his left wrist in a bandage. He looked at her for a moment and then abruptly looked away.

More than ever she wanted to talk to him and tell him she was sorry, but he had chosen a seat far from her and she would have to wait until recess. Jahal was sitting at his seat in front of her, and he had not said anything or turned around. She wished she was sitting somewhere away from him.

Miss Zarina was curious to see Junaid not occupy his usual seat. This seat was farther away and as she preferred to keep her eyes on him, she told him to move back to his customary place behind Nyla. Neither Nyla nor Jahal moved, but they could hear Junaid get up slowly, collect his books, and take his old seat behind them.

The three, sitting one behind the other had never felt as tense as they did today but none showed it. Jahal in front, Nyla in between, and Junaid at the rear. Miss Zarina collected the homework and then started writing the day's math problems on the board. She taught them what she had prepared, and as the students started solving the problems, she began scoring their homework. She was delighted that Junaid had submitted a complete and almost perfect assignment. She looked toward him and smiled, but he was busy with his work. She noticed the bandaged left hand and raised an eyebrow, calling him to her desk. Junaid looked up, butterflies fluttered in his stomach. What was she calling him to the desk for? Did he do something wrong again? Was the homework very badly done, worse even than usual?

"Yes, Miss," he said as he got up and walked over to her desk. She asked him to come around beside her and asked him gently what had happened to his hand and why he had a bandage on it. Jahal and Nyla were close enough in front of the classroom to hear what was being said. Nyla, sitting behind Jahal, saw his ears turn red as he stared at Junaid and his teacher.

Junaid knew he had to tell the truth but in a way that was not going to get him or anyone else in trouble, especially not Nyla or her special friend Jahal.

"I fell, Miss," he replied, not lying but not telling the entire truth as to how he had come to fall.

"Are you hurting bad, Junaid? Did you break anything? Can you stay or do you need to go home?" she asked.

"Only when I move it. I don't know. And I can stay. Mom said if it is not getting better by tomorrow she will take me to Dr. Marwani in the morning, Miss," he said, feeling relieved that it was just about his hand and not about something wrong he had done or the homework that he had spent so much time on after school yesterday. He had not been able to go to the woods because he could not climb a tree nor use his slingshot. So he had stayed home and done schoolwork instead. That is when his mother had found out about the hand injury and put a bandage on his wrist and hand. He had told her the same story about the fall, and she was surprised that he had fallen walking home when he could climb trees, run across rough ground in the woods, and jump over fallen logs with the ease of a deer. She was pleased that he was studying however and did not question him any further. She would take him to the doctor if he was still hurting after another day or two.

Nyla could sense Jahal take a deep breath and felt his body slump into an easy posture. She saw Junaid start to walk back to his seat and heard Miss Zarina say to him with a smile, "And, Junaid, good job on the math homework."

"Thanks, Miss," he said almost inaudibly as he walked back to his seat.

Nyla could hear his breathing settle down in a few moments as he started scribbling again.

She was pleasantly surprised at her teacher's comment about Junaid's homework and wondered what had inspired him to work at it seriously.

During recess when all the children picked up their lunch boxes and went outdoors, she waited to see if Junaid would stay or leave too. He waited for her to stay or leave so he could do the opposite. Jahal finally got up and left, glancing at the two as they sat in their seats.

"Aren't you going to go have your lunch, Junaid?" she finally asked.

"Yes, but why are you not going out to eat? Jahal is waiting for you," he said as she turned to face him.

"Do you want me to go and eat outside or here with you?" she questioned with her eyebrows raised, looking intently into his soft brown eyes.

Here was a tough question for Junaid. Much more difficult than the most difficult question Miss Zarina could ever ask him. He squirmed in his seat, looked at the door, expecting Jahal to come in any moment.

"Does not matter what I want I guess, but your friend wants you to eat with him, and I don't want him to be upset," he replied finally.

"Would you like to go and sit out in the sun and eat together? No one will be upset. I want you to," she said with a little smile.

"Really! I thought you were upset that I wrote the thank you note?" he said with his innocent eyes staring at her.

"No, I am not. And I am sorry you hurt your hand. Be careful and don't go around falling all over the place, OK?" she teased him smiling, not wanting him to know that she knew what had really happened to his hand.

"OK!" he said as he finally smiled back, getting out of his seat.

They picked up their lunch boxes and went to the playground together. There was an empty bench on the other side, and they walked through the playground between their classmates and sat down to eat. Jahal and Parveen were sitting together on a bench with some other students and seemed to not look in their direction.

Junaid was having a little trouble opening his lunch box with one hand, and Nyla helped him with it. After eating his sandwich, Junaid picked up his apple and offered it to Nyla who was done with her lunch too. She thanked him, asking him to eat the apple himself, but he persisted.

"Can we share it then?" he asked candidly, taking a bite and holding it up for her to now take a bite too.

Nyla looked around and felt uneasy. She had wanted to sit and talk and eat with Junaid and was glad to have done it but sharing an apple, eating it from his hand, was a little different and she knew it. But looking at his guileless face, the apple held out inches from her face was impossible to refuse.

"OK, just one bite, I am really full," she said softly, taking a little bite of the apple. This little bite was seen around the playground and caused one little girl to drop her spoon and another to forget to close her mouth. Jahal and Parveen looked at each other and got up to go back to the classroom.

"I am going to go back to the class now. You go ahead and finish your lunch. See you inside," Nyla said and got up, looking a little flustered. Junaid's mouth was full as he shook his head up and down to say yes.

As she turned and walked off, Junaid threw the half-eaten apple into the bushes behind him and walked after Nyla, entering the classroom just a few steps behind her.

All eyes were glued on them, and Nyla was blushing as she got to her seat and sat down. Junaid was comfortable and easy in his demeanor. He looked back at the staring children as he sat down with just a little more enthusiasm than usual. Some of the girls giggled, but soon the class went back to the normal routine of the afternoon.

After the school was over and the classroom emptied, Miss Zarina sat at her desk thinking about Junaid, the boy who had remained something of an enigma to her and who she had been unable to understand fully. She liked the fact that he seemed to be inherently well behaved and polite. She was happy to see him turn in the first properly completed assignment ever. His injured hand had brought forth in her a protective instinct that she had for all her students, whether they seemed to be performing well academically or not. She was looking forward to next week's exams and wanted to see how Junaid would do. She wanted all her students to do well, particularly those who were struggling.

Junaid walked home today with a little spring in his step, forgetting for the moment the pain in his left hand. He hesitated slightly as he walked beyond the bushes where he had been attacked yesterday and looked to the right and left, half expecting Jahal to appear out of thin air.

He walked beyond the bushes and only then heard quick steps behind him. Not wanting to let Jahal get the jump on him today, he turned around swiftly, dropping the backpack to his right arm. But instead of Jahal, he saw Nyla's friendly face as she stepped up to him. She had been standing behind a tree waiting for him to pass where she had seen him on the ground yesterday and where she had later learned he had been attacked by Jahal. Once she saw that he was safely clear of the bushes, she had come forward to join him in the walk home. They smiled at each other and walked together without saying a word. He walked with Nyla to the end of her street and stood there watching as she then continued on to her home. She glanced back and saw him standing there looking at her. They waved at each other, and she went inside.

Junaid knew next week was exam week. He had done poorly the last time, and when Miss Zarina had posted the grades and rankings of the students, he had been at the very bottom of the class and barely passing. He intended to not suffer the embarrassment of having his classmates, his parents, Zarina Begum, and most of all Nyla see him at the bottom of the rankings ever again. After a quick snack, his mother saw him sit down at his desk against a window overlooking his beloved woods.

The trees and the berries, the birds and their nests, the calls of the jackals and the antics of the squirrels, and most of all the varied and sundry songs of the mockingbird from the oak tree just outside the window would all just have to wait. His hand was hurt, and he could do little about that but wait for it to heal. But more importantly, he suddenly felt self-reproach and remorse for having neglected his schoolwork for which he had suffered the consequence of humiliation and that was something he intended to do something about.

Why he felt this in his heart now and not before he could not understand nor associate with anyone yet. He just no longer wanted to look bad or be ridiculed in front of people anymore.

He would realize in time that he had the same teacher, the same parents, and the same classmates as before but that something had changed within him and that someone had caused it to change. Much later would he realize that if there had never been a Nyla, if she had never existed or if he never knew her, that he would not have felt the need to change. Deep within his heart was the desire for him to look good in her eyes, for her to be proud of him. That this change in him would matter to her was shown by her having stood up for him when he was being ridiculed.

Junaid was motivated for the sake of two people more than for anyone else—for his own pride and for that of Nyla.

# Chapter 5

It had taken Junaid a long time to finish the homework that night. Determined not to give Miss Zarina any excuse to pick on him or to punish him, he had started working on his homework immediately after getting home from school. It was past midnight by the time he had completed it to his liking and had fallen asleep sitting at his desk, which is where his mother had found him when she came to check on him the next morning when he had not come down for breakfast.

Ignoring breakfast, usually his heaviest meal, he had hastily washed, changed, and grabbing his backpack was out the door in a few minutes, hoping to get to class before Miss Zarina.

Miss Zarina had just entered the class and was settling down at the desk when Junaid rushed in, panting and out of breath. He was pleased to not have missed the roll call as he took his seat behind Nyla.

Before beginning the day's work, Miss Zarina asked for the students to bring their homework to her desk one by one in the order they were seated. As his classmates began to submit their work, Junaid looked inside his backpack, first calmly and then frantically as he could not find his homework that he had spent so much time and effort on the previous night. As Nyla got up and brought her homework to the teacher's desk, Junaid's frenzied search for his homework reached a climax and just as his teacher asked him to bring his assignment to her, he had a startling recollection. He had forgotten the homework on his desk in his haste to get ready and get to school on time!

He now stopped searching and stood up, distraught and pale with anguish as his classmates looked on.

"Junaid, do you have your homework?" asked Miss Zarina.

"Yes, Miss. I mean no, Miss," stammered Junaid.

"Junaid! Either you have done your homework or you have not. Now which is it?" his teacher asked sternly.

"I have done the homework, Miss, but I left it at my desk last night," a haltering response came from a petrified Junaid.

"I see! You left it at home! Again!" his grim-faced teacher said for all to hear.

There were no giggles or smart comments from anyone as Miss Zarina was visibly too upset to allow that to happen. The deathly quiet made Junaid feel even worse than if someone had said something to take the focus even slightly off him. Nyla sitting in front of him and facing forward could not see him but could feel his misery and pain as if she was herself the recipient of Miss Zarina's ire. She could do nothing however to help him or say anything to comfort him at this time.

Miss Zarina had felt that he might be becoming more serious with schoolwork. She had hoped that Junaid would try to do better, to at the least make an effort and attempt to be more responsible. Today she seemed to have come to the end of her rope. Perhaps he just did not respond to her teaching. Perhaps he needed a different teacher to bring out the responsible side in him. She felt hurt and angry at the same time; she had tried her best.

"Junaid, do you not like to be in my class? Do you not like the way I teach?" she asked, no longer sounding angry.

"No, Miss. I mean yes, Miss. I like to be in your…," replied a meek voice, from a confused Junaid.

"Maybe you would like to be in Miss Gulbadan's class, Junaid?" she asked, looking more hurt than she sounded.

"You mean the pretty teacher?" asked a befuddled Junaid, whose only concern at this point was to not make his teacher any more upset and to agree with anything she suggested.

Despite the tension that had built up to a breaking point or perhaps even because of it and hearing Junaid's spontaneous response, the class finally broke out first in insuppressible giggles and then uncontrolled guffaws and laughter as Miss Zarina herself could not help but smile at the comment made by the innocent and bewildered child standing in front of her.

She excused herself from the classroom for several minutes and returned to find Junaid still standing and the remainder of the class talking animatedly about Junaid and his comment about Miss Gulbadan.

Miss Zarina looked light of heart and of a much sunnier disposition when she returned.

"Yes, Junaid, the pretty teacher. Would you like to be in her class instead?" she inquired, without sounding bitter.

Junaid, now somewhat comforted by not seeing his teacher angry at him, pondered the question and after he had come to a conclusion, replied, "No, Miss, I want to stay in this class."

"Why is that, Junaid? Why would you not want to go to the class of a teacher you find so very pretty?" asked Miss Zarina with a barely concealed look of amusement.

"Well, Miss…because…" Junaid seemed to be having trouble saying what was in his mind.

"Yes?" encouraged his teacher.

"Well, because there is no Nyla in that class," muttered Junaid in a soft and barely audible voice.

The howls of laughter that followed this remark were heard across the hallway in Miss Gulbadan's class and occasioned Nyla, who was sitting in front of the standing Junaid, to turn around and give him a quick look of frustrated indignation that made Miss Zarina's anger look like playful cheer in comparison. She then turned around to hide her painfully embarrassed face in her hands as she absorbed the teasing comments from her classmates.

"Junaid thinks Miss Gulbadan is pretty *but* not as pretty as Nyla!" said one shrill voice.

"Junaid *loves* Nyla!" said another voice with a musical lilt.

These and other appropriately timed comments generated much hilarity and merriment in the classroom at the expense of Junaid and especially Nyla, who were both nonetheless unable to help look somewhat amused at their own discomfiture.

Miss Zarina and Miss Gulbadan, who had come out of her class to inquire about the cause of the festivities in her colleague's class, had a private meeting in the hallway. Presently, and with a look of attempted earnestness, Miss Zarina returned to her class and raised her hand to quite down the jocularity so she could talk. As the class simmered down, she told Junaid that for not submitting the homework and for making comments that caused Nyla to suffer the chaffing of her classmates, he was to stand in the corner for the remainder of the day and not just during the morning. Junaid, happy to see a resolution to his plight, albeit at his own expense and now realizing the discomfort he had caused Nyla, was only too eager to go stand in the corner at the back of the class. He was glad to no longer have his classmates stare at him or make comments to add to his misery. As he stood staring at the corner, his teacher told him to turn around and face the front so he could follow what she was teaching the class.

Junaid had been standing in the corner for over two hours, and there was still another hour to go before the lunch break when there was a knock on the door and the principal Mr. Pervez entered the classroom. He had some papers in his hand and he beckoned the teacher to come out and speak with him. Miss Zarina returned after a few minutes and sat down at her desk reading the papers in her hand that the principal had handed to her.

"Junaid!" she said aloud, still looking at the papers in her hands.

The poor child, standing in the corner had a look of utter and complete exasperation as he stared at his teacher, his heart aflutter and his lack of having had a breakfast after a long night and then having to stand for hours was now causing him to feel close to passing out.

"Yes, Miss," he whimpered.

Even those of his classmates who did not care much for him were starting to feel sympathy for Junaid as he was summoned to the teacher's desk.

"Did you have your breakfast this morning, Junaid?" asked Miss Zarina with concern showing in her kindly eyes.

"No, Miss," replied Junaid with surprise and relief in his voice and a confused look on his face.

"Why?" asked his teacher as she stood up and put her arm over his shoulders.

"I was rushing to get to class on time, Miss," replied Junaid, looking down at his shoes, one of which had an untied lace.

"Your mother found and brought your homework that you had forgotten on your desk, Junaid," she said loud enough to let the class hear her.

"So you *were* telling the truth this morning. I am also proud of you for doing a great job with the homework!" She beamed.

"Thank you, Miss," Junaid replied with a faint smile on his dry lips.

"Now, I want you to take out your lunch box and go eat before you faint!" she said with a loving smile. "And, Junaid, never miss your breakfast again!" she added sternly. "Class, you can have your lunch a little early too, thanks to Junaid. I will see you after lunch," she declared.

Junaid, too tired and hungry to go out to eat, sat at his desk and gulped down his lunch as quickly as he could. With his nerves no longer on edge and his hunger finally sated, he could not help falling asleep as he lay down his head on his arms on top of the desk. This is how his classmates and teacher found him when they returned after lunch.

He woke up with a start when he heard Miss Zarina talking. Looking around he saw his classmates focused on what was being taught and was surprised that no one had attempted to wake him up or teased him for falling asleep. He then remembered something and got up out of his chair and walked back to the corner he had been standing that entire morning. Miss Zarina, seeing him stand in the corner, stopped talking and told him he could have his seat.

Junaid hesitated and stayed where he stood.

"Junaid, you can have your seat now. I know you did your homework," she ordered.

"But, Miss, you told me to stand in the corner for two reasons. For not turning in my homework and for making Nyla feel bad," replied Junaid, standing his ground.

"I see, as you wish. I cannot speak for Nyla," said Miss Zarina, as she glanced at Nyla, who seemed oblivious to the conversation.

Miss Zarina sighed and continued with her talk on the basics of chemistry.

Nyla knew Junaid had said something that had embarrassed her in front of her classmates and her teacher. Thinking back at his comment, she also now realized he had not said anything negative about her or even suggested that *she* liked him. All he had said was that he did not want to be in a class if Nyla was not there and that was a roundabout way for a ten-year-old to say that he liked her in some manner. If anything, this was a compliment and not an insult and for that he was now standing in the corner. She felt some of her classmates looking at her and whether it was their looks that had the message or whether she was feeling guilty for being the cause of Junaid still standing in the corner, she had to do something to make this feeling go away.

So after thinking about this for some time, she finally raised her hand.

"What is your question, Nyla?" asked her teacher.

"Miss, Junaid can sit down if that is all right with you," replied Nyla politely.

"Miss, if it is all right with you, I would like to stand for a while longer," said Junaid before Miss Zarina had the chance to answer.

"Why would you like to keep standing in the corner, Junaid?" asked his surprised teacher, as his classmates also turned around to look at him for making his unusual request.

"Because I am already standing in the corner in case I do something wrong again, Miss," Junaid replied calmly.

Miss Zarina wanted to tell him that he had done nothing wrong to deserve standing in the corner as far as she was concerned. Nyla wanted to tell him the same thing, and yet he had been made to stand in the corner, a punishment he had not earned but perhaps deserved for saying what he felt within. It was his lack of tact that had once again landed him in trouble, this time with Nyla.

At the end of the school day, after she had given her class the assignments for their homework, Miss Zarina sat down to review the homework from yesterday and as she sat at her desk she promised herself she would never make Junaid stand in the corner again; little did she know that he was never again to give her the excuse.

After school, a tired Junaid with achy legs and feet and a heavy backpack limped away toward his home. Though physically exhausted, he was in high spirits and felt an unexplained elation. As he limped by Nyla who was sitting on a bench talking to her friend Farah, he acted as if he had not noticed her. The two girls waved at him, and he responded by quickening his pace and nodding in acknowledgement. Nyla said a quick goodbye to Farah and told Junaid to stop walking so she could join him.

"Sorry," said Junaid, as Nyla came next to him.

"Don't be. I am the one who should be sorry," she replied sheepishly.

"For what?" he asked, his eyes wide open.

"For being so upset at what you said," she said, looking apologetic.

"Why were you upset at what I said?" asked Junaid without a hint of anger or frustration.

"Well, I guess because you are a boy, Junaid," she said after pausing to think a bit.

"And?" He looked at her quizzically.

"And I am a girl," she said in a haltering manner, trying to understand it herself before replying to his question.

"And when a boy says he likes to be friends with a girl it is different than when a girl says the same thing, especially the way you said it in front of the teacher and the class," she added demurely, unconsciously batting her long eyelashes as she looked down and then looked up at him.

"I guess you are right," said Junaid with a shrug of his shoulders as he tried to digest that.

"I will not say that again in front of anyone again!" he said as they started walking.

"You already said it, so it does not matter if you say it again or not," replied Nyla smiling, not looking annoyed in the least.

"And you are OK with that?" asked Junaid with an unbelieving expression as they continued to walk.

"Yes, I am OK with that," said Nyla with a smile, as she playfully bumped into his side.

He looked at her face that he thought was rather cute but bit his tongue before he could tell her that, in case she got mad at him again. Girls were different that way, he told himself, weird even, but in a good way. They were hard to understand but easy to like. They were definitely not like boys, that was for sure. They looked different, but they were also a lot more complicated. If a boy was angry at you for something you said, he would stay mad until you said sorry or gave him your best marble or half of your peanut butter and jelly sandwich; but if you said something that made a girl angry, she was as likely to stay mad at you as to actually like you for having said what had made her upset with you in the first place! Yes, they were hard to figure out sometimes, most of the time even. But he liked the way he felt when they smiled at you, especially when Nyla smiled at him, it made his heart go a bit faster and flutter like it was going to fly out of his chest if she did not stop smiling. He figured that was because girls could smile with their eyes and not just their lips.

And when they did stuff like bump into him, which no girl had ever done except Nyla, even though it made him almost lose his balance and nearly fall, he felt like he could stand her bumping into him for the rest of his life and still not be upset with her. He felt that it made him nearly lose his balance as if he was going to fall but it also made him lose his balance as if he was going to stop walking and start flying. It made him feel off balance in the way he had seen kites and eagles seem a bit off balance in strong wind, but they seemed to be having fun and never fell or stopped flying. He wondered if he would feel the same way if another girl smiled at him or bumped into him. Then he felt strangely guilty for thinking that and furtively glanced at Nyla to see if she had noticed. He would *never* want another girl to smile at him, smile at him that is with her lips *and* her eyes, and for sure he would not want another girl to bump into him! Then he wondered about Nyla smiling at another boy, like Jahal, with her eyes and bumping into another boy and he felt so bad inside that he just had to stop thinking about it. Girls could do that to you without even saying anything. How could they be so different? He wondered as he looked at Nyla walking next to him. She moved so much more than he did while walking, he noticed.

They walked to her home, and as Junaid was about to leave, he thought of something. "You know, what I said about Miss Gulbadan! You think Miss Zarina told her? You think Miss Gulbadan is going to be mad at me for saying it?" he asked with genuine concern.

"She is not going to be *mad* at you. She will probably be *happy* to hear it! All girls like it when they are told they are pretty," replied Nyla, trying to comfort him.

"Even you?"

"What do you mean even me?"

"That you would like it if someone told you that you were pretty?"

She rolled her eyes, cranked her neck forward, put her hands on her hips, and said, "Duh! I am a girl, aren't I?"

Taken a bit by surprise at her question, he quickly looked away over her head as if he had spotted a sparrow hawk.

"Yes, you are a girl all right. Never said you weren't," he stammered.

"And?" she asked, maintaining her posture, but cocking her head instead of craning her neck now.

"And what?" he asked.

"Really?"

"You are confusing me, Nyla!"

"I am confusing you? Don't you want to tell me something that all girls like to hear?"

He thought about the question. How did she always come up with the most difficult questions?

"You already know I want to be in the same class as you," he said, refusing to meet her stare.

"So! What does that mean? That does not mean you think I am pretty!"

She looked at him biting the corner of his upper lip and looking everywhere except at her.

"Goodbye Junaid, see you tomorrow," she finally said with resignation and a trace of a smile, as Junaid waved at her amiably and walked off with a relieved expression on his face. Sometimes it was better to not say anything and let them figure it out since they always figured it out anyway. If it was the truth it was bound to come out.

Later, after he was done studying in preparation for the next day, he thought about the eventful day. Initially, he had felt bad for having said something that had made Nyla so unhappy. He had told himself that he was going to have to be careful and not say anything about wanting to be in the same class as Nyla or wanting her to be his friend. He had concluded that there was little point in being someone's friend if it only made that person feel bad and hurt their feelings. After talking to Nyla on the way back home, however, he felt differently. Once again he was convinced of the validity of his assumption that speaking the truth about one's feelings was always the best thing to do, at least in the long term, even though it was not always the easiest or sometimes the safest in the near term, especially when girls were involved or even teachers for that matter. He had told his teacher the truth and once she had realized that to be the case, she had treated him accordingly. He had told the teacher and his class the reason for his not wanting to go to Miss Gulbadan's class, and while Nyla was initially upset with his declaration, she had eventually changed her opinion and feelings and seemed happy with what he had said. So he figured that with girls, all girls and especially the ones that you liked, it was best to tell them the truth and then let them figure out if they liked what you said or not. It appeared to him that girls were real smart and they always figured out, sooner or later, what was really said to them, even if it was not said with words but by just the way one acted around them and whether it was worth liking or not.

As Nyla lay in bed ready to sleep that night, she thought back about the day. She blamed herself for being so upset when Junaid had made his comment. She thought about his remark; and in the calm before sleep, she felt the sweetness and inno-cence of those words he had said in front of their teacher, their friends, and classmates. As she slipped deeper into slumber she imagined how it would feel to be in a class without Junaid and the thought was strangely abhorrent to her and she banished it from her mind.

# Chapter 6

Nyla could not stand to see Junaid's name at the bottom of the class rankings again. She knew he was not applying himself and in time she intended to encourage him to devote more time to his schoolwork. She did not know how to approach him in this regard but now was not the time, and it would not do him any good as today they were all sitting in the class waiting for Miss Zarina to hand out the test. She did want to do something however and had struggled with whether she should help him with the exam today. The questions were in a multiple choice answer format, and Junaid sitting directly behind could easily see her answers if she were to just move her body slightly to the left. She looked back at him, smiled, and asked if he was ready. "I hope so," he replied, nervously twirling a short blunt pencil in his hands.

He had studied every day of the week, after school and during most of the weekend. He wanted to do as well as he could in this exam and to be more conscientious about his studies in the future.

The exam notebooks were passed out, and the students started answering the questions. Junaid bent forward with determination, focused and confident. He noticed nothing of the classroom but the task at hand. Nyla, as she quickly dispensed with the first page, leaned a little to her left and moved the exam notebook slightly to the right, clearing her throat softly to attract Junaid's attention. She could not see Junaid but heard him flip to the next page and quickly turned to the next page herself. She repeated the performance after finishing the next five pages until she came to the end of the questions. Junaid did not notice her moving to the left until he was himself on the last page and felt that she was letting him see her answers. Now he could hardly focus on the last few questions and thoughts raced in his head as his ears turned red with equal parts of shame and humiliation. Finishing the exam, he calmly reviewed his answers, closed the notebook, and sat back in his seat just as the time was called, and Miss Zarina started going around the class collecting the exam notebooks.

It was a half day at school and by recess time the children were free to go home. Junaid picked up his backpack, and as he was leaving, Nyla asked him how it went. Unable to look her in the eye and fidgeting uncomfortably he told her he did not know but that they would find out tomorrow. He then said he had to go home now and left. Nyla was a bit surprised that he did not walk back home with her but was happy that she had helped him and that his ranking tomorrow should be at or near the top of the class.

The next day, Miss Zarina posted the results and the rankings of the students in the hallway outside the classroom and the children gathered around looking for their scores. Nyla noticed her name and that of Parveen at the top of the list. She glanced at the bottom of the rankings and was relieved to find Junaid not occupying his usual spot. His name was instead near the middle of the list and his score was far better than anyone had seen in the past. He was sitting in the classroom waiting for the other student to come back in so Miss Zarina could begin teaching.

Miss Zarina asked him with a smile if he wanted to check his score, and he replied that he would but later.

Nyla was taken by surprise at Junaid's ranking and things were starting to make sense to her as she thought back about yesterday. Clearly Junaid had not copied her answers and had done all he could to prepare for the exam and do his very best. He had obviously also noticed that she had tried to help him by letting him see her answers, which had upset him and that explained his behavior after the test yesterday. She felt that in an effort to help someone she cared for, she had in fact ended up hurting him. Nyla realized that she must have insulted Junaid by assuming that he would be interested in seeing a better ranking for himself by any means.

It comforted her however that her goal was simply to help someone who she was concerned about, and it made her proud that the boy she had taken a certain liking to was beyond using any means to achieve an end. She was happy that Junaid had the honesty and integrity to try to do for himself whatever he could rather than take the easy way out of relying on someone else to do the work for him. She wanted to let Junaid know this, that she was proud of him.

At recess she saw him leave with his lunch box and make his way to the lunch room instead of the playground where their other classmates were sitting on the benches. She went straight to him and sat down opposite him.

"Hi, Junaid. Are you mad at me?" she asked directly looking at his eyes.

Junaid was taken aback by her straightforward question. Sure he was upset with her effort to help him in the exam yesterday, and he felt a loss of face by her assumption that he would copy her answers. He felt that if she thought he would copy her answers then he must not be a very honest boy.

"A little," he said quietly, looking down at the table.

"I am so happy that you studied for the exam and did so well, Junaid!" she said. "I am proud that you did it yourself and did not need anyone's help."

"I am happy you were trying to help me, Nyla."

"I only did it because I would feel bad if I did not even try to help. So I guess, I was really doing it for myself. You are smart enough to help yourself."

Thinking hard, he looked up. "I do not know if I am smart or not, but I like to get a grade that I deserve, so I can feel good." Junaid's eyes brightened up and he smiled genuinely. He seemed to relax where he sat.

Nyla smiled and held his hand in hers for a moment.

"You want half an apple?" he asked.

"Yes, but only if you eat it with me at the playground and not here. I love to be in the sun when it is a bit cold."

They walked happily into the playground amongst their classmates. As they walked by where Jahal and Parveen were sitting, she called out and said, "Hey, Junaid, we saw your ranking! Wow, it looks like you are getting help from somewhere special!" Parveen looked at Jahal and they both winked at each other. "It must feel good to not be dead last again! Huh, Junaid? Mr. Go-stand-in-the-corner!" They both laughed but were not joined in the merriment by Farooq or Fowzia or Ozair, who were sitting close enough to hear everything. Nyla turned to answer Parveen but Junaid told her with his eyes to not say anything. Instead, he looked at Parveen and Jahal, smiled, and walked on. There was fire in Nyla's eyes as she devoured Parveen with her gaze, but she did not say a word.

"Do you wanna go out to the woods with me this weekend, Nyla?" Junaid asked, munching on his half of the apple.

"Sure. Do you go to the woods a lot?" she asked.

"Sometimes. When I do not have anything else fun to do. I have not gone in a week, but the exam is over and the woods are pretty with leaves turning colors. We can just go for a few hours," he replied.

They stood talking in front of her home for a few minutes and parted with the agreement that she would try to make it by nine and if not he would go alone.

Junaid walked home happier than he had been in a long time. He wanted to show Nyla the blackberry tree and his secret tree house that no one knew existed, but most of all, he wanted to show her the stream and the hidden pond where he swam and fished. It was a very special place for him, and he would only share it with someone very special. Someone like Nyla.

# Chapter 7

She arrived at Junaid's home at nine in the morning as planned, just as he was leaving out of the front door. His mom waved at her and called out to Junaid, reminding him not to make Nyla walk too much and to be back well before dark. They waved back and then walked together on the narrow dirt path that led to the tree line and the woods beyond.

Over the past two years Junaid's diligent schoolwork had made him happier and more comfortable at school. Now in the seventh grade and almost thirteen years old, he was still more at ease when not sitting in class, but it had been a while since he had said to his mother that, "I don't wanna go to school." His parents, teachers and Nyla felt proud of this change in him. He was as always happy in his beloved woods and would take time to go hiking alone every chance he could, which was now only one or two weekends a month. He was delighted that Nyla finally had the time and the desire to come with him today.

Nyla had grown in the past two years. She was almost as tall as her mother now and starting to look like a young lady. Her schoolwork was always her first priority, and she found great pleasure in it. She had become close to Junaid over the past almost three years and was glad and relieved to see him perform so well in class. They had become good friends but rarely had the chance to see each other outside of school. She had been wanting to spend time with him, especially in the woods, and was thrilled to finally be able to do so today. He had not mentioned or asked her to do so in a while now, and she knew he would let her decide when she was ready. When she asked him after school yesterday if he was going hiking this weekend and he had said yes, she remembered his excitement when she told him she wanted to join him.

The sun had been up for nearly an hour now and its warmth was starting to take the chill out of the crisp November morning. The dense fog that lay close to the dry brown grass was lifting away as the sparrows and spotted starlings were beginning to chirp and stir about. The tops of the Margalla hills that stood to the north of the city were covered with clouds still and would be covered with snow in a few months.

Nyla was wearing her walking shoes, dark wool leggings, and a short warm jacket that came down to her hips. A purple scarf kept cold air away from her neck, and her shiny black hair gently blowing in the morning breeze fell loosely around her face and shoulders. The tip of her nose was a bit red due to the cold air; both her hands were in the pockets of her jacket and a small basket dangled from her left arm.

Junaid looked at her as they walked together and smiled; she looked cute, he thought. He was wearing his well worn hiking shoes, light blue jeans, and the old denim jacket over a full sleeve warm shirt. His trusty slingshot was tucked out of view beneath the jacket in the right rear pocket of his jeans. He had grown taller and was strong and lean with all the hiking and climbing he had done over the years.

"Hey, Junaid, THIS today!" Nyla said, looking at him with an amused expression.

"What today?" he replied, looking a bit confused.

"Thank heavens it's Saturday today!" she said with a giggle.

"OH!" He chuckled, walked a few steps, and said, "Hey, Nyla, THIS tomorrow!"

"No, silly, THIS today!" she said, continuing to walk.

No, THIS tomorrow. Thank heavens it's Sunday, tomorrow!" It was his turn to giggle.

She punched him a friendly little punch on his right shoulder, and they laughed happily.

"Good one, Junaid, know any more acronyms?"

"Not really, you?"

"Sure, I make them up myself all the time," she said then added, "You are JAB and I am JAG and we are BF!"

"Wow, that is tough, I give up," he said after scratching his head for a while.

"You are just a boy, I am just a girl and we are best friends!" she said excitedly.

"Does anyone else use JAB and JAG or only you?" he asked.

"As far as I know, just me," she said with a little hint of innocent pride. "But I will tell my friends Rehana and Fareeda."

"And I am your BF?" he asked, looking straight ahead, not smiling.

"Yes, my BF," she replied, thinking a bit, looking at him from the corner of her eye for a second, then added, "You are my BF and I am your BF, but you are not my BF and I am not your GF, right, Junaid?"

Junaid kept looking forward, "Of course," he said with a little chuckle then he took a deep breath, shook his head as if to clear it, and looked ahead to spending some good time with his BF.

Just beyond the tree line, Junaid took her through a hidden path between some dense bushes laden with wild berries. This narrow path that went west, took off from that point upward and to the left, climbing some of the lower Margalla hills, a part of the lesser Himalayas.

They walked over dry crunchy grass and red, yellow and orange leaves that made a colorful blanket under towering euca-lyptus and peepul trees.

It was clear to Junaid after they had walked for almost half an hour that not only was Nyla able to keep up with him but was actually enjoying every minute of the hike. They some-times went over and sometimes under fallen logs and branches, through thick thorny bushes of a tasty purple-black wild berry, and jumped from one round slippery rock to another as they crossed murmuring mountain streams. He only helped her across the most difficult terrain by holding her hand for balance or pulling her over a slippery rock that she could not get a good foothold on.

Junaid was making for one of his favorite spots where he had never seen another human being and where he loved to swim during the hot summer months. He had kept this spot his secret but was only too happy and excited to show it to Nyla. Centuries of rushing water coming down the rocky surface of this particular mountain stream had hollowed out a smooth walled pool the size of a house. The cold clear water entered through a narrow channel in the North and exited through another opening at the other end. Small round pebbles of various colors formed the floor of the pool and minnows with glittering sides swam in small schools over these pebbles. Tall pine and sheesham trees lined the sides of the pool and wild pink rose, dandelion, blue milk thistle, and purple hyacinths were sprinkled amongst the trees. In different seasons, the different colors of the flowers and leaves and the ever changing shrubbery around the pool made this a lovely place that Junaid could not resist visiting every chance he could.

Now, after an over two-hour hike and standing in front of the stem of a mighty sheesham tree, Junaid asked Nyla to close her eyes and took her right hand in his left, guiding her around the tree and beyond to a flat rock at the edge of the pond. Opening her eyes as he let go of her hand, Nyla gasped with surprise and pleasure as she took in the crystal clear pool hidden in the most beautiful natural setting she had ever beheld. She looked at all this spellbound and without knowing her right hand sought and found Junaid's left hand as they stood together; she squeezed his hand tight and turned toward him and hugged him with glee.

The sun was now high in the eastern sky and its warm rays lit up the pool and warmed the rocks around it. Sitting on one of these rocks with their feet dangling down, they could see schools of small fish darting to and fro.

"Do you know how to swim?" asked Junaid.

"No, I don't," she replied with a pout, looking at the inviting water and imagining how it would feel to be able to swim.

"I learned to swim in this pool a few years ago. Would you like to learn to swim? Not now, it is too cold, but when it is warm this coming summer?" he asked.

"Yes! Could you teach me?" Nyla pleaded, turning toward him and holding his hands.

"Yes. It would be fun!" replied Junaid. He looked into her almond brown eyes that radiated warmth and fondness but perhaps most of all trust, a little longer than usual and then feeling uneasy, looked away at a pine tree across the pool. Nyla leaned toward him and kissed him on his left cheek. "Thanks!" she said and let go of his arm, getting her legs under her to stand up.

Junaid was surprised and elated at the same time. It felt good to get a kiss, a friendly peck from Nyla, it made him just a little dizzy as if he was standing on top of a high mountain cliff. It made him feel like all was right with the world. She was his friend and yet she was more. Ordinary friends did not make him feel as she did. He wondered if being with him made her feel the same way. If it did she certainly did not show it. He wondered if she could tell just by looking at him what a little peck from her on his cheek could do to him. He hoped that she could not.

He looked at the sun directly over their heads now and then looked at his watch; high noon, just as he thought. They were getting a little hungry with all the hiking this morning. Washing their hands in the stream as it left the pool, they sat down on a flat rock and Nyla opened her basket to produce orange marmalade sandwiches, cashews, bananas, and two small bottles of water. She spread this on a red-and-white cloth from the basket, and they sat down cross-legged on each side to eat with relish. Having finished eating first, he drank some water and burped contentedly, smiling at Nyla, who burped a little burp, and they giggled and laughed happily.

Looking up across the stream, Junaid spotted a mulberry tree, which still had some dark juicy-looking berries on the higher branches. Taking the now empty basket in his hand, he crossed over to the other side and climbed the tree with ease, going up toward the branches which held the sweet treats. He looked down at Nyla on the other side of the pool, sitting on her bottom, knees bent against her chest, legs held together by her arms in front of her. Her chin rested on her knees, as she watched him climb the tree and start putting the berries in the basket. Their eyes met; she smiled and he waved. Once he had collected enough mulberries, Junaid clambered down the tree, jumped over the narrow channel at the bottom of the pool and placed the half-full basket in front of Nyla.

He asked if she wanted to go on and hike a little farther, but she wanted to just stay here, at his favorite spot in the woods. The flat rocks were a perfect place to rest after a satisfying lunch, and they both lay down on their backs looking up at the deep blue sky and the towering trees that rimmed it. As they rested on the warm sandstone rock a family of chukar partridge walked out to the clearing on the other side of the pool, scratching the ground and the dry leaves looking for seeds and fallen berries. Junaid quietly pointed out to Nyla a pair of gray doves sunning on a rock not twenty yards away, all but invisible against the rocks they sat on, nibbling on each other's beaks playfully. A brightly colored rose-ringed parakeet flitted across the blue sky above and circled once, coming down on the branch of a sheesham tree above them. Nyla knew this was not the last time she would come here to this serene place with

Junaid. She did not know she would like this hidden paradise as much as she did. She did not think Junaid knew how much she loved being there. She wondered if this place would feel just as special without Junaid. She knew the answer as soon as she had asked it. It made her smile and made her feel funny inside. She knew she would never come here without him; she knew that would make her so very sad.

She wondered why she felt that way.

As the sun crossed the western edge of the rim of trees above them, Junaid sat up; it was time to start the walk back. He looked at Nyla as she lay on her back with her eyes closed, hands on her belly and her chest gently rising and falling as she breathed peacefully. He was glad he had brought her here, but he also knew that it would be very difficult for him to come here again alone, without her. This place, his private hideout, had somehow changed just as he had changed. It was not going to be the same ever again. He looked about him and the very thought of coming back here without Nyla made him sad beyond imagination. His special place had become even more special but only if she was here with him. She had somehow taken this place away from Junaid and made it Junaid and Nyla's place instead; it was no longer his place, it was theirs.

She felt his eyes upon her and opened her eyes just as he looked away. This was the same boy she had known for almost three years now, but somehow he was different. At school he was shy, quiet, and somewhat uncomfortable among their class-mates. Here she could sense a confidence in him that she found attractive. There was a strength about him that was new to her and a gentleness that she had always known; these two qualities together gave her comfort and were reassuring to her maturing mind.

He stood up and looked down at her with a smile. "We should start heading for home now," he said, giving her his right hand and helping her get up to stand next to him.

"OK," she said, smiling back at him and brushing her hair with her fingers, tilting her head forward and to the side. Junaid picked up the basket and they started to climb off the flat rock toward the sheesham tree at the head of the narrow path that had brought them to the pool.

As they reached the giant tree, Junaid realized that he could not feel his slingshot in its usual place in his right back pocket. They both looked back at the rock they had been sitting on and not finding the slingshot on the rock Junaid thought he must have dropped it when climbing the mulberry tree on the other side of the pool. Asking Nyla to stay where they stood, he scrambled down loose shale and stones to the narrow channel on the exit side of the pool and jumped across to the other side. Within a few minutes he found the slingshot under the tree partly covered with some leaves and having retrieved it he looked back toward Nyla and waved, smiling happily. He made his way back to the channel and as he was about to leap across to the other side, he looked down and saw the pug marks of a large cat superimposed upon his own footprints in the soft wet ground at the edge of the water. He froze where he was and looked at Nyla as she stood where he had left her under the tree.

He had seen the rare Margalla leopard only twice before and only when he had hiked several miles up the hill. He had never seen it this far down and certainly not during this time of the year. Junaid could tell that the leopard had crossed over to Nyla's side of the pool after he himself had gone the other way in search of his slingshot. He knew that leopards fed on the rhesus monkeys that abounded in these hills and did not attack humans unless they felt threatened or were forced by extreme hunger. He could not see or hear anything of the leopard but that the cat was near at hand was beyond doubt. He wanted to warn Nyla but shouting and screaming across the twenty yards was ill advised as the noise and the possible panicky reaction from Nyla could trigger a response from the cat.

Standing on his side of the pool, Junaid scanned the opposite side from the edge of the pool to the rocks and beyond to the trees and where Nyla now stood for any movement or sign of the leopard. Having seen Junaid come to a sudden halt and freeze had confused Nyla, and she had stopped waving. Junaid put his right index finger in front of his lips to tell Nyla to stay quiet just as she called out to him. In that same instant Junaid heard an angry growl from his left and Nyla's right, about fifteen yards from each. It was Nyla's turn to freeze as she looked to her right and saw a big spotted cat, partly hidden within the branches of a large fallen tree.

Junaid saw the big male leopard as it crouched low, belly to the ground, gaze locked on Nyla and its hind legs coiled underneath it, ready to launch. He could see the hindquarters and the head and part of the chest of the cat, its midsection hidden behind a thick branch. Junaid was too far to get to Nyla in time. He would have to jump over the stream and then climb up the steep rocky side to get in between her and the leopard. Staying quiet was no longer of any use, and he shouted telling Nyla to not move an inch and to not look anywhere but straight at the cat's eyes. He needed to distract the leopard from its laser like focus on Nyla, and there was only one thing he could do besides shouting. In a smooth quick motion, he reached in and took out a large marble from his jacket's right pocket. Without looking away from the leopard, he loaded the heavy marble in the leather pouch of his slingshot and brought it up to aim at the leopard fifteen yards away. This movement was detected by Nyla, and she looked away from the leopard toward Junaid just as he let loose the shot. As if in slow motion and with his senses heightened, the boy saw the missile leave and go straight and strike true, on the leopard's neck. More from surprise than injury, the leopard sprang straight up, striking at an invisible enemy with his right paw. Growling savagely the cat came down on all four legs just as another stinging marble caught it on the right shoulder. Confused and having lost its focus, the leopard performed an acrobatic somersault, landed behind the fallen tree and disappeared in the thick bushes with a smooth and lightning fast movement.

As if awakened from a dream and back into reality, Junaid jumped across the pool, over the rocks, climbed up the embankment and to Nyla's side as swiftly as he could. Nyla stood against the sheesham tree, pale and trembling as he rushed to her. She was just a young girl who had never seen a leopard much less be within a few yards from one that seemed intent on getting much closer. She had seen the glaring amber eyes, the long fangs, and heard the fearsome growls at very close range only seconds ago, and while she had been as brave as any human could under the circumstances, now suddenly her mind and body felt numb and weak.

Her unblinking eyes were wide open with fright as he came forward to hold her. They hugged each other tightly until she stopped trembling.

Junaid heard the rhesus monkeys scolding the leopard a hundred yards away up the hill, and he knew the cat had left and that they were safe now. It was very unusual to have come across a leopard this far down the hills and this early in winter. Perhaps it had been following the monkeys or perhaps it was colder than usual this year; nevertheless, Junaid was not coming back into the woods even this far until well into summer next year. These thoughts and a feeling of guilt assailed him as he led Nyla back, holding her left hand in his right and clutching her basket tightly in his left hand.

As they walked briskly through some tall dry grass, a large partridge took to the air with loud whistling wings, from almost under their feet, first startling them with fear and then making them laugh out with relief. Thereafter they were much more at ease, and Nyla started enjoying the hike back home again.

As they got close to home and the fright the leopard had given them began to fade away, they talked of the wonderful time they had and what they had seen together. Nyla told Junaid how much fun she had and that she wished they could go back to the pool one day. He said they could safely go next summer but that they should avoid going too far into the woods during the winter months.

Nyla seemed to remember something and stopped as they left the woods and stood on the track that would take them the last few hundred yards to Junaid's home. She remembered seeing Junaid standing on the other side of the pool motion-less, arms holding the slingshot steady, head tilted slightly as he aimed, and fired twice in the blink of an eye, striking each time and making the cat go away. She remembered how he had reached her within seconds of making the cat run away, but she could now see how that would not have been quick enough had he not used his slingshot instead. She was amazed at how he acted so grown up and brave and how he had made her feel safe.

"Junaid, I saw what you did back there with your sling-shot!" she said with wonder.

Junaid looked down for a moment and then swallowing, he again looked into her unquestioning eyes. "I am sorry I took you so far into the woods. I am sorry the leopard got so close to you. I did not think that would ever happen."

"Stop! I had a wonderful time today, especially at the pool! I know you would not have taken me if you knew this could have happened. I would love to go back with you when you think it is safe. If you don't take me back, I will be really mad at you! OK?" she said with a pout that assuaged Junaid's feelings and lessened his self-reproach.

"OK, if you really want me to," he said.

"I do. And what were you shooting at the leopard with your slingshot? I saw you take it out of your jacket pocket," she asked with her big eyes open wide.

"Oh, just these," he said, taking out a fistful of glass marbles of different sizes and colors for her to see.

"Wow!" she exclaimed, looking at his open hand with the pretty marbles shining brightly.

He picked one with a pink flower design inside it and held it out for her. "Here, I want you to have this one," he said.

She took the marble and put it in the palm of her left hand. "Thanks!" she said as she closed her fist and put her hand in the pocket of her jacket, still holding the marble in her hand, as they started walking back home.

The sun was still an hour from setting when Junaid walked Nyla to her home safely, handing her basket back to her and thanking her for bringing the lunch. He waited in front of her home until her mother opened the door, and she turned to wave at him.

He felt relieved as he walked back home after dropping Nyla off. He was upset at himself for not thinking about the danger he had exposed Nyla to in his excitement to show her what he loved so much about the woods. He knew he had to be more careful when she was alone with him. He was glad that she was safe. He was thankful that she was not hurt and he refused to think what he would have done or how he would have felt had she been harmed in anyway. The thought was too painful to even entertain.

That night he was a bit quiet at dinner. That night he prayed a little longer than usual; a prayer of thanks and gratitude. Exhausted after a full day, Junaid fell asleep quickly and dreamed of a blue sky, rimmed by tall pine trees and a warm hand holding his.

Nyla lay on the bed on her side with her eyes closed as she thought about the day, the birds on the Mulberry tree, the fish in the streams, the pool, and how it must look now in the dark of the night even though there was no one there to see it. Her eyes suddenly opened wide as she remembered the essay on nature that Junaid had written over two years ago and that she had read after their teacher had posted all the essays on the classroom wall. Nyla had liked the simple clear sentences that seemed to speak to her and she had told Junaid this. At the end of the school year, he had given her his essay as a little parting gift. She got out of her bed, went to her desk, and found the folded page. She remembered and once again read the few lines and saw once again the big red circled letter *C* that Miss Zarina had written on the top of the page. She knew now why the simple words of that essay held so much meaning to Junaid and now to her as well.

*"Nature is a blackberry tree with a cardinal on one branch and a blue jay on another. Nature is a snapping turtle waiting for the minnow to pass close enough. It is also a squirrel hiding dry seeds in an empty woodpecker nest for winter. Nature is autumn when the leaves turn golden and red and make a carpet for the woods. Nature is all of this and many other beautiful things that happen even when no one is looking."*

She lay down again and closed her eyes. A smile was on her lips as she fell asleep soon after, holding a pink marble in the palm of her right hand.

# Chapter 8

It was two weeks before the finals, and Junaid was feeling excited. He had been focused on his studies as he never had in the past and felt that he was ready. Nyla was getting ready for the finals as well and was devoting extra time to her studies. There had been an undeclared competition between her and Parveen since the beginning of the school year, but that battle had lately been joined by her friend Junaid and she was happy for that.

Miss Zarina had seen the change in his schoolwork and Junaid had over the past several months become one of her most responsible students. She had spoken with his parents the previous week during the parent-teacher conference day and had learned how his study habits had changed for the better. She was proud of his work and felt that he would do well from this point onward.

She was surprised therefore when he did not show up for school on Monday and genuinely worried when he was once again absent on Tuesday. She called and spoke with Mrs. Kafrooni during the lunch hour on Tuesday and learned why he had been absent and would most likely be absent for several days, possibly even weeks, and would therefore miss the final exams. He had acquired malaria and was quite ill in bed since Sunday morning.

Zarina Begum was saddened by the news and announced it to the class. Nyla was shocked to hear of Junaid's illness and wanted to go see him. She went home after school and told her mother about Junaid and asked her to call Junaid's mother to see if she could visit him that evening. Mrs. Ibrahim was informed by Mrs. Kafrooni that Junaid was spiking fevers up to and sometimes beyond 105 degrees Fahrenheit and that unfortunately he was not able to see anyone for at least a few days, she would however call and let her know when Nyla could come visit him. Nyla was greatly disappointed and was now even more worried about Junaid's illness. She just wanted to see him if only for a few minutes but understood why that would not be possible at this time.

The next day she was quiet at school and at home later. It was difficult for her to focus on anything but the thought of Junaid suffering in bed since Sunday, four days ago. Nyla knew Junaid loved carrot cake, and she helped her mother make it for him and then brought it to his home. She knocked and Mrs. Kafrooni opened the door, surprised to see her standing with a dish in her hands. Before she could say anything, Nyla said, "I know I cannot see Junaid, but I just brought him this carrot cake in case he feels like eating." And she handed the dish to his mother, stepping back to leave, saying, "Please tell him to get better quickly and that I miss him." Mrs. Kafrooni, seeing the drooping shoulders, the sad eyes and hearing the flat tone of her voice, came forward and gave Nyla a hug and holding her hand she brought her inside. She had Nyla sit while she went upstairs into Junaid's bedroom. Coming back in a few minutes she told Nyla to come with her, and they both entered Junaid's room together.

Junaid was lying on his back with a sheet covering his body. The window against which his desk stood was open and trees were visible in the fading light of the day. There were Junaid's books piled up on top of the desk but it was quite clear that he had not opened these in a few days. As he lay motionless on the bed, only his face and arms were visible, and Nyla was dismayed to see how pale and weak he looked. He struggled to turn his head to the door and managed the faintest of smiles on his dry lips. Nyla came toward him and stood next to his bed, looking at his yellowed eyes she put-on an encouraging smile as he beheld her worried expression. She glanced back toward his mother who smiled and nodded her head encouraging her to sit down on the bed. Nyla sat down facing him and reached out to hold his left hand. She was startled to see how warm, almost hot his hand was and looked up quickly to see him staring at her face. He tried to open his mouth and say something but she put her finger to his lips and told him, "Shhhh…Just rest, Junaid. Don't worry, you will be well soon. Don't worry about anything, especially school."

Mrs. Kafrooni brought carrot cake for each of them and set the plates on the bed next to Nyla. "He just does not want to eat anything, Nyla. Has not had anything since a few sips of soup this morning," she said. Nyla took a little bit of the carrot cake on a spoon and held it near his mouth, asking him to eat. He pleaded with his eyes that he could not and refused to open his mouth. "Junaid, if you do not eat this, I will never eat an apple from your hand again, ever!" She threatened, feigning anger. "I mean it!" she added. Junaid stared at her face and then closed his eyes as a hot tear dropped to his left ear. She saw his lips tremble as she placed the tip of the spoon in his partly open mouth. With much effort, he started to chew the cake and then swallowed it as if he was swallowing dry sand. He managed to finish half of the small amount of cake on his plate and then could no longer continue. Nyla did not push him for any more. "Good job!" she said and squeezed his hand.

Mrs. Kafrooni was surprised and delighted to see her son eat. As treatment for malaria, he had been forced to eat quinine pills every few hours, and everything he ate or drank tasted horribly bitter to him. She told Nyla about this and saw her cringe.

Nyla left soon thereafter to let Junaid rest, promising to return to visit him again.

Her mother, Mrs. Ibrahim, saw her walk into the house sluggishly; her puffy eyes and cheerless expression told her what Nyla could not. She came forward and held her daughter against her chest, gently rubbing her back as Nyla started sobbing, tears wetting her tightly closed eyelids.

"He is... very sick... Ammi," Nyla managed to say, her chin trembling and swollen lips desperately trying to keep from crying openly.

"Yes, my daughter, he is, but he will be better soon, you watch...shhhh...shhhh."

Then thinking of something, Nyla suddenly pulled away and looked into her mother's eyes. "But he ate Ammi, he ate from my hand! The carrot cake, he ate some!" said Nyla excitedly, tears wetting her flushed cheeks, as her eyes searched her mother's face.

"I know, Junaid's mother called me, she told me how you fed him, how no one else could make him eat," said her mother, looking at her daughter with pride, trying to hold back her own tears.

"If he eats he will get better! Right mom? Right Ammi? He just has to eat! I miss him so much, I just want him to get better quickly."

"Yes, he will daughter, he just has to eat," replied her mother, trying to comfort her.

Nyla sniffled, wiping her tears with the fingers of both her hands; she then smiled and nodded her head, reassuring herself and feeling confident.

From that day forth Nyla came to see Junaid after school every day and had him eat something from her hand. Mrs. Kafrooni was happy to see her son eat and was deeply affected by Nyla's caring manner and the affectionate way the two interacted with each other. Every day Junaid would wait patiently for the highlight of his day, for Nyla to come and sit with him for a few minutes on her way back from school. On some days when she was late it was because she would go home and bring him some tasty dish or treat that she then shared with him as her dinner.

He had acquired the illness once before a few years ago and had suffered from it horribly. After that initial episode, he had tried to learn about malaria by reading and from his parents. He had learned how the bite of a particular type of mosquito was responsible for the disease that made hundreds of thousands of people around the world sick every year and how thousands of those who had no medication died each year. The only treatment for it in those days was the bitter quinine pill, and he sometimes wondered if the treatment was worse than the illness itself. Dr. Marwani had come to see him at home on Monday and prescribed the treatment, encouraging him to eat as much as he could to keep his strength up.

Within a few days, the illness had sapped his strength and the medicine had taken away his appetite. He lost the ability to walk or even sit up by himself in the bed. His mother would bring him his favorite dishes for breakfast and lunch and dinner, but he could not bring himself to eat. He would drink some water and eat a few grapes during the day and then wait patiently for Nyla to come and sit with him. He had learned that the illness did not go from one person to another and so was not worried about Nyla getting ill from being near him.

Today was Friday, and Nyla took a little longer than usual to come and see him. She had brought his favorite dish of all, chicken karhai with some chapatis that she had made herself with a little help from her mother. She now sat next to Junaid, feeding him the warm aromatic dish with her own hands as usual. He ate an entire chapati with some chicken and the effort was enough to cause him to perspire. The food that he usually found delicious was today barely palatable but his motivation was not the food itself but the girl who had cooked and was now feeding it to him. He thanked her with his eyes after every morsel she fed him. Nyla gave him strength and motivation to get better that the food and medicine alone could not.

A week had passed and while he could still not sit up by himself, he was now able to say a few words before losing his breath.

"Thanks for coming every day," he almost whispered through dry lips.

"It makes me feel good to come, so thanks for letting me come see you even though you must feel so tired," she replied with a warm smile as she sat next to him, holding his left hand in her two hands.

"I feel better when you come. Are you ready for the final exams?" he asked.

"I think so. You can always take the makeup exam if you are not much better soon, so don't worry," she encouraged him.

Junaid nodded as he turned his head to look at his books.

"Do you want me to put your books on the bed?" Nyla asked with her eyebrows raised.

"Yes. Maybe I will try to study later," he said softly.

"OK, I will, but don't tire yourself too much. You need to get better first," she said as she put some of his books on the bed within his reach and promising to visit again tomorrow she left soon afterwards.

Junaid lay on his back with his eyes closed for several minutes gathering strength before he could reach for a book and pulled it close to himself. He then struggled to move the book onto his belly and propped the book against his drawn up legs. Opening to the first page he started to read slowly and deliberately. Before long his eyes got heavy and he fell asleep peacefully.

For the first time since he had taken ill, he slept well and woke up in the morning feeling a bit more energetic. His mother brought him his breakfast and was pleasantly surprised to find him sitting on the bed reading. She was even more encouraged to see him eat a slice of buttered toast and drink half a glass of milk. Junaid read purposefully until lunchtime and continued after he had eaten some rice and kababs. He realized that time passed more tolerably when he was studying and that he was beginning to regain his energy and appetite.

Nyla came to see him Saturday and then again Sunday afternoon and each day she was delighted to see him doing better. On Sunday he was able to sit at his desk for over an hour and as he gazed out the window he saw a cardinal in the oak tree singing lustily. He had the hope that by Friday he would have the energy to go to school and not have to miss the finals. That would require him to not only continue to recover from his illness but also to review enough to be able to pass the exam. He studied day and night to the extent that he was physically able to.

Nyla, seeing that he was feeling better, instead of coming and staying for an hour, during most of which she had been patiently feeding him, began instead to visit him for just a few minutes on the way home from school in order to give him more time to review for the exam.

On Thursday she came to see him for the last time and found him in the living room waiting for her. She placed her backpack down, and they sat having a snack and talked for a while before she was ready to leave. Junaid had studied all he could and wanted to relax before the big day tomorrow. He also wanted to walk Nyla to her home despite her objections. It was a slow and tiresome walk, but Junaid did it with great pleasure and arrived back home feeling exhausted but in high spirits. Later that night when Nyla opened her backpack she was pleased and surprised to find a big red apple and a little note from Junaid saying, "Thank You." She was happy to have been able to help and encourage him when he was ill and happier still that he was feeling better now.

Miss Zarina sat at her desk the next morning waiting for the students to take their seats. She saw the empty seat behind Nyla as she started distributing the exam notebooks to the class and wondered when Junaid would be able to take the makeup test for the finals. As she handed Nyla her notebook, she looked up to see Junaid slowly walking toward his seat. He appeared pale and thin, but his eyes were bright as he took his seat and smiled as she handed him the test. Miss Zarina was amazed and gladdened at Junaid's unexpected return. She now sat watching him take the test with his classmates and wondered how well he was prepared and whether it would have been better for him to have waited for the makeup test instead.

Miss Zarina collected the notebooks back and talked to her students about the year that had come to an end. She told them she was proud to have been their teacher and expected great things from each of her students in the future and that the scores and the rankings will be posted by the middle of the next week. She then wished them a safe and happy summer vacation and the class was dismissed. Junaid was not really interested in the rankings. He was just glad he had been able to take the test and start the summer break with his classmates.

Nyla looked back at Junaid and said, "Thanks, it was delicious!" and they both smiled at each other. Jahal turned around to see as Nyla helped Junaid get out of his seat after the long and tiring test.

As they were walking out of the classroom, Junaid stopped and looked back at Miss Zarina, who beckoned him to come to her. Leaving Nyla at the door, he walked back to his teacher who stood up and came forward to meet him.

"Thank you, Miss," he said.

"You are a good boy, Junaid. Keep up the great work," she replied with a warm smile.

"And, Miss," he added as he was turning to leave, as if he remembered something.

"Yes, Junaid?" she asked.

"Thank you for calling Mom to ask about me when I was ill," he said and walked back to join Nyla at the door.

They both waved at their teacher and walked off into the sunny afternoon.

# Chapter 9

It had almost been a month into the summer vacation. The eleventh grade was history and the final year of high school was just a few months away. Junaid had taken a few short hiking trips into the woods but had not been able to make himself go to what he now considered to be "their" special mountain stream hideout where Nyla had the scare with the leopard a few years ago.

Two years ago Junaid's father had given him a telescope for his birthday, and he would spend hours poring over the sky charts during the day and at night he would try and find the different constellations, planets, and even faraway galaxies. The roof of their house was a flat platform that was safely accessible from stairs on the side of their home, and this was where he spent hours at night with his telescope and sky charts. One of his favorite sights in the sky however did not need the help of a telescope to appreciate. On particularly dark nights and during the right time he was able to look up and see the glorious Milky Way without the aid of a telescope. He had learned that it was our galaxy and was made up of hundreds of billions of stars of which the sun was just one average star. He learned that there were millions of other galaxies that made up the universe and the size and the distances between the stars and the galaxies made him wonder with awe.

On one such dark, warm summer night as he sat on the terraced roof, peering into his telescope looking at the rings of Saturn, he heard voices coming from the direction of the woods. It was nearly midnight, and he was surprised to hear Jahal and Parveen talking loud enough for him to hear them quite clearly. He saw Jahal's big dog, Shaytan, before he saw the two of them coming toward him on the dirt path. As it was pitch-dark they could not see him and continued as if unseen. Jahal had his left arm around Parveen's waist, and he was kissing her on the neck and face every few steps as they both laughed with merriment. As they came alongside his home on the path, Jahal turned his face and sneered. "That's where that wimp Junaid lives. I wish I could catch him in the woods one day with Shaytan," he said, as he spat scornfully on the ground. "You are so strong, Jahal, so much like a man!" said Parveen, moving her hands over his shoulders and arms. "I wish you would too. Even better if that goody-two shoes Nyla would be with him when you do!" They both howled and roared with mirth at the thought and walked on beyond his hearing range.

Junaid watched them walk away and pondered the prospect of meeting with Jahal and his vicious dog in the woods. During the previous year, students took elective classes and Nyla and Junaid were no longer in any of the classes with Jahal and Parveen. It was therefore surprising to Junaid that Jahal should harbor such resentment and ill will toward them. He made a mental note of doing everything to not expose himself and particularly Nyla to any danger. Junaid looked at the ringed planet for a little longer and having lost his appetite for more stargazing he went down to sleep.

The next time he met Nyla he thought about telling her what he had seen and heard that night but then decided not to worry her needlessly and kept it to himself. She had not forgotten about the woods and the lovely natural pool that they had visited during the winter a few years ago. The memory of the encounter with the leopard had also lost its edge in the three intervening years and so she asked him if he was finally going to keep his promise and teach her how to swim. He had been wanting to go swimming himself and thinking that it was highly unlikely for them to run into a leopard during the middle of summer he agreed to take her back into the woods. He knew that leopards stayed high in the Margalla hills and the more remote mountains beyond during the warm summer months. He was a little concerned about what Jahal had said but was not willing to allow that to deprive Nyla and himself of the joy of a hike in the woods, something they had been looking forward to for so long.

Two days later they were both walking into the woods together just as the sun was coming up in the east. Junaid was carrying a heavy walking stick for added protection in addition to his slingshot, and Nyla had her picnic basket in her hand and a small backpack on her back. They walked briskly and were at their favorite spot in just over an hour. To Nyla the place looked even more wondrous than before. Bright yellow dandelions and light purple hyacinths were covering the ground where the water entered and exited the deep pool. Giant Himalayan lilies sprouted out from tall slender stems on the ground beyond the rocks and pink wild roses were sprinkled between the trees. The towering trees made the place feel secluded and safe.

Throwing off his clothes and walking stick on the granite rock they had sat on previously, Junaid canonballed into the deepest part of the pool in his swimming trunks. He stayed submerged for almost two minutes and just when Nyla was getting worried about him, he could no longer hold his breath and splattered out joyfully, gulping air as he caught his breath. Beckoning her to join him he saw her shyly remove her shirt and pants and walk toward the shallow end of the pool in her modest one-peace white bathing suit. Junaid gulped with concealed nervous excitement, pretending not to notice her shapely form and her smooth golden skin.

She stood in ankle deep water with her arms across her chest, as he came toward her and taking her hand took her into knee deep water and made her sit down so that only her face was above the water. Encouraging her to hold her breath and become used to putting her face in the water he was able to get her to control her fear and then as he held her afloat with his arms under her, she practiced thrashing her arms and kicking her legs. Before long the desperate need to breathe and the rigid posture gave way to more relaxed movements, and she began to breathe more easily. By lunch time she was able to swim doggy style from one side of the pool to the other some fifteen feet away and by the time the sun was getting close to the western edge of the tree tops above, she was able to swim the thirty feet length of the pool. At all times Junaid was next to her, guiding and encouraging her. By the time she swam the second length of the pool she was utterly exhausted, and he helped her out and onto the warm flat rock.

They had a little snack of sweet mangoes that Nyla had brought and that Junaid cut with his pocket knife. By the time her swim suit and hair were dry, and she had put on her clothes the sun was no longer visible in the blue tree-ringed opening above them. This was summer however and they had several hours before the sun would set. They started the walk back at a leisurely pace talking and joking happily about the day so far. Junaid was impressed with Nyla's ability to learn to swim so quickly, and she felt that he had been a great teacher.

They were about halfway back to the dirt path and fifty yards from the tree house that Junaid had yet to show Nyla when he heard the dog barking in the distance. At first Junaid ignored the barking, but as it continued to come closer and became more distinct, he was able to distinguish the peculiar hollow honking sound that he had heard before and was therefore able to identify with increasing unease. Shaytan was no more than a hundred yards away, between them and the dirt path, and was closing rapidly. Considering his options given that Nyla was with him, Junaid decided to make a run for the tree house. He took Nyla's backpack and told her to run as fast as she could after him and make for the line of trees on the other side of the flat grass covered ground to their left.

Jahal had sent Shaytan, barking fiercely, after a rabbit which had managed to escape and the dog had then instinctively chased after the running Junaid and Nyla instead.

They were about twenty yards from the tree house when looking back he saw Shaytan entering the open ground they were on. Encouraging Nyla to run to the towering peepul tree from which a rope ladder could be seen dangling, he started to run behind her keeping an eye on the fast gaining dog. Just as they reached the ladder, Junaid looked back and saw Jahal walking toward them at the edge of the open grassy field with Shaytan now a mere fifteen yards away. Jahal was calling Shaytan to come back and was not aware of Junaid and Nyla.

Helping Nyla climb the rope ladder, Junaid himself followed and did so just as the big dog jumped up snapping his jaws inches from his left foot. They climbed to the tree house over fifty-five feet from the ground just about half the way to the top of the tree, and Junaid pulled up the ladder after them as Nyla lay gasping for breath on the wooden floor. The branches and thick covering of leaves made the tree house completely invisible from the ground. They heard Shaytan barking furiously to the point of getting hoarse and then heard Jahal as he shouted at the dog to shut up and stop running after squirrels. Jahal looked up at the peepul tree and without the ladder was completely unaware of the tree house. Not long after they heard Parveen's voice as she joined Jahal under the tree in an effort to calm the dog down.

Eventually Shaytan, tired of barking and now panting with exhaustion, lay down with his head on his front paws next to Jahal and Parveen in the cool shade of the tree. Occasionally, he would look up and whimper but soon lost focus as a particularly adventurous squirrel came down a nearby tree and stood on its hind legs, teasing the dog from not more than five yards away. One stern word from Jahal however and Shaytan put his head down on its paws again.

The tree house had a small window opening on the side opposite the door, and Junaid and Nyla having caught their breath and upon hearing a shriek from Parveen were now able to look down through this window and see the two with their dog directly underneath. Jahal was struggling with the giggling and laughing girl's shirt as she was playfully holding him off. She eventually stopped resisting and lay down on her back with her arms around his neck as she faced up looking at the towering tree above. Seeing this, Nyla quickly moved away from the window and this movement caught Parveen's eye who then clearly saw Junaid's head move and disappear far above her between the leaves and branches of the peepul tree. Shocked, she uttered a cry of surprise and pushed Jahal off her chest. Jahal was bewildered upon seeing Parveen push him off abruptly and start running away from him. He ran and caught up with her just as she reached the grassy clearing beyond the tree line some twenty yards away. She told him what she had seen and was very upset about having been caught in a most compromising position by Nyla and Junaid. She was shaking with anguish, and he was not having any success calming her down.

She eventually stopped quavering as Jahal told her that it was Junaid and Nyla's word against theirs, and no one would believe it anyway. Jahal held her arm and dragged her back to the tree again. "We know you two are hiding up there, Junaid! And you better not say anything about us or we can say the same about you. I don't think Nyla would like that!" he shouted, looking up, trying to find them.

Nyla and Junaid were shocked by the turn of events and by what they had seen. They had not had the time to think about what if anything they were to tell anyone. Now hearing Jahal's words, they looked at each other and knew they had no intention or desire to tell anyone anything whether or not Jahal had made his threat. Their presence was known however, and there was no point in staying quiet now. Junaid came out of the door of the tree house onto a large branch from where he could look down and be seen from below. "We have nothing to say to anyone. Go away and leave us alone," he said loudly, looking down and holding a branch with his right hand, as Nyla stood rigidly at the door, nervously looking down at a scowling Jahal and a seemingly defiant Parveen who held her arms tightly around her chest, clutching her shirt with both her hands.

Shaytan now seeing Junaid started barking and running around the tree once again. The four stood for a few moments staring at each other and then Jahal and Parveen turned around and started walking away, calling Shaytan after them.

Junaid had no intention of exposing Nyla to any risk from Shaytan, and he waited until he could see the dog and its owner walk away well to the dirt path on the way back home. He then threw down the rope ladder, and they both came down off the tree. It was only now they realized that Nyla in all the rush and excitement of climbing up the ladder had still held on to her basket. With Junaid alongside her, she had never really panicked and had her wits about her even when they were running and then clambering up the ladder. She now reflected on whether it would have been better if she had actually dropped the basket on the way up and allowed themselves to be discovered and so kept Jahal and Parveen from acting as if they were alone and unobserved. Junaid's stick that he had carried all day was recovered in some tall grass a few feet from the tree.

As they walked back toward home, the sun was getting low in the western sky and the shadows of the tall trees were getting longer. They were both quiet during the walk back and each had unsettling thoughts about the events of the latter part of the day.

Nyla was feeling somewhat guilty for having seen what she had seen and embarrassed that Junaid had seen the same. Lately, she had felt confused about how she really felt about Junaid and the obvious physical intimacy between Parveen and Jahal compounded the turbulence and commotion within her. She knew she would rather be with Junaid than with anyone else but did not know what that meant with certainty. She felt special in a certain way when she was with him that was new to her. She had become more aware of the fact that she was now a young woman and that Junaid, her friend, was a young man who may justifiably harbor feelings only natural to his age that any young man may possess. While she was aware that being a woman and close to Junaid meant that she would likely be the object of those natural feelings, she also felt that she was safe with him. She did not want to change her relationship with Junaid in any adverse way due to what they had seen and therefore decided to try and not act differently around him.

Junaid cared deeply for Nyla and felt happier in her presence. He had felt an attraction toward her as a friend and lately as a young man and that physical attraction had become even more evident to him earlier that very day when he was helping her learn how to swim. He had however not disclosed that affection to Nyla beyond showing that he was her friend who happened to be of the opposite sex. What he saw happen under the tree with Nyla by his side had affected and perplexed him. He felt embarrassed just like Nyla but more than that he felt an agitation and a stirring that confused and frustrated him. Having never come across this in his life and only now experiencing the difficult transition that all young people must make as they arrive at the junction where they become young adults, he did not know with confidence where the exact boundaries lay, which must not be crossed and those that needed to be crossed or indeed that he was expected to cross. He had seen Jahal cross certain boundaries of physical intimacy with Parveen and had seen how she had not only allowed him the liberty of this but had clearly enjoyed it as well. Furthermore, Junaid knew that Nyla had seen another young man act in a physically intimate way with who was evidently his girlfriend. As he struggled with these thoughts, Junaid felt some solace from the realization that Nyla was not his girlfriend in the common sense of the word and therefore he must maintain their usual and comfortable relationship of being friends.

Therefore both felt tolerably relieved in their own mind as to the role the other played in their life. Whether this was a convenient way to help deal with difficult questions that neither was able to answer at this time was yet to be seen.

They arrived at Junaid's home just as the sun was about to set. He walked Nyla to her home and as she unlocked the door to go inside he took a step backward and then remembered to ask what he had almost forgotten.

"Nyla, would you like to come to my place tomorrow night around 10:00 p.m.?" he asked hesitatingly.

"At ten at night?" she said, looking quizzically at him.

"Yes, I want to show you something. If you don't have any other plans that is. It will only take a few minutes and you can leave if you do not like it," he said, looking at her hopefully.

Nyla thought about this invitation from Junaid to visit her late at night at his home and her hesitation was sensed by him. He felt that she was not comfortable coming to see him that late and so he backed away saying they could think about it for another time.

Nyla looked at Junaid as he turned to leave and she all of a sudden realized that had he asked her this very question yesterday, she would not have hesitated for a second and would have said yes. She knew she had allowed what they had seen earlier that day to affect the way she treated him.

"Wait, Junaid! I would love to come and see what you have to show me!" she said with a smile. "I will be there tomorrow night at ten," she added.

"Great!" He smiled back and waved, leaving Nyla wondering about tomorrow.

As he slept that night, Junaid was at ease. He was glad he had found the courage to ask Nyla to come see him late at night despite the hesitation he had felt. He was happy that Nyla, even though at first she had acted uncertain, had finally accepted his invitation; that meant a great deal to him. It meant that she was comfortable with him.

Nyla was exhausted after a physically and emotionally draining day. She showered, ate, and fell asleep quickly, comfortable in the knowledge that she had not allowed her friendship with Junaid to be compromised due to something neither one of them had any control over. She was nevertheless curious as to the reason Junaid would invite her to his home so late at night, and she would have to let her mother know of her whereabouts.

The next day Nyla told her mother over lunch that she was going to meet Junaid at his home at 10:00 p.m. later that night and would be back by midnight if not sooner. Mrs. Ibrahim knew Junaid and his parents well and had little problem with this although she wondered why they had to meet that late. Most of the day she read and relaxed and after dinner she changed into her denim jeans and a cotton T-shirt. The walk to Junaid's home was only five minutes, but she decided to ride her bike as she did not want to walk so late at night.

As she got out and was about to get on her bike, she saw Junaid outside on his bike waiting for her. She smiled and knew that he had come to accompany her to his place as he did not want her coming alone at this time of the night.

They rode beside each other and talked about what they had done that day. It was a cloudless night and while the day had been quite warm, it was now almost chilly. As they arrived at his home, Junaid stood his bike on the side of the house and instead of inviting her inside, asked Nyla to follow him up the stairs to the terraced roof. She was surprised at this as she had thought they would go inside the house and not be alone on the roof. Without showing any outward concern however, she followed Junaid to the terrace that was bordered by a metal fence on all sides. There was no moon that night and it was very dark. Before her eyes could get used to the dark, Junaid took her hand and guided her forward and had her sit down on a reclining chair in the middle of the platform.

He then told her to close her eyes and recline back and relax.

"Junaid, what are you doing?" she asked with a little apprehension in her voice.

"Nothing, just sit back and close your eyes, Nyla. And don't open them until I ask you to," he replied.

Despite feeling a bit uneasy, Nyla closed her eyes and sat back on the chair. She heard Junaid walk away and then walk back moments later. She heard him fumbling with something and then he asked her to open her eyes.

"I want you to look through this eyepiece, Nyla," he said with some excitement.

The fear that was inching into Nyla's heart was gone as she saw a telescope in front of her and an eyepiece within inches of her face.

And as she looked through the eyepiece, she saw what she would never forget as long as she lived.

In the darkness of the sky she saw an utterly indescribable light show. She was immobilized as she tried to take it all in and was frozen at the eyepiece, her mouth open with wonder. She finally looked away and saw Junaid standing next to her with a pleased and expectant look on his face.

"I love it! What is this? Is it the Milky Way? It is beautiful!" she exclaimed, her eyes wide open with amazement.

"Yes, it is! So you like it then?" he asked, knowing the answer already.

"Yes I do like it, very much!" she said, as she bent her head down once again to look through the telescope.

"So all those tiny dots are stars! So many and so beautiful! Why are so many of the stars gathered mainly in the middle?" she asked.

Junaid beamed as he answered, "Yes those are all stars just like our sun and there are several billion of them in our galaxy, the Milky Way. The Milky way is shaped like a disc with several arms or spirals and our sun and solar system are near the outer third of one of those spirals. So when we look toward the center of the galaxy we are looking at most of the stars that make up the Milky Way."

"Ours is not the only galaxy, right?" she asked again, getting more interested every second.

"Right, there are millions of other galaxies in the universe," he replied, happy to see that she was intrigued.

"So our solar system is just a speck in just one of these galaxies?" she asked, captivated by what she was seeing.

"Yes, just a dot in the billions of dots in this galaxy, which is just a speck among the millions of other galaxies," said Junaid slowly, looking at the sky with wonder.

Nyla looked up and could see untold numbers of stars in the dark moonless sky. She knew now why he had asked her to come to see him this late at night, to let her see the greatest show on earth with him. She felt warm and wonderful in the knowledge that Junaid was a genuine, caring, and thoughtful young man and that he had proved and earned her trust in him, once again. She was just a bit ashamed for having allowed a tiny bit of doubt in her mind about him. As she thought of this, she turned toward him and hugged him tightly. "Never change, Junaid. I love you!" she said and then a moment later she whispered, "You are the best friend ever."

Junaid was thrilled to see how much Nyla seemed to have enjoyed what he had hoped would interest her. He knew they would be talking and learning of the heavens together in the future. Even more than all this however he was glad to see that they were both comfortable and at ease with each other as friends.

When therefore Nyla hugged him tightly against her warm and soft body, he felt relief rather than any sensual feeling go through him. It was when she said, "I love you!" that his eyes opened wide and his heart skipped a beat or two, but before he could say anything in response, she had told him that he was her best friend ever. He closed his eyes and clenched his teeth just for a moment, imperceptibly shaking his head, scolding himself for feeling jubilant for even a second and for almost responding to her before she had said all she was going to say in the next breath. He knew he would have made a big blunder if he had said what he felt inside. He knew now that as far as she was concerned he was no more than a friend, a good one, and one that she trusted. He must not destroy her trust in this friendship. He must never betray his true feelings and deep affection for her. He must stay for her as she liked, even loved him to be, her best friend ever, and nothing more.

The turmoil she had caused in his soul by saying those few words was unknown to her as she finally pulled away from him, holding his hands in hers and smiling at his suddenly somewhat somber face.

"Do you want to show me more through your telescope?" she asked brightly.

"Well, the moon is not up yet tonight. It is getting a little late, and I want you home by eleven. Maybe we can look at the moon another night," he replied with a slightly flat tone that surprised Nyla a little but she knew it would be best for her to be home before it was too late.

"OK, sounds good," she said.

They came down the stairs and rode their bikes back to her home. Nyla thanked him for asking her over to show her the Milky Way.

"What are friends for, thanks for coming, and I am glad it was not a waste of your time," he said.

"Of course it was not a waste of my time! How can you even think that?" she said, poking his ribs with her forefinger, trying to make him smile. "And why are you so serious all of a sudden, mister?" she added when he refused to smile.

"Oh nothing, just a bit tired I guess," he lied. Angry at himself for lying and even angrier for letting Nyla see that he was not his usual self.

She moved forward to hug him good night, but Junaid backed away as if he had not seen her and got on his bike.

"Good night, Nyla," he said, looking back toward her.

"Good night, Junaid," she replied and walked into her home without looking back as he paddled off hastily.

Junaid felt he could not have allowed Nyla to hug him again, tonight. It was too difficult for him to get so close to her knowing that he was so far from her. It would have made him feel like a hypocrite for the second time that night, and he was not going to do that to Nyla or to himself.

Nyla now felt that something was not right with the way Junaid was acting. She thought about the night and pinpointed almost the exact moment when his behavior had changed. He was his usual cheerful self until the moment she had hugged him after seeing the Milky Way. Thinking back now, she remembered what she had said to him, "I love you!" and recalled how his body had tensed for just a fleeting second. From that point he had become a bit aloof and had brought her back to her home shortly thereafter. She had ignored it at the time but when he had avoided her hugging him goodbye she was forced to think back.

Nyla assumed from his behavior that he was offended by what he must have thought was her declaration of love for him. She concluded that he must not have similar feelings for her or he would have been happy to hear her say those words. However, she knew there was truth in those words she had uttered, but there was also the fear of a lack of reciprocation from his side and so within a moment of having said that "I love you" and before giving him a chance to respond, she had added, "You are the best friend ever." She knew she had been overly cautious if not outright cowardly in what amounted to saying those precious words and then taking them back before she could be hurt by the possibility that he may not voice similar sentiments toward her. She had decided, in the passing of a moment, that she would be more comfortable at that time to just remain in the gray zone where she could sense and explore her way around his feelings before making a declaration of this magnitude.

She was an astute young lady who could now conceive that Junaid could be acting in this cold manner for two different and indeed completely opposing reasons. Her saying those three words of love could be distressing to him if he had no such feelings toward her and that would explain his desire to make short of their time together that night and his avoidance of her hugging him.

On the other hand there was a small chance that he had actually loved to hear her say those three words. There was a chance that when she had felt his body tense slightly upon hearing those words that it was not because he was alarmed or disturbed but because he was elated and had not expected to hear what he had heard at that moment. His aloofness and cold behavior then could be explained not by her having said, "I love you," but rather by her having added, "You are the best friend ever." If that was the case, she had hurt him grievously.

Here was an enigma she was not at the moment able to solve, and it was a consequence of her split second decision earlier that night to avoid confronting the possibility of a rejection of her declaration of love.

This was a most uncomfortable position for her to be in, and she did not know how she could know what was in Junaid's heart now that she had denied him the chance to tell her. Had she known that not knowing causes more misery than knowing the truth, whatever it may be, she would have not said a word after saying, I love you. She thought of all this and tossed and turned in her bed as sleep eluded her.

There was a different tempest robbing Junaid of his sleep that night and for many nights to come. He had convinced himself the day before that he was able to keep his liking for Nyla to just that and be her friend as he always had been. That conviction had given him the will to ask Nyla to come see him late at night to show her the heavens through his telescope. That will and conviction had gone out the door very quickly when Nyla had hugged him tightly and uttered those magical words. Instantly upon hearing those powerful words that all love thrives on, his resolve had broken and he was on the verge of uttering the same words for Nyla to hear when she had taken him from the top of the world and thrust him down lower than he had ever felt before.

Whereas he had convinced himself that while he liked her very much that he was able to and was comfortable with maintaining that affection at the level of friendship, she had in an instant made it clear to him that he in fact loved her and was not satisfied with nor able to hide that love. What's more, in the very next moment she had told him that she on the other hand did not love him; he was her best friend however. That was a consolation prize Junaid did not need or care for. This double dose of cruel awareness was too much for his young mind to handle, and he was unable to maintain his usual composure. The only way he could deal with the pain at that moment was to try and get away from the source of that agonizing distress. He had therefore done exactly that. It would have been impossible for him to have hugged Nyla at that time as it was all he could do to get away from her as soon as possible. Not because he hated her, but precisely because the opposite was true and he loved her.

Neither Nyla nor Junaid knew how they would feel or act the next time they met. For the first time in their young lives they hated the thought of seeing each other. For the first time in their lives each knew that they were deeply in love with the other.

# Chapter 10

The last two months of the summer vacation were agonizingly slow for Junaid. While ordinarily he would have gone hiking, fishing, biking, and kite flying at every opportunity, he instead had just mostly stayed up late reading and preparing for the next school year. He would sometimes watch TV when he could not read anymore. Reading, he had discovered was the best way to keep his thoughts diverted and lessened his misery to some extent. He had not done much star gazing since that night with Nyla almost two months ago.

Junaid's parents were a little concerned about this change in him. Instead of being outgoing and cheerful, he had kept to himself in his room for most of the past several weeks. They were also somewhat puzzled by the fact that his good friend Nyla had not been by to visit and when they had inquired about her he had just shrugged his shoulders. Unable to account for it, they had finally blamed this change in him to just being a teenager. They were nevertheless glad that he was not doing anything to harm himself or someone else and was quite focused on studying to prepare for the final year in high school.

While initially after that fateful night, she had not wanted to see him, Nyla had wondered about Junaid every day and not hearing from him, she had passed by his home on her bike to see if she could run into him. She had also gone walking a short way into the woods over the dirt path hoping to find him on one of his hiking trips. On two occasions, on cloudless nights, she had even gone to see if she could catch him stargazing but he seemed to have disappeared from the face of the earth.

With just two weeks before school and on the first day of enrollment she had gone to the school and chosen her classes; of the electives she picked, one was astronomy.

The first day of the last year of school was here. But while Nyla went to school hoping to run into Junaid in one of her classes, he himself was petrified by the very thought of seeing her. Junaid's first class was calculus, a subject he loved. The entrance was through a door at the back of the class, and he saw Nyla sitting facing forward near the middle of the classroom. There was one empty seat next to her and two up near the front of the class in the second row. Junaid took one of the two seats and opened his book on the desk in front of him as the last of the students trickled in to occupy the remaining seats.

Nyla saw him walk by her row to the front of the classroom to sit away from her even though there was an open seat next to her. He looked a bit thin but other than the fact that he seemed not to have shaved in a week or so, he appeared well.

There were some new students that had enrolled, and they were particularly lost this first day of school. One such student was Jameela, a new girl from out of town, and she took the last seat next to Junaid.

Junaid was engrossed in the book and did not notice who was sitting next to him until Jameela touched his right elbow. "What are you reading?" she asked.

"The textbook," replied Junaid without looking at her.

"Why are you reading from the middle of the book and not the first chapter?" she inquired.

"Why do you care?" said Junaid with a little irritation as he finally looked sideways at her.

He noticed that she was wearing red lipstick and little lady bug–shaped red earrings. She had uncommonly large eyes, and he could not help but think that she was extraordinarily pretty. Be that as it may, he was in no mood to let her bother him any further, and he turned back to his book with renewed attention.

"I don't have the textbook yet. Where do I get one?" she asked without batting an eye.

"What? You don't have a book? How are you going to follow the teacher and know what he is talking about?" He looked at her with incredulity.

"I don't know. Could I share your book, today?" she asked with a smile, unfazed by his obvious annoyance.

"I guess. Just today. The bookstore is next to the library," he said with a shrug.

"Where is the library?" she inquired, rising her eyebrows and tilting her head flirtatiously.

Junaid turned in his seat and faced her with a frown on his face. "I guess I will show you where after the class. Now keep quiet," he hissed.

"Jameela, that is my name. What is yours?" she asked, smiling and clearly enjoying his exasperation.

"Junaid. Don't say a word more," he said, turning to his book again as the professor, Mr. Bhatt cleared his throat and started to speak to the class.

Nyla saw the new girl with the red lipstick sitting next to Junaid and noticed how she kept talking to him and touching his elbow and batting her beautiful eyes at him while he was clearly trying to get back to reading. She saw his face when he turned to look at the girl and thought he looked handsome and annoyed. It was when he pushed his book to share between himself and the new girl that Nyla was surprised, as she could clearly see a textbook in the girl's bag that she had set on the ground to her right. Despite her best effort, Nyla could not help feel a wee bit of jealousy in her heart. She wanted to get up and take out the girl's text book from her bag and slam it down on her head. The thought amused her, and she smiled a little smile.

Mr. Bhatt taught the first lesson of the year to his new students and in the end assigned the homework and dismissed the class. Jameela had continued to pester Junaid with questions during the lecture. She made comments about how difficult calculus was and stated in an exaggerated manner how amazed she was at how Junaid found it all so easy and explained everything to her so clearly.

"You are going to get an A+ in this class for sure, Junaid! It is like you have taken this class before and you already know everything!" she alleged with amazement.

"Sure I will get an A+, especially if you keep badgering me during the lecture!" he said with with a flat tone, as he closed the book and looked at his watch.

"Do me a favor and sit somewhere else tomorrow. OK, Jameela?" he told her.

"Why? You think I disturb you? I won't say a word tomorrow! Promise!" she pleaded.

"You better not. I am trying to get a good grade so I can keep my GPA high and get into a good college," he said, getting off the chair and walking toward the door.

"You have to show me where the library and the bookstore are, Junaid!" she called after him, picking up her bag and hurriedly getting up to join him.

"OK, let's go. But hurry up I need to get to the next class, and it is all the way on the other side of the school," he told her.

Nyla heard the girl pleading with Junaid to let her sit with him again tomorrow and not able to stomach any more of her, she got up and left the classroom. Being a girl and especially one who cared for Junaid however, she turned to look back from down the hallway and saw the two walking toward the library. She frowned at the new girl who seemed unable to wipe that smile off her face. And what a face, too round and too much makeup for sure, no one has skin that flawless!

And surely there should be a limit on how big your eyes can be in relation to your face! Good heavens, if she swayed her hips anymore while walking, she was surely in danger of slipping a disk! Is that what men—no, not men, *boys*—like in women these days? And she walked off, with not too slight swaying of her own fine figure, to her astronomy class, that was on the other side of the building. She had on very light makeup and had chosen clothes that enhanced her feminine figure in a subtle way. She knew she looked attractive but was a bit annoyed that Junaid had apparently not noticed her at all. At the same time she felt he seemed to have his hands full of this new girl with too much makeup and clothes that were too tightly fitting in her estimation.

Junaid barely made it to the astronomy class and as the door was near the front of the amphitheater shaped classroom, everyone, including the teacher Miss Gulbadan, saw him burst through the door breathing heavily as though he had to run to get to the class. Miss Gulbadan knew most of the class and knew him particularly well. She used to teach fifth grade a few years ago along with Miss Zarina and was now teaching astronomy after having completed a two-year course at a college abroad. She recalled the story Miss Zarina had told her about Junaid and she smiled at the recollection.

"Find a seat, Junaid, and stop staring at me even though I am so pretty!" she said with a mischievous grin and the entire class burst out laughing. They had either been in the class at the time of the incident or had been told of it by their classmates and friends.

"Yes, Miss," said Junaid blushing furiously as he sat down on the nearest seat he could find.

"Now, Junaid already has an A in this class since he thinks I am pretty, but the rest of you will have to work to deserve it!" she continued teasing him as the class dissolved into yet another round of roars and howls.

"But, but"—she raised her hands to quiet down the uproar—"we must remember that Junaid, even though he finds me to be very beautiful, would only attend my class if a certain Miss Ibrahim was also in my class…and voila, there she is sitting right behind him!" The screams and whoops that now erupted must have been heard across the building and now Junaid and Nyla were both blushing and being lovingly tormented by their classmates and their jovial teacher.

As the merriment died down Miss Gulbadan got down to teaching her students about the wonders of the heavens.

She posed questions about the planets and the stars to gauge the general level of knowledge of her class. For her next question she arbitrarily pointed to Nyla and said, "Would Miss Ibrahim share with us what she knows and thinks about the stars?"

Nyla, sitting directly behind and slightly above Junaid, was quiet for a moment as she looked at his back and then she stood up to answer. "On a night when there are no clouds, if you go to a place where there are no bright street lights to dim the view, you can look up and see millions of shiny diamonds glittering in the sky. If you are lucky, you would have a telescope to look through and if you are so fortunate as to have a friend point out the Milky Way to you, you would learn that there are billions of stars in our galaxy and that our star the Sun is but one of those billions of stars. You would learn that your galaxy is just one of millions that make up the universe. This is what I know of the stars, and I am glad to have been shown this by a very special person. And that is why I am in this class today trying to learn more about the heavens."

There was momentary silence and then claps of approval as she sat down. "There is definitely an astronomer in the making in our class today! Thank you, Miss Ibrahim, and well said indeed!" Miss Gulbadan said, beaming with pride as she gazed at the young enthusiastic faces surrounding her.

Nyla looked at the back of Junaid's head and noticed that his ears had turned red, and he was staring at the floor in front of him.

"Would Mr. Kafrooni care to add something to what Miss Ibrahim has stated so beautifully?" Miss Gulbadan said, looking at Junaid with a smile.

He hesitated not knowing if he had a choice in the matter or if his teacher was actually asking him to say something. When Miss Gulbadan continued to look at him expectantly with her hands clasped in front of her, he knew he had no choice but to say something. He stood up slowly and said, "I think Miss Ibrahim said it all about the stars. She is right about good friends being very important but sometimes friendship alone is not enough." As he took his seat, there were no claps and Miss Gulbadan raised her eyebrows. "And I think we have a philosopher in the making in this class as well!" she said, and this garnered a few chuckles from the class. "I suppose he means that friends can only teach you so much and you need to then study and read on your own to learn more," she added.

Nyla knew he did not mean what Miss Gulbadan had assumed he had meant. It made her think back on that night two months ago. What did he mean when he said sometimes friendship is not enough? Could he mean that he wanted and had hoped that they had been more than friends? What is more than best friends? Could it be? Was this the answer she had been seeking? She wondered still.

They had been together in both of their morning classes, and they had still not had the chance to speak to each other. Nyla could no longer wait. She needed to end the torment that consumed her soul. She needed to talk to Junaid.

The classroom emptied promptly at lunchtime, and Junaid was about to get up and leave when Nyla's hand on his shoulder made him stay where he was. He turned around and looked at her face for the first time in too long. As they stood facing each other, she noticed anew his face which she had missed seeing and that she now realized she had always found so attractive and what she loved most about it, his deep set soft yet piercing brown eyes; eyes which even now stared, unblinking, at what was for him the most bewitchingly fair and at the same time an agonizingly difficult face to behold. They said nothing and just stared at the other's eyes seeking to learn what they had been unable to with words, searching for the answers that had eluded them and perhaps most of all looking to find the strength in the other's eyes that they felt they needed so desperately themselves. Then in an instant when each knew what was sought was found, the eyes saw and the mind deciphered, this could not be anything but love.

She leaned forward toward him, and he lifted her off her feet and brought her to stand next to him. Without saying a word, he placed his arms around her back and pulling her to himself he kissed her. She moved her head back to look at his face and then pulled his head toward her kissing him passionately. The first time either one had ever kissed and it only felt right.

It was as if the turmoil of their tortured souls, over those eternally long months was a dark cloud that had suddenly lifted and the day was bright and the colors vivid again.

Junaid had not been aware of Nyla's feelings for him and had suffered greatly while trying in vain to forget how he felt about her. He had essentially isolated himself in his room but the more he tried to fall out of love with her, the more he seemed to have fallen in deeper. The despair he had felt in his heart minutes ago was now replaced by a joy and exhilaration he had never experienced before.

Nyla felt like a woman who was no longer afraid. She was no longer afraid because she knew the answer to the question she had pondered and lost sleep over for so long. She now knew what she could have known sixty long days ago. Having had to wait so long made it so much the sweeter and gave her the reassurance that it had been real. It had been real because despite not seeing him or hearing from Junaid for all this time, she had not lost what she felt for him. And having seen him today she knew she loved him and needed to know how he felt about her. She had looked in his eyes for the answer she had deprived him from giving her with his tongue. She searched for the answer she sought so ardently and then suddenly, without a shadow of a doubt she knew that she had found it. Now, feeling an euphoria she could not believe she was capable of, she kissed the shy uncertain boy she had seen grow into a loving and trustworthy young man.

Feeling like the luckiest man alive, Junaid took Nyla's hand in his and walked out into the hallway. Barely aware of the people around them, and as if walking on air, they made their way to the little playground besides the school and found a bench under the shade of a tree. They sat there for a long time talking as if for the very first time. Seeing each other afresh with the eyes of lovers. Eager to hear what the other had to say and even more eager to tell why they had acted the way they had, falling in love ever deeper with every new explanation and every new hurt that love unidentified had caused unknowingly. Crying and laughing with untold happiness they sat together, unaware of anyone and everyone. For hours they sat and felt as though only a moment they had been together and each convinced that they must tell the other everything they felt now and not wait for tomorrow.

Only when the light of day was giving way to the dark of the evening did they realize what time it was and marveled at how quickly it had passed. They laughed with feigned guilt but showed no remorse as they realized they had missed the afternoon class. Picking up their books, together they walked in blissful happiness. They had walked home together untold number of times before but today each felt as though it was the very first. Arriving at Nyla's home, they continued talking and lingered, unable to part from each other, dreading that they would not see each other until the next morning. It was only when Mrs. Ibrahim called Nyla to come in as it was already quite dark and time for dinner that they reluctantly said their final goodbyes first with words and then with eyes locked onto the other's. As she walked to the door looking back at Junaid, she nearly stumbled at the doorstep and Junaid, standing fifteen feet away, involuntarily reached out with his right hand as if to keep her from falling, and they both laughed with relief and happy cheer. Mrs. Ibrahim finally came forward, let Nyla in, smiled and waved at Junaid, and closed the door. Junaid stood where he was for a few moments and then exultant and with a spring in his step he jaunted homeward.

Mrs. Ibrahim noticed something different about Nyla and did not need to be told that her daughter was in love or with whom. Nyla was seventeen, trim and slim and every bit a very attractive young lady. She was intelligent, serious about her education, and had been taught well at home and at school. Having guided her well, Mr. and Mrs. Ibrahim trusted her judgment and therefore respected her decisions, always keeping the watchful eye of a trusting but attentive parent on their one and only treasure. The Ibrahims knew Junaid as an outstanding young man of good character and polite manners who was keen on the outdoors but over the past several years had turned to his education and future with singular diligence. They knew that it was only a matter of time before their beautiful daughter would have a suitor, and they had both secretly wished that it would be someone like Junaid. They had enough experience and had lived long enough to know that love can make an otherwise rational person irrational. They had always hoped for their daughter the joy of being in love but with someone equally special.

Therefore when that night Mrs. Ibrahim broke the news to her husband it was with a sense of barely concealed jubilation rather than dread. As she had expected, he was initially hesitant and uncertain of how he should react to this news of his daughter showing clear evidence of becoming a young woman with her own insight and ability to make life-changing decisions. Seeing his confusion, she reminded her husband of how they had taught, guided, and instilled in their daughter the qualities to prepare her to make her own determinations in matters that would affect her own future and that her choice in this most critical matter had been nothing less than what they had both secretly hoped and longed for. Being a man of consideration and one possessing an open mind and perhaps more importantly one with the grace and wisdom to know when and where to pick his battles, and in the end being relieved in his daughter's choice in love, he joined his wife in supporting and standing by his little girl. There was one other factor however that they both had failed to consider at this moment and that would become evident in the not too distant future. Presently however they were blissfully oblivious to it.

Nyla, now in her bedroom and getting ready to sleep, had little doubt that her mother had seen and realized the difference in her behavior toward Junaid. She was also relieved to see that her mother had seemed pleased that night and had not said anything that could signal her displeasure either with the fact that she had come home very late or that she had lingered talking to Junaid for a long time outside. Nyla was certain that her parents were talking about her and Junaid that very moment alone in their bedroom. Nyla knew they liked him and his parents, but she was not entirely convinced that her father would not raise any objections of his precious daughter falling in love at a relatively young age. His main objection, in her judgment, could only be that she must not deviate from her goal of educating herself. She was however prepared and comfortable in her ability to help ease that potential objection by reassuring him that she had no desire to do anything to compromise that end.

Junaid arrived back home after the first day of school very late, just as his parents were sitting down to dinner and starting to worry about his whereabouts. However seeing his good humor and high spirits alleviated their concern, and they were happy to see him join them for dinner with a hearty appetite that had been missing of late. They were unable to account for his new found cheer but were nevertheless comforted by it and decided not to pry into it at this time. The cause would become evident soon enough if it was significant enough and more importantly if it had the staying power to keep him so elated. They would let him disclose it to them in due time.

The next morning as Nyla was about to leave for school after having her breakfast, her father came down to go to work. He was a tall and personable, clean-shaven man, who Nyla had clearly taken after. He looked at her, from top to bottom, and beamed a little. She thought she saw just a little wetness in his eyes as he turned to leave.

"You know I love you, Daddy," she called after him.

"I know. I love you too," he replied without looking back as he left for work.

Nyla looked at her reflection in the full-length mirror near the door. She could see her father in herself. His reaction this morning, after what he must have heard from her mother last night allayed any fears Nyla had and she felt proud of her parents for trusting her.

She felt blessed and left for school with excitement in her heart at the prospect of seeing Junaid, *her* Junaid.

# *Chapter 11*

Nyla arrived in Mr. Bhatt's calculus class early but a few minutes after Junaid had already taken his seat. She gave him a warm smile and took the seat next to him where Jameela had been sitting the day before. As she opened her book and placed it on the desk in front of her, Junaid reached to his right and held her left hand gently for a moment, making her blush.

As they talked about what Mr. Bhatt was to discuss today, Jameela walked in and seemed visibly upset upon seeing Nyla sitting next to Junaid.

She came over and asked Nyla to move.

"Excuse me?" said Nyla, her brow furrowed, as she looked incredulously at Jameela standing in front of them.

"This is my seat. I sat here yesterday. You need to sit somewhere else!" replied Jameela stubbornly, not moving an inch.

Nyla and Junaid looked at each other amazed at Jameela's audacity.

"Jameela, this is my girlfriend Nyla, and she will sit next to me. There are many empty seats for you to pick," Junaid said softly but firmly, as he reached for and took Nyla's hand in his.

"This is your girlfriend?" asked Jameela with her big eyes open wide.

"Yes, she is. Now please go sit somewhere, OK?" replied Junaid as he looked at Nyla and smiled.

"I see, but I will tell you something about your *girlfriend* later," said Jameela as she tilted her head and walked to a seat in a row behind them.

After the class was over, Nyla and Junaid walked to their next class together hoping that Miss Gulbadan would not tease or pick on either one of them today.

Junaid sat in the seat next to Nyla, and they both talked about how neither one of them would ever forget this class for as long as they lived. They thought back about the eventful night they had looked at the Milky Way, the night they would always remember and how that night had affected both of them in so many ways. Nyla had chosen this elective only because she had become intrigued and fascinated by the universe that night. When Miss Gulbadan had asked her to say something about the stars, Nyla had stated what she had experienced that night and what she had said had in turn caused Junaid to reply in such a way that she knew he wanted more than to just be her friend. That was the answer she had sought and in this classroom and with Miss Gulbadan's unintentional mediation they had come to know that they both had loved each other. Miss Gulbadan had become a very special person for them both, and they looked at her with much appreciation and delight as she walked into the classroom.

Their teacher stood in front, looking at her students, waiting for everyone to settle down.

"I see that the astronomer and the philosopher are sitting together today," she said with a smile. But after that brief comment, she turned the lights off and started to show the students slides of some amazing pictures of the universe taken by the Hubble telescope that was in orbit around the earth. She commented on each of the pictures and gave brief descriptions. The stunned response from the students clearly showed that they were as astounded by what they saw and heard as she was when she had first seen these pictures. It was indeed some of these very pictures that had affected her to the extent that she had gone to the effort of obtaining a scholarship to enroll in a college program abroad and decided to return to teach what she loved so much to her students, hoping to get some of them interested in this most fascinating field.

Turning the lights back on after the slideshow was over, she started asking her students what they found most fascinating about what they had seen. Sajjad, his eyeglasses almost at the tip of his nose, said he liked the picture of the Andromeda galaxy, the nearest galaxy to the Milky Way. Farah, tall and slender and one of Nyla's friends, picked as her favorite the close up pictures of the surface of the sun with the giant flares shooting out into space. Junaid thought the picture of the supernova that had exploded millions of years ago and the wave of dust that was still traveling out from it at incredible speed was most fascinating while Nyla thought the Sombrero galaxy was an amazingly beautiful sight to behold.

Now Miss Gulbadan, having asked each of her students about his or her favorite picture, told them to write a paper on that topic and submit it by next Monday.

The morning classes over, they picked up something to eat from the cafeteria and went to sit under the shade of a tree in the playground. It was not very long before Jameela showed up and walked straight up to them.

"Junaid, yesterday when you ran away to your class after showing me the library, I followed you. After the class was over, I waited for a while and then I went inside to look for you," she said with a pout of her thick red lips.

"Why did you follow me to my class?" asked a surprised Junaid.

"Because you were so sweet to me and I wanted to thank you and maybe have lunch with you!" she replied, batting her eyes and acting kittenish as though Nyla was not there at all.

"I was barely civil to you and I feel badly about it. You have no reason to thank me, Jameela," said Junaid with a shallow forced smile, his toes curling inside his shoes.

"Well, guess what *I* saw when I went inside the classroom, Junaid," she continued to speak, with a roll of her eyes toward Nyla.

"I don't know, what *did* you see?" asked Junaid, sounding a bit irritated by Jameela not leaving them alone to themselves.

"I saw your *girlfriend* kissing a boy! That's what!" she said with her hands on her hips and her neck stretched forward as she glared at Nyla who could barely conceal her laughter.

"Oh! OK! Jameela, thanks for looking out for me. You are a good friend, and I will have to have a talk with her," said Junaid with a heroic effort at looking as serious as he could. And when he saw that Jameela was not moving, he added, "I will need to have a serious talk with her in *private*, Jameela, so please go on now."

At this Jameela finally budged and started to move away saying, "I will see you in calculus tomorrow, Junaid, keep the seat for me. I am so glad I was able to see what I saw, for your sake!" And she was gone after giving Nyla a parting poisonous stare.

"I think she has a big crush on you, Junaid," said Nyla with a laugh.

"You think!" Junaid chuckled with a frown. "That girl needs to leave me alone. She is all over me. I am already dreading seeing her again tomorrow."

"Don't worry, Junaid, I think I have an easy solution to the problem of the seating arrangement," reassured Nyla with a smile on her lips.

"Now let us go to our history class that we missed yesterday. I cannot believe you have picked the same classes as I did!" she added.

"It was no accident," said Junaid with a sly grin. And hearing this, she punched him playfully on his shoulder with as much love as surprise.

"Careful, Nyla, or I will tell Jameela you have been physically assaulting me!" said Junaid with a fake sob.

"Go ahead! I am just dying to get a chance to give her a good thrashing!" she replied with feigned anger.

They burst out laughing and got up to go to their history class together.

The history class was being taught by a handsome young man who had just recently finished his education in England and had moved back to his native land. He looked somewhat familiar to Nyla, but she could not decide if she had seen him before and if so where. It was when he wrote his name, Tahir

Ayoub, on the blackboard that she suddenly remembered who he was and why he had looked so familiar. She now remembered that he was the son of one of her father's good friends from Lahore, who had come with his family to visit and had stayed with them for a few weeks during a summer vacation when she was about ten years old. He was seven years older than her while his sister Tara was about her own age. Nyla remembered playing with him and his sister Tara during that summer a long time ago.

While they were waiting for Mr. Ayoub to take the roll call, Nyla told Junaid about her recollection and he was quite surprised by it. Their teacher started to call out the names of the students, and when he called out her name, he paused and smiled at her. Clearly he had recognized her name and face. Nyla smiled back at him, eager to talk to him about those long ago years.

After the class was over, Junaid accompanied Nyla when she went up to their teacher's desk. Tahir and Nyla talked animatedly for several minutes while Junaid, not having any of these memories to share with them was essentially sidelined. Junaid finally cleared his throat and Nyla felt bad about having not introduced him. She introduced Junaid as her friend to Tahir and the two shook hands and looked at each other briefly before Tahir turned once again to Nyla and they continued talking about Tara, their parents, when he had returned from England and where he was now living, etc.

Finally, with the next class already filing in, Nyla and Junaid said goodbye to Tahir and left the classroom.

"Well, he seems pleasant enough," said Junaid.

"Yes, he is! We had so much fun when they were here that summer!" said Nyla enthusiastically.

"I can see you two remember each other very well," remarked a somewhat subdued Junaid.

"I know, I cannot believe he remembers me so well!" exclaimed Nyla. "I have to tell Mom and Dad about him tonight," she added.

Junaid did not reply and they walked out of the school campus toward home.

As they walked, Nyla turned to Junaid and said, "I am sorry I did not introduce you right away, Junaid. You must have felt left out."

"Just a little," said Junaid quietly. He did feel left out and more than a little jealous that another man, a good-looking man, knew Nyla well enough to keep her occupied with interesting memories. Nor was it lost on him that he himself had been introduced as her "friend" and not her boyfriend.

"Why did you tell him I was your friend instead of your boyfriend?" asked Junaid, as he stopped walking.

"I don't know. Maybe because he is almost like family?" she said, looking confused.

"You don't know? You said your mother and father both think we are in love, right?" he said, looking at her eyes.

"Yes. That's right. But no one else in the family knows yet," she said, looking a little uncomfortable.

Junaid started walking again. He was in deep thought and looked agitated and hurt.

"No, I think you just did not want *him* to know. You have not seen him in seven years and suddenly you seem all gaga over him!" Said Junaid, looking straight ahead and sounding miffed.

"I am not all gaga over him, Junaid!" It was Nyla's turn to stop walking, a hint of annoyance showed in her voice.

"If you say so, Nyla," Junaid replied, regaining his calm.

"You seem jealous of him, Junaid," she accused.

"If I was acting as you did, you would be jealous too, Nyla," he retorted.

"I did not act jealous when that loon Jameela was acting cuckoo around you," Nyla reminded Junaid.

"You said it. Jameela was acting that way toward me, not the other way around," responded Junaid with the slightest hint of a smile.

Nyla looked at his face and saw the hurt in his eyes. "I think we both get a little jealous…," she started to say.

"Because we don't want anyone to come between us," he finished her sentence, smiling as she came forward and took both his hands in hers.

"I am sorry. I should have been more sensitive," she confessed.

"And I am sorry, I should have been less sensitive," he replied, as they stood gently holding hands.

"Can we do some stargazing tonight, Junaid?" asked Nyla with a twinkle in her eye.

"You bet. I will pick you up at ten tonight," he answered as they started walking again.

Junaid dropped Nyla off at her door and wanted badly to kiss her but Nyla pushed him off, telling him with her eyes that her mom was going to see them. "Tonight!" she promised as she puckered her lips, blew him a kiss, and closed the door behind her.

She saw her mother preparing dinner and went up to her quietly and hugged her from behind, scaring the poor woman half to death.

"You look very happy today, Nyla," she said, looking pleased.

"I am Mother! I don't believe I was every happy before the way I am now!" she said honestly.

"I know. Nyla, I have to talk to you about something. Come sit with me," said Mrs. Ibrahim, looking a bit grim.

"Ammi, you are making me feel worried! What is it? Is Dad all right?" asked Nyla, as she sat up straight and leaned forward, holding her mother's left arm in both her hands.

"Yes, yes, your dad is fine. Nyla, do you remember when you were ten years old and one of your dad's friends had come to stay with us over a summer break for a short while?" she asked her daughter.

"Yes, Mother. I was about to tell you! You remember Tahir, the brother of Tara? Well, guess what! He is the new history teacher at school, and Junaid and I are both in his class!" said Nyla with obvious excitement.

"Let me finish, daughter," said Mrs. Ibrahim, patting Nyla's knee.

"Mr. Ayoub, Tahir's father, is a very conventional man from a very traditional family. He is close friends with your father and when he had come to visit us, Mr. Ayoub and his wife Nusrat both liked you. They had liked you enough in fact to ask that we accept their son for you once he was old enough to have finished his education and was working to support a family."

"Accept him for *me*? What do you mean, Mother?" asked Nyla, looking very confused.

"I mean, they asked us, your father and myself, to agree to give your hand in marriage to Tahir when he was ready to get married," said Mrs. Ibrahim.

"And you said no, of course! Right, Mother?" asked Nyla abruptly before letting her mother finish.

"No, Nyla. We told them *we* had no objection to it," replied her mother.

"What! You had no objection to my getting married to someone without letting me decide whether I wanted to or not! I cannot believe this!" Nyla said testily, as she sat on the sofa next to her mother with her arms folded.

"Nyla, you have to understand, it was a long time ago and the offer to us was made about their son. It would have looked very rude to tell them that we did not want their son, that he was not good enough for our daughter even though they were our close friends, close enough to come and stay with us in our home for three weeks! And it was about the remote future," Mrs. Ibrahim, looking apologetic, tried to explain.

"So is that why Tahir has moved here, to take a teaching job in this city of all the places he could have gone to teach? So that he can marry me as his parents and my parents had decided for us close to a decade ago?" asked Nyla bitterly.

"I assume his father told him to, Nyla. He is a man bound to tradition, and he remembers the word he gave us and our response that we had no objection," replied her mother.

"But *I* have an objection, Mother! I *do not* want to marry someone I do not love. I love Junaid and you and Dad both know that!" said Nyla as she stood up, her voice shaking with emotion.

"I know, Nyla, and your father knows that too. Sit down, daughter. Your father came home early today, and we had a long talk this afternoon about this. Mr. Ayoub called your father earlier today and informed him about his son starting a teaching job at your school and reminded him of the arrangement we had. Your father was quite taken by surprise, and he told Mr. Ayoub that you were still in school and not quite ready for marriage. Mr. Ayoub is a determined man however, and he replied that you can become engaged and then get married in a few years when in college and that Tahir will have no problem with you continuing your education. Your father respects and cares for his long standing friendship with Mr. Ayoub, but he also loves you and does not want to force you into a marriage that you are not happy with," explained Mrs. Ibrahim to a now somewhat calmer Nyla.

"Good, so no one is going to try and force me to marry Tahir," said Nyla, as she sat down again and placing her right hand on her chest breathed a sigh of relief.

"Let me ask you. If you were not in love with Junaid or anyone else for that matter, would you have an objection to marrying Tahir? Knowing that he is educated, good-looking, and a good man and the son of your father's dear friend?" Nyla's mother asked with a benign expression.

"No, I would not marry anyone that I did not love, Mother!" replied Nyla with confidence and finality.

"Do you not think that people can fall in love after they get married?" asked her mother.

"They could I guess, but maybe and maybe not. What if they get married and never fall in love, never get that special feeling, then what? They are stuck with each other for life!" replied Nyla thoughtfully.

Mrs. Ibrahim could not help but smile at the conviction of her daughter. She had herself had an arranged marriage, like most of her friends, and was happily married to a man she had respected initially and then had fallen in love with.

"Well, Tahir's father and mother are coming to visit a week from today. They will have dinner with us together with Tahir and will want to discuss things in more detail," Mrs. Ibrahim broke the news to Nyla.

"Mother, I will not be part of these discussions and refuse to be present for the dinner. You and father will have to tell Mr. and Mrs. Ayoub that I am able to and *will* make my own decisions about my own marriage in due time, when I am good and ready," said Nyla with a stony calm in her voice.

"I will be going to Junaid's home after dinner and will be back before midnight. We want to do some stargazing," she added.

"All right, I will let your father know about your decision. I am on your side, daughter. I just wish there was a painless way to resolve this," said her tired-looking mother.

Junaid rode his bike to Nyla's home at ten and found her waiting for him. They rode back to his place, and Junaid took her inside where his parents were waiting to see her. They talked pleasantries for a few minutes and then while his parents retired to their bedroom, Nyla and Junaid went up to the terraced roof.

Junaid had noticed that Nyla was a little quiet and not her usual self since he had picked her up from her home. Now alone on the platform, he asked her why she looked glum. After some hesitation and resistance and especially remembering the conversation they had earlier on the way back from school about Tahir, she finally divulged everything she had talked about with her mother that evening.

Junaid looked stunned for a moment and then realized that both Nyla and her mother were on his side. He was relieved and proud that Nyla had argued and fought for them. He was happy that she had stood firm and had proclaimed her love for him in front of her mother. He was not sure how to proceed from this point however.

"I am so proud of you. I love you, Nyla," he said softly as they sat together, leaning back on the reclining chair.

"I love you too. But I am afraid about the coming days, Junaid. I am worried about us going to the history class. I am worried about my parents telling Mr. Ayoub what he would not want to hear. I am worried about this damaging their long friendship," she said, sounding clearly distraught.

"I know, but as long as we do what is right, we should not feel responsible for what others may or may not want us to do. They have every right to make decisions for themselves as do we," reassured Junaid, feeling conviction and strength building within himself.

They smiled at each other, and she leaned closer to put her head against his chest as he closed his arms around her and held her close. Junaid looked up at the stars and realized once again their place in the infinite universe. The cold immensity of the heavens made him even more aware of the love he felt for Nyla, whose warm body he held close to his. He kissed the top of her head gently, and she looked up at him. He bent his head down as she reached up and they kissed a soft, warm, and passionate kiss; an unhurried and patient kiss; a kiss of giving and taking, of gentle encouragement and assurance; a kiss to affirm and seal their love.

It was close to midnight when Junaid finally dropped Nyla off to her home and despite her resistance he kissed her goodbye at the door.

She stood at the door watching as he paddled off, waving until she could no longer see him in the enveloping darkness.

# Chapter 12

Despite the troubling news they had both received, Nyla and Junaid both slept well after having spent some time together that night.

Nyla did not see her father before leaving for school the following morning and felt that may have something to do with what her mother must have told him the previous night. Nevertheless, she was confident and happy as she walked to school that morning.

Junaid arrived at Mr. Bhatt's class and found Nyla sitting at a seat near the middle of the classroom. She had saved a seat for Junaid who joined her, smiling at her simple solution to the vexing problem of Jameela not wanting her to sit in her seat in the front of the class. Soon Mr. Bhatt walked in and finally as he was about to start the lecture, Jameela came in and sat down in the front seat. She looked back, saw Junaid sitting with Nyla, and then turned around, shaking her head.

The astronomy class of Miss Gulbadan was always entertaining and informative, but Nyla and Junaid were both dreading the history class they had to attend after lunch that day. During lunch, they discussed and mutually decided to not say or do anything to offend Tahir but also to make clear to him at the first opportunity that they were a couple, a couple in love.

They walked to the history class and took their usual seats together, feeling tension building, as Tahir, their teacher walked in. They tried to focus on the lecture and took notes as well as they could. With the class finally dismissed, they were about to get up and leave when they heard their teacher say, "Miss Ibrahim, please see me after school for a few minutes in my office."

They were now doubting their decision to continue to come to the history class. There was nothing to do now but to go see Tahir after school and Junaid insisted that he go with her. Nyla had no objection to this and actually felt relieved at avoiding the prospect of having to face Tahir alone. They felt that he may have something to say about the arrangement their parents had made for their marriage long ago but wanted to hear it from him and were prepared to make it clear to him that it was not acceptable.

If he was anything like his father however, or if he was intimidated enough by him, then they had little hope of making Tahir understand and accept Nyla's total rejection of the idea of marrying him.

It was therefore with a sense of great foreboding that they walked to his office and knocked at the door. Presently he opened the door and smiled as he saw Nyla standing there with her books held in front of her chest. Tahir seemed a little uncomfortable seeing Junaid standing next to her and looked at him quizzically.

"Mr. Ayoub, Tahir, this is Junaid, my boyfriend," said Nyla with calm confidence. "What did you need to talk to me about?" she asked.

"This is your boyfriend?" asked a surprised looking Tahir.

"Yes, Mr. Ayoub. We love each other," Junaid responded before Nyla could answer.

"Well, I guess both of you should come inside then," said Tahir, as he held the door open and then closed it behind them, pointing to a pair of chairs in front of his office desk.

"I do not know where to begin, so I will just start talking," he said as he sat down behind his desk.

"Nyla, have your parents, uncle, and auntie Ibrahim talked to you about us?" he asked.

"Yes, my mother told me last night about the arrangement they had made over seven years ago. I had no idea they had such an agreement or even that there was any talk about such a thing until just yesterday!" Sitting up straight in the chair, she responded with patience, not showing her emotions that were boiling just under the surface.

"So you were unaware of this arrangement, which explains Mr. Kafrooni here being your boyfriend?" he asked again.

"Yes, of course!" she answered.

"Miss Ibrahim, Nyla, what have you told your parents and what was their response to your decision?" inquired Tahir, his eyes gleaming, as he leaned forward with his elbows on the top of the desk.

"She told them she wants nothing to do with this arranged marriage with you or anyone else, Mr. Ayoub!" Junaid interrupted, clearly frustrated with having to listen patiently to another man interrogate and possibly try to persuade Nyla to uphold their parents' decision.

"Miss Ibrahim, if you would please. I need to know in your words and I need to know their response, in their words." Said Tahir, looking at Junaid but clearly addressing Nyla.

"Exactly what Junaid said. I told my mother I could not marry someone I did not love. I told her they had no right to arrange my marriage to anyone without my approval. I did not talk to my father, but my mother told him what my decision was," said Nyla with firm determination.

"And your mother was in agreement with your decision? She had no objection despite the word they had given my parents?" asked Tahir with eyes wide open and curiosity painted on his face.

"She told me all about the traditional man your father is and how he feels that the word given about such a marriage must be carried out even though the two people getting married had no say in the decision. But she said that my father would not force me to marry anyone against my wish and that she was going to stand by my side in my decision," declared Nyla with grit in her voice.

Junaid and Nyla looked at each other and smiled a sober smile, reaching out to hold each other's hand. They looked at Tahir, who had slumped back in his leather chair, the fingers of his right hand rubbing his chin as he looked up at the ceiling in deep thought.

He now looked at the two of them with relief.

"Thank God!" he said with an obvious alleviation of the burden he had been carrying.

"What! You are not upset or angry?" asked a surprised Junaid.

"Not at all! I could not be more happy or relieved!" said Tahir, smiling at Junaid.

"Let me tell you two!" he exclaimed.

"You have made me happy beyond your wildest imagination! I have been studying in England over the past several years and during the course of my stay, I met and fell in love with a girl, a student just like myself, from Pakistan."

He continued, talking rapidly, looking at Junaid and then at Nyla.

"I have told my parents about her, but my father is adamant that I must marry you because of the word he had given your father. I had felt that your parents and you were expecting me to carry out my father's wishes and to keep his honor and your parents' I decided to come here in hopes of convincing you and your family to not bind me to a decision I had no say in. That is why I asked you to come see me today. So you can imagine my joy when I learned from you that you felt just as I did about this matter!" exulted Tahir, his eyes sparkling with jubilation.

"But I will need your help in convincing my father," he asked, looking hopeful.

It was the best possible reason Junaid and Nyla could have heard for Tahir to want to talk to Nyla and the most painless solution to a problem that seemed very difficult to resolve if not insurmountable not long ago. They now looked at each other with cheer and a sense of deliverance. A great weight was off their chest as well.

Now when they looked at Tahir, they saw a friend who needed their help and not someone who was threatening to try to tear them apart. They saw a man who was trying desperately to be with someone he loved just as they themselves wanted to be with each other. They felt his pain and anguish just as they had felt their own, and they both were eager to help him in any way they could.

"How can we be of help, Mr. Ayoub?" asked Junaid sincerely.

"Tahir, please call me Tahir. I think we are friends more than anything else," replied Tahir, adding, "You can help me, both of you, by letting my father understand that while Nyla's parents have no objection to our arranged marriage, that you certainly do. Once he realizes that his word of honor and that of his friend are not in jeopardy and that both, you Nyla and I are happy with the dissolution of the arrangement they had made in good faith so long ago, I think he will be able to accept it."

"I do want to help you, Tahir, we both do, but I don't think I will feel comfortable sitting with your family and mine, talking about why we do not want to carry out their wishes. I think I have made clear to my parents what I cannot do, and they need to explain that to your parents. I feel that our parents decided something for us without our input and now they need to decide to change that and make it right," argued Nyla, voicing the faith of her conviction.

"I cannot argue with that. My father and mother are arriving in a few days. I will tell them all we have discussed and ask them to meet with your parents and work out a solution," replied Tahir, agreeing with Nyla's reasoning.

With that, Junaid and Nyla got up, they shook Tahir's hand, wished him the best in his effort to do what he had to do, and turned to leave.

Just as they left the office with Tahir about to close the door, Nyla turned around and asked him, "What is the name of the lady you said you are in love with?"

"Gul, I call her Gul. Gulbadan is her name," replied Tahir with an exultant smile as he closed the door.

# Chapter 13

There could have been no better way to end the week for Junaid and Nyla. They had suffered the anguish of the news Nyla's mother had given them, but Tahir's resolve to his love and his objections to the arrangement their parents had made greatly relieved their distress.

Nyla wanted to spend time with Junaid this weekend, and she could think of no more secluded and tranquil place than the tree house. They decided to spend most of the afternoon there and to write the essays on the topics of their interest that Miss Gulbadan had assigned to them.

She arrived at Junaid's place with a picnic basket and her notebook before lunch time, and they hiked to the tree house in less than half an hour. Junaid was carrying his backpack with his and Nyla's notebooks and a book on astronomy. It was not too many months ago that they had climbed up the tree in haste to escape Shaytan. The memory of that day was still fresh, but they were now more than mere friends. Junaid took the picnic basket from Nyla as she climbed up the rope ladder and followed close behind her.

Once in the tree house and not harried as they were the last time they were there, Nyla did a little exploring and was delighted with the view from this high vantage point. She noticed how the floor of the tree house was made of panels of solid wood closely joined together and the roof was of a similar construction but the walls were made of loosely fitting branches some of which were actually part of the tree and had luxuriant leaves protruding into the tree house. There was a flattop panel of wood a foot and a half wide by six foot long that was attached two feet from the floor and below the window on the side of the wall opposite the door, and it served as a table or work surface. It had sturdy legs supporting it and Junaid arranged the notebooks and the picnic basket along with the water bottles on this bench. He untied a thick rug from underneath the bench and unrolled it on the flat floor to make a comfortable seating surface.

They blissfully sat on the floor together, enjoying the sandwiches and snacks Nyla had brought, and then spent the next few hours talking about every little thing they could think of.

They expressed glee at the happy chance that had brought Miss Gulbadan and Tahir together in a far off land. Nyla thought they were a perfect match and teased Junaid that Tahir had made off with his first love! Junaid responded with a laugh that had she but waited for him to finish his college education just a few years hence, he would have made a great match for her. He added that he was reasonably happy with his second choice in Nyla, which made her punch his shoulder with all her might causing him to scream out for Jameela to come help him, necessitating another punch from Nyla on his other shoulder. Rolling on the floor together laughing until their sides hurt,

Nyla hugged Junaid tightly and whispered in his ear that he was her teddy bear and that she loved him. Junaid kissed her eyes softly and told her that was nice but that her teddy bear was famished and needed food. Pushing him away with mock exasperation, she took out two samosas and made him eat both since he was so hungry!

Eventually they spent some time reading the book Junaid had brought with him and got around to writing the paper for Miss Gulbadan's class.

It was shortly before sunset when they climbed down from their tree house and made their way back home listening to the songs and calls of the birds all around them.

They did not see each other on Sunday as they woke up late and did some chores around the house in addition to finalizing their papers and getting ready for school Monday. Cell phones were not common then and Junaid called Nyla on her home phone, and they talked for over an hour before falling asleep.

Monday morning they saw each other in Mr. Bhatt's class and then eagerly walked to Miss Gulbadan's class, excited to see her and possibly talk with her about what they had heard from Tahir.

Miss Gulbadan was a little late coming to her class, and when she arrived, they were quick to recognize that she was not her usual jovial self. She did not make any funny remarks during the entire session, kept strictly to her lecture, and avoided any personal remarks about Junaid or Nyla, her favorite students. She particularly avoided eye contact with Nyla, which surprised and confused her. After collecting the homework from her students

Miss Gulbadan left the classroom without giving any assignment for the next day.

They were unable to explain her behavior until it finally dawned upon them that Tahir must have seen her over the weekend and finally told her about the arrangement his parents had made for him and Nyla all those many years ago. This must have come as a shock to her even though he must have also told her about his and Nyla's very strong position against this arrangement. Miss Gulbadan, Gul as he called her, must be painfully aware that the parents of the man she loved were adamant that he marry someone else, someone that she herself knew very well. All his reassurances to the contrary must have provided little comfort to Gul, and it was unlikely that she would feel better unless Nyla herself spoke with her. Nyla was the one person she was loathe to see at this time and the one person who could give her the peace of mind she so desperately needed.

They discussed this likely explanation for Miss Gulbadan's behavior over lunch and decided to speak with her after school. They were unable to find her however as she had left to go home early that day and had cancelled her afternoon classes.

That evening Miss Gulbadan lay on her bed sobbing, her lovely eyes pouring out the tears that soaked her pillow, her long raven hair matted on her rosy wet cheeks. She was not Miss Gulbadan the teacher, but rather the little girl Gul who was in need of a friend to hold her hand and tell her that all will be well. Her parents were in far away Peshawar and even if they were here she would have no way to explain to them that she was in love with a man she had met on her own, while in London, a man who was to marry someone else as arranged by his parents a long time ago, a man who had not told her that until just yesterday! How could she tell them what they would not understand and what would only bring their displeasure upon her.

Tahir had tried to explain to her many times since yesterday that he was not aware of this arrangement until just a few weeks ago, that he had come to the city to be with her, Gul, and that it just so happened, by some infinitesimally improbable chance that the girl he was arranged to have married also lived in the same city. He had told Gul that he had not told her sooner because he wanted to speak with Nyla and her parents to try to convince them to change their position and disallow the arranged marriage and only when he had that assurance and good news was he planning to tell her. But she would not listen to his reasoning for the hurt was too much, the pain too unbearable. The fact that he had not told her until yesterday, less than a week from the time his parents were to arrive from Lahore to speak with Nyla's parents; the fact that this other woman, Nyla, just happened to live in the same city; the fact that his parents strongly desired that he marry this other woman despite him having told them that he loved someone else, all this was too much for this young woman to come to terms with so soon after it had come to her awareness. The more she thought about this, the more she felt unable to console herself. Even though she loved Tahir and even though she felt loved by him, her biggest fear was that his parents would not change their rigidly held convictions and that he will therefore not be able to marry her after all.

It was this storm of unbearable and irresolvable thoughts that were assailing her when she heard a knock on the door. Powerless to contain her sobs, she asked who was at the door and hearing that it was Tahir, she told him to go away.

"I have someone here who wants to speak with you," he said adamantly, showing no inclination to go away.

"I cannot speak with anyone right now, Tahir. Please leave." She sobbed.

"And I cannot leave until I have seen my Gul. Open the door or I will have to break it down!" he threatened, hoping that she would not call his bluff.

There was quiet for a minute or two and then the door slowly opened. It was dark inside, and Tahir entered followed by Nyla and Junaid. Gul went back to her bed and lay down on her pillow face down, not willing to let anyone see her tears.

Tahir led Nyla and Junaid into Gul's bedroom and sat down next to her while they stood together near the entrance to the room.

"Gul, I need you to think about what I have told you. I know it is too much and too painful, but I promise to you that every word of it is true and I want to make it right for us," he implored.

"I don't know how to stop thinking about all that you have told me, Tahir. I don't know how to suppose that all that can go wrong will not go wrong. I have given you my love and I have nothing left to give. What will I do if you are taken from me?!" She sobbed as she answered, her voice muffled by the pillow.

"I know, Gul, I know. I wish I did not have to tell you all this. I wish I could have solved all this myself and never had to trouble your heart with the pain this has caused you. Trust me that I could not possibly bring myself to telling you until I had spoken with Nyla and had a solution and an answer to the anguish that I have myself suffered through alone. I did not want to lay at your lap the news of this hardship without also giving you the comfort of a resolution to this nightmare," he said, speaking gently and holding her hand, as he sat on her bed.

"Nyla! She is here?" asked Gul abruptly.

"Yes, and Junaid. They are here," answered Tahir, looking at the two and gesturing for them to come near.

"Why did you bring them?" asked Gul with an accusing tone.

"I did not call them. They came on their own," replied Tahir as he stood up and asked Nyla to come and sit next to Gul.

Nyla moved forward and sat down on the bed, as Miss Gulbadan wiped her tears and sat up with her arms around her drawn up legs.

"Miss Gulbadan, both Junaid and I care for you and for Mr. Ayoub. We care for you and look up to you." said Nyla softly.

Gul sniffled and rubbed her nose, not saying anything.

"Junaid and I love each other, and we know how it feels to be in love. We also know how it feels when there is a chance of losing that love, Miss Gulbadan." Nyla continued, "Junaid and I want to be with each other just as much as you and Mr. Ayoub want to be together."

Gul, upon hearing these heartfelt words, gave Nyla a rueful smile with her soft, wet eyes and reached forward to clasp her hand. Presently she leaned forward and the two young women hugged each other whereupon both of them started to shed tears, but this time these were tears of happiness and appeasement. Miss Gulbadan whispered just two words, "Thank you," into Nyla's ear but she said these with such feeling and sincerity that no other words or explanation of her feelings of gratitude were needed.

She now looked up at Tahir and Junaid, and it was clear to them that the smile on her face was a genuine expression of the amelioration of her affliction. She reached her arms toward Tahir even as she climbed out of the bed and they hugged affectionately, giving each other comfort and strength.

Miss Gulbadan finally looked at Junaid who felt sorry and a little embarrassed to see his favorite teacher cry.

"You look pretty even when you cry, Miss Gulbadan," Junaid said with such sincerity that she beamed and blushed self-consciously.

"Thank you, both of you," said Miss Gulbadan as she stood close to Tahir, holding his right arm in her hands.

"One day we will tell you how you helped bring the two of us together without even knowing it, Miss Gulbadan," Nyla said cheerily as she walked up to stand next to Junaid.

"We should be going now and will see you in class tomorrow!" said Junaid with a smile as he held Nyla's hand and they all walked to the door.

"I am glad our astronomy teacher did not give us any homework for tonight!" said Nyla as she winked at Junaid.

"I am glad I did not give any homework assignment either, I have yet to read and grade your papers from today!" said Miss Gulbadan with an alarmed look as she remembered what she needed to do tonight in addition to prepare for the class the next day.

They rode their bikes home, feeling confident about the coming days and the ability of the four of them to stand firm together.

Gul felt reassured of the inviolability of her love as she witnessed that its sanctity was as precious to Tahir as it was to her. She had always assumed that to be the case but witnessing Nyla and Junaid longing for what she herself desired so ardently had comforted her and given her the assurance that she was not alone in this effort. She was grateful to Junaid and especially to Nyla for taking the initiative to come and see her tonight. She knew that the solace which had replaced the discord in her soul was in a large part due to their coming and saying what she needed desperately to hear.

Feeling a bit remorseful for not trusting Tahir after hearing all he had told her yesterday, she was nevertheless able to forgive herself since he had not placed blame upon her for a natural response to overwhelming news. She was now determined to stand by him and to forever be the support he could lean on and the strength he could trust.

Later that night as she was reading and grading the assignments submitted by her class, she came across some lines that Junaid had written in his paper on supernovas that she found uplifting and inspiring.

> It is fascinating to learn that some of the atoms that make up the complex human body can only be forged in the incredible heat of a super-

nova, the monumental paroxysm that marks the death of a massive star. So forged in one such catastrophic explosion, the newly formed particles travelled at millions of miles an hour across a galaxy and became part of the wonder that is our planet and more amazingly our own bodies. So it is that our bodies are made of particles and elements that were born from and why we are indeed stardust.

So when we look up with wonder at the beauty and expanse of the heavens and feel small and insignificant, we should try and remember that we are not irrelevant or trifling and are rather the stuff that stars are made of.

She felt that the young Junaid that Miss Zarina used to tell stories about and who had made the innocent comment about her being the pretty teacher, had grown up to be a keen and reflective young man and that from how he wrote about the heavens he might be a good candidate to pursue this field of learning. If even only one of her students was so inclined, she would consider that rewarding and worth the effort of teaching what she loved. Her personal liking for Junaid over the years was now augmented by her respect for his ability as a student.

Miss Gulbadan decided that she would share Junaid's essay with Miss Zarina, the teacher who had longed over the years to see Junaid do well in school and who had played an important role in his transformation.

She knew she would have to encourage Junaid to consider astronomy as he entered college next year and that would mean he would have to go abroad to England or to the United States. How that would play out with Nyla also ready for college next year was a consideration she was not in a position to adequately gauge at this time.

# Chapter 14

The news had spread like jungle fire. A group of nine children between the ages of seven and fourteen had gone hiking in the hills and a ten-year-old boy had not returned.

Nyla and Junaid were at school on Monday when during the morning assembly the principal Mr. Pervez had made the troubling announcement. Apparently the children, all of whom lived in the neighborhood, had decided to go hiking together on Sunday. They had hiked and swam all day, and it was not until they were already on their way back home that the fourteen-year-old boy Nadir had realized that Gulzar was not amongst them. They had all gone back to look for him, and it was only when it was dark that they decided to go home and had told their parents. A group of these parents had then gone in search of the missing boy and returned empty-handed just that morning and notified the police.

The children were all students at the school and while Junaid and Nyla did not know them personally, they had seen them around the school. The principal and the teachers had decided to end the school early to be able to help look for

Gulzar, the missing boy, one of Miss Zarina's students from the fifth grade.

During the assembly, the children and the parents of these children who had gone hiking were all present. The plan was simply to find out where exactly the nine children had gone hiking the previous day and then go look for Gulzar.

There was a large map in front and on it the principal had drawn with a red marker the path the children had taken into the woods, where they had gone, where they swam and the path they had taken back home. Junaid, sitting with Nyla near the front, knew the area intimately and after seeing the picture of the missing child he left the school with her.

The two decided to leave for the woods early in the day to give them as much time to search for Gulzar as possible before sunset. Nyla was to change into her hiking clothes and shoes and bring lunch and meet Junaid in front of his home in one hour.

After changing and putting in his backpack whatever he thought could come in handy, Junaid took a map of the Margalla hills and marked the areas the boys had said they had been to yesterday, making mental notes of any places where there was a chance for them to have separated without noticing their missing friend.

Nyla arrived a few minutes early and they said goodbye to Mrs. Kafrooni who made them promise to come back before sunset.

It was a pleasantly cool mid-morning in early October and the leaves were already beginning to change colors. Junaid was carrying a backpack and a walking stick while Nyla had a pair of small binoculars that she used every now and then to scan the woods and hills around them.

Junaid had one major concern and it was leopards; although it was still too early in the cool season for that to be likely. The other concern was the snakes that were common in these hills although they were more active during the summer months. Last night the temperature dropped into the mid forties, cold enough to endanger hypothermia in the child and without food, water, and shelter he would not survive too many nights in the hills. Junaid had planned to go as far as the swimming hole and then instead of tracing their way back, he intended to make a large semicircular path farther north and then east toward and beyond the tree house and then south toward the dirt path that would take them home. He showed Nyla his plan on the small map he was carrying, and she was game and willing to do what would amount to several miles of hiking through difficult terrain. Besides, as she said sounding very hopeful, they would find him well before covering all that ground. Junaid smiled and acknowledged that as the best possible scenario.

Hiking expeditiously over open country but carefully scanning and investigating every possible place that little Gulzar could have fallen into or could be hiding in, they made their way deeper into the woods. Progress was oftentimes slow as they looked carefully for any sign of the missing boy, and it was not before early afternoon that they finally arrived at their favorite swimming hole. It was a good time to take a break, and they sat on the flat limestone rock over the water and ate the tasty sandwiches that Nyla had brought. Having fortified themselves and not finding any sign of Gulzar, they now crossed over to the other side of the pool and ventured deeper into the woods that formed the foothills of the larger Margalla hills.

Nadir had not included this area as part of where they had hiked, but Junaid thought the boy could have wandered a good distance in any direction once getting lost, during the past twenty-four hours.

As they hiked along the sides of the mountain stream they called out Gulzar's name every now and then. After another hour of walking they came to a large limestone hill that went more or less straight up two hundred feet and from the bottom of this hill through an opening lined with rocks of various sizes gushed out the cold water of a mountain stream. The hill, covered with only sparse vegetation, was about a hundred yards wide, and Junaid never having seen it before decided to go around it to see if there was a convenient place to climb it. They turned to their right to walk along the side of the hill. After going more than seventy-five yards they came to a large pine tree that had fallen and was propped up against the side of the hill about sixty feet up at a not very steep angle. Junaid and Nyla climbed up this tree and onto the hill, which was relatively easy to climb from this point up. Arriving finally at the top they realized that the ground around it had gradually risen to the level of the hill on the other side and they could have walked on to the top quite easily. The top of the hill was a nearly flat rock where some grass and hardy bushes had taken hold wherever enough soil had accumulated in crevices and depressions. As they walked across this hilltop, Nyla was slightly behind and to the left of Junaid.

"I guess we should make a turn to the east now, Nyla," said Junaid, looking forward.

He heard her utter a cry, and turning to look, he found that Nyla had disappeared and just then he heard a splash. Hastening to where she was standing before disappearing, he found a hole about three feet in diameter in a patch of long grass. Peering down this hole he could barely make out ripples of water a hundred feet or more below the opening.

He could hear Nyla splashing in the water as he quickly threw the backpack in and jumped feet first through the opening.

Junaid fell for a few seconds before hitting the water and swam back up after going in several feet. The cold water made him gasp as he came to the surface and frantically looked around himself for Nyla who was a few feet away and staying afloat by thrashing her arms and legs.

He swam to her and grabbed her around the waist with his right arm.

"You OK?"

"Yes, but it is cold!" she managed to spurt out, gasping and choking, her lips turning blue.

Junaid looked around and saw his backpack floating not far from them. He could barely make out the sides of this subterranean pool of water. Holding Nyla by her waist, he started swimming with powerful strokes of his legs and left arm. He swam to the side where he could barely see some large rocks jutting out of the water and getting to the nearest he helped Nyla grab onto and climb it first before getting out of the cold water himself. The only source of light were two holes in the ceiling, one through which Nyla had fallen and another a dozen yards to the right next to the wall of this yawning enclosure. As their eyes became accustomed to the darkness, they were able to see that there were two other larger rocks around them and then closer to the inside wall of the chamber was a few feet of sandy ground above the level of the water. On this ground they saw a little boy sitting on his knees, staring at them as if in a trance.

"Gulzar! Are you all right?" Nyla called out with excitement, forgetting her cold.

"Are you hurt, Gulzar?" shouted Junaid.

Not hearing a response, Junaid jumped into the water and swam rapidly to the little boy who seemed to be in a state of shock.

He was cold and unable to talk although his eyes moved and followed Junaid's every move; he seemed otherwise unhurt.

Nyla saw Junaid's backpack float by the rock she was sitting on, and she grabbed it out of the water. She then threw it to Junaid and jumped onto the next big rock and then walked in waist-deep water to Junaid and Gulzar. As she put her arm around Gulzar, Junaid opened the backpack and took out a bar of chocolate that he unwrapped for the little boy whose eyes opened wide and grabbing the bar he started to bite off large chunks hungrily.

Gulzar recalled how he had been hiking with his friends and how he had gone behind a bush to urinate, and not finding his friends upon returning, he had walked in the direction where he thought he heard their voices. After walking for several minutes he could no longer hear them, and he had become frightened and started running in one direction until he had come to the vertical side of a large hill. He had gone around the hill and climbed it to see if he could look for his friends from the top. He had been running to get to the front side of the hill when he had suddenly fallen through the hole.

The ten-year-old had been alone for almost twenty-four hours in this dark, cold, and utterly quiet place. Gulzar had fallen through the same opening as Nyla and then managed to swim to the sandbar and had shouted for help for hours until the sun had set and whatever little light was coming through the two holes in the ceiling was gone. The night had been pitch dark and very cold. He had been hungry and cried for his mother and father. In the absolute darkness of the chamber he imagined ghosts and goblins all around him as he lay shivering on his side with his head bent close to his chest, his knees drawn up, and his arms covering his head. He had awakened several times during the night and thinking that he was having a nightmare had cried himself to sleep, hoping that when he woke up he would be in his warm bed, smelling the eggs his mother was frying for his breakfast.

Gulzar had awakened in the morning to the same cruel reality. While at night the monsters of his imagination assailed him, now the reality of complete isolation terrified him. In desperation, he shouted for help for a long time before losing the energy and hope to continue.

He had given up the belief that someone would find him when he had heard a loud splash and saw Nyla and then Junaid. He was too weak and too much in a state of shock to call out to them and had sat where he was, thinking that he was imagining things. It was only when Nyla had put her arm around him and when he was offered the chocolate that he knew this to be real. As his strength returned and his fear subsided, he was able to tell Nyla and Junaid what had happened to him.

Having found the lost child unhurt, Junaid and Nyla now turned their attention to the not trifling matter of getting out of this enormous cavern that amounted to being a burial chamber for all three of them, if they failed to find a way out.

Digging into his backpack Junaid found his waterproof flashlight and hoping that the bulb had survived the fall into the water from well over a hundred feet, he turned it on. A narrow beam of yellow light illuminated their surroundings and the size of the enormous chamber now became evident to them. The enclosure was roughly rectangular in shape and about two hundred feet from the ceiling to the floor which itself was under about fifty feet of crystal clear water. The walls were mainly limestone with some outcropping of sandstone and on one sandstone rock that was partly submerged in the water they found two human footprints that were made eons ago. Not wanting to use up the batteries too quickly, Junaid turned off the flashlight and they sat talking while Gulzar now no longer alone or hungry began exploring.

Nyla saw Gulzar standing in the ancient footprints and a thought came to her.

"So people used to live in this underground cavern at one time in the past. And they left the footprints we see over there," she said thoughtfully.

"I guess so," replied Junaid.

"Well, if they lived here they must have had an easy way to come and go from this place!" said Nyla with excitement.

"There must be some way and we need to find it," she added, standing up and looking around.

"You are right! There must be a way, and I hope it is still present and usable!" Junaid said enthusiastically.

Taking the flashlight from Junaid's hand, Nyla turned it on the walls of the cavern and not fifteen yards away they saw a narrow stone stairway that started at the water line and went up along the wall but only to about half the way toward the second opening in the ceiling that was close to that wall.

It was clearly the way that had been used a very long time ago to come in and out of the cavern but unfortunately with the top half of the stone stairway now broken off it was no longer useful. That was demoralizing especially if there was no other way out.

Judging from the fading light coming through the two holes in the ceiling, it was now late afternoon and the sun would be setting in another hour or two. They knew the search parties would have concentrated their efforts to the areas that Nadir and the other children had hiked in and that they were unlikely to search this far north. The search would likely be called off at sunset, and it could be restarted tomorrow or left to the authorities.

Their parents were expecting them to return by sunset, and if they failed to return, they would be considered missing as well.

"Nyla, remember we saw the mountain stream coming out from near the very bottom of the hill when we were outside?" asked Junaid, looking at that end of the rectangular cavern.

"Yes, I do," replied Nyla, already beginning to guess what Junaid was thinking.

"Well, I wonder if I could dive down to the opening from inside and find a way out," said Junaid, confirming what Nyla suspected he was contemplating.

"But you yourself said this water is about fifty or sixty feet deep! You will have to dive all the way down in this cold water, try to find the opening, and follow it out while holding your breath! Even if you hold your breath long enough to find the inside opening and follow it, there is no guarantee there will not be any rocks blocking the way out!" She said, as she stood with her arms around her chest, shivering a little in her damp clothes and looking concerned and clearly unhappy with his risky suggestion.

Junaid moved forward and held her tightly against him, rubbing her back vigorously to try to keep her warm. He thought about her argument and looked up at the ceiling with the fading light of the setting sun seeping through; he looked at the broken off stone stairway and he looked at Nyla and Gulzar. He knew the chances of a search party finding them were extremely remote; as it was, they had only found Gulzar completely accidentally. He considered the options and felt that they could all stay together and slowly starve to death waiting for help to arrive or he could try to do something while he still had the energy and strength to do it before it was too late. He knew Nyla and Gulzar had no chance to survive without his own effort to find a way out and if that meant his life was in danger, then it was of little matter as it was forfeit in any event, while he tried to find a way out or while he sat and allowed death to come slowly from starvation and exposure.

"The alternative is for us to wait here and hope someone will come and find us. I think the chances of that happening, given where we are and how we got to this hidden chamber, are very slim to none," reasoned Junaid with conviction, adding, "I think I should at the least dive down and see if I can find an opening to the outside, Nyla."

"I do not agree, but if you want to dive down to just try to find the opening, I guess you could try. Remember that the water is very cold, and you will have to swim in darkness to find the opening," she said with resignation in her voice as Junaid took a step back and taking off his denim jacket he put it over her shoulders.

"I will be careful and use the flashlight to find my way," promised Junaid as he removed his sweater and jeans. He placed his clothes on top of the backpack and taking off his watch he handed it to Nyla saying, "Here, put it on. I wind it every morning." Then he hugged and kissed Nyla and telling Gulzar to take care of her, he took the flashlight and plunged into the cold water.

He swam with the current to the narrower end of the chamber and then turning on the flashlight and holding it in his mouth he took a deep breath and dove straight down. The pale beam of light probed the cold, dark water in front of him as the water pressure on his eardrums increased with his descent deeper. He was eventually able to see rocks and boulders at the end of the beam of light and now propelling himself with renewed energy, he eventually came to what was the tunnel-like opening that led to the outside. Over thousands of years larger and smaller rocks had accumulated in this area and had made something of a tunnel. For Junaid, it was impossible to tell how long this passage was as shining a light within it did not reveal anything but boulders and rocks with spaces in between, some of which were wide enough to accommodate him and others were too narrow. How long this rock strewn channel was or whether it narrowed or was blocked once he was already underway through it was impossible to guess without actually attempting the passage. No longer able to hold his breath and still having to swim back up some sixty feet, Junaid pushed off the rocky floor with all his strength and made desperately for the surface, kicking as hard as he could with his legs.

Nyla and Gulzar had been staring at the surface of the water where Junaid had disappeared near the other end of the pool for over two minutes now and were becoming worried. Nyla held Gulzar next to her, with an arm tightly around him as she hoped and prayed for Junaid to reappear. When almost three minutes had passed and panic was starting to take the place of concern, Junaid finally broke through the surface of the water gasping for breath and unable to say anything for a half minute as he held on to the wall under which he had found the possible opening.

Junaid knew that if he swam back to Nyla and told her what he had seen below, she would not let him go back down and risk his life. He also knew that if he did not risk his life in that tunnel, all three of them were likely going to die in this cavern. Banishing that thought, he regained his breath and visualized where he must dive to get to the passage in the least time while covering the shortest distance. He waved to Nyla and shouted, "I love you, Nyla!" and as she waved back shouting "I love you too," but before she had a chance to tell him to come back, he took a deep breath to fill his lungs and once again disappeared from her view. With strength and determination born of the conviction that the life of someone he loved depended on him, Junaid forced his way to the bottom of the lake and without waiting to consider whether he would be able to find a way to the outside or die trapped in the tunnel, he swam through the opening and disappeared within.

Nyla saw Junaid come up and after catching his breath instead of swimming back to her, he had stayed where he was, he had waved to her and she had heard him shout, "I love you," whereupon she had waved and shouted the same declaration of love to him but he had then disappeared under the water before she could urge him to come back.

Thoughts were aplenty in her mind which was now fraught with apprehension and laden with dread.

Had he found an opening?

If he had found an opening, he would have been ecstatic and would have shouted and told her that as soon as he had come up.

Had he not found an opening?

If so, he would have come back to her and then told her that.

Had he gone down and still did not know if there was an opening?

That is what Nyla's heart told her was the case.

He did not know if there was an opening and the only way for him to know was for him to go in farther. He would either find it or he would not. If he did not, he would die trying to find out.

That is why he had come up and stayed where he was to catch his breath before making the attempt.

That is why he had shouted his love for her, for her to hear, for possibly the last time.

She now began to see why he had insisted on going to find a way out.

If he failed, he would die.

If he failed, they would die as well.

If he never tried, all three would die together.

If there was the slimmest chance that he could find a way out, then he was willing to risk his own life to discover it for all of them.

She was glad to have shouted out her love for him. She was hoping that those were not the last words he ever heard in his life. She was glad that if he was never to hear any other words in his life, that the very last three words were "I love you" from her, his Nyla. Tears streamed down her cheeks onto Gulzar's head and he looked up at her.

"Why are you crying, Nyla?" asked Gulzar, afraid to see her cry.

"Because…because I love Junaid," answered Nyla, wiping her tears and attempting a smile for the benefit of the child staring at her face.

"But love is supposed to be good and makes you smile!" he said, trying to make her realize the fact he knew.

"Yes, it is good. Sometimes something good can make you even sadder than something bad. That is when you really know it is truly good," she said as she bent down and hugged him.

"I know this is all very confusing, but I promise you will know exactly what I mean one day when you are older." She then stood up straight and wrapped Junaid's jacket around herself tightly, clutching the lapels firmly in her cold, trembling hands.

As Junaid entered the tunnel, he took the flashlight out of his mouth and grabbed it in his left hand, pointing it in front of him and using his right hand to hold and maneuver around the rocks while his legs propelled him forward, his feet pushing against the rocks. Some ten feet ahead he saw a large boulder in the middle of the tunnel with a path on each side, forming a Y. Just then, his left hand hit and was badly scraped by a rock that was jutting out, causing him to let go of the flashlight that immediately floated up and to the ceiling of the tunnel, seven feet above him. For a moment he thought about going after the flashlight but then seeing that the ceiling of the tunnel was slanted upward toward the main cavern and the flashlight was rapidly following this slant higher, he decided to let it go and stay focused on his goal of finding a path through the tunnel.

Noticing that the entrance to the path on the left of the boulder was wider, he swam vigorously toward the junction and turned left. It was only now he realized that losing the flashlight may have been a blessing in disguise. While the passage was ink black and he was able to make progress only by feeling with his hands, as his eyes became better accustomed to this darkness he could see a faint blue light coming from beyond the rocks and this light guided him forward. A few more minutes and the sun would be below the tall trees. Another ten feet were covered slowly, almost inch by inch and as he arrived at what appeared to be a flat rock obstructing his path, he knew he could not hold his breath much longer. Unable to find a way beyond the flat rock, in desperation, he instinctively and forcefully went upward as if trying to get his head out of water and as he did this his forehead came in contact with a sharp rock on the ceiling of the narrow conduit, which was only about five feet high here. Unable to hold his breath any longer he exhaled forcefully, expecting now to inhale water but was shocked to suck in air instead. Astonishment and disbelief turned into jubilation as cold life-giving air found the deepest parts of his lungs. Using his hands to feel around, he learned that quite by a miracle he had surfaced into a small air pocket no more than a foot wide by two feet long and about six inches deep. He was standing on the rocky bottom of the tunnel with his head in the air pocket as the blood trickled from the gash in his forehead between his eyes and into his mouth. He felt the gash with his right hand, the taste of blood metallic in his mouth and clearing his head.

He had been given a second chance by the accidental finding of the air pocket, and he needed to make the most of it. He took a deep breath and submerged into the water, feeling around the rock to see if an opening large enough for him to pass was present. After a second gulp of air and trying once again he became certain that water was flowing around this rock through small crevices and openings that would not accommodate him. There was only one thing to do now. Go back to the junction and take the other path on the right this time and hope that he could find an opening large enough to let him through.

The oxygen in the air pocket was essentially used up by now and inhaling as much air as his lungs would hold, he dove, swimming against the current and toward the junction some ten feet away. Facing away from the light as he was now, he had to use his hands to guide himself forward around the rocks while propelling with his legs.

Nyla glanced at Junaid's watch on her left wrist. He had been gone about ten minutes when Nyla saw his flashlight come up to the surface of the water near where he had disappeared from view. She shouted his name excitedly and waited for him to show himself. After another minute it became quite apparent to Nyla that Junaid was not holding his flashlight, which was now bobbing near the wall, its anemic light throwing ghostly images onto the ceiling and the walls of the cavern.

The worst possible thoughts now assailed her. The fact the flashlight had come up without him. The fact that it had been at least ten minutes since he had gone underwater before the flashlight had appeared. Both these facts pointed to just one possibility.

Junaid had gone down to look for the passage amongst the rocks in the tunnel, and he had become trapped. When his hands were no longer able to hold the flashlight, it had floated up and finally popped up where she had seen it. Junaid had given his life in an attempt to save her and Gulzar. She felt an emptiness within, as if a part of her body was missing, as if her mind was a bit loose from its normal moorings, as if whether she made it out of this trap was no longer all that important or even desirable. The energy in her limbs ebbed and the brightness in her eyes faded away even as the last rays of light coming through the ceiling holes died out. But the darkness in the vast underground chamber paled in comparison to the gloom and murkiness within her young heart, now barren and desolate, fate having cruelly wrenched from it the object and source of its love.

She did not say any of this to Gulzar and instead automatically opened the backpack and took out the last two chocolate bars, giving one to Gulzar to eat now and keeping the other for him to eat in the morning. They had no shortage of fresh water and drank from the clear pool whenever they felt thirsty.

Junaid arrived at the junction and moving with agility born of desperation, he turned onto the path to the right. The urgency to breathe burning in his lungs, he swam as fast as his vision would allow, guided by the sallowest and barely perceptible glow that was now more a difference in the degree of darkness than even the dimmest beacon. He arrived now at a point, roughly the same distance as where his progress was halted in the other passageway, and three rocks now hindered his way. He felt rather than saw, a triangular opening in the middle of these three rocks and went headlong into it with his arms stretched out ahead of his head, his chest snug in the impossibly small opening and his feet scratching for purchase and then kicking viciously against the sharp rocky outcroppings. The prospect of getting caught in this position was too horrible for him to imagine as he kicked and struggled ignoring the sharp pain in his sides until finally his chest and then his belly and legs were beyond the slabs of limestone. Another few seconds and he would have to breathe, his eyes bulging with the strain and his cheeks and lips barely holding in the stale air that was desperately trying to blow out of his lungs, he exerted with all his might what he felt was his final effort and as his body lunged forward, he felt as though the water was pulling him forward faster than he was swimming.

Seeking what he could not yet see, he shot forward and as he finally exhaled the air he had inhaled over three minutes and an eternity ago, he was spat out of the opening with a torrent of water like an insignificant twig. He splashed onto a small pool of water and breathed the cool fresh air his body was starving for. Collecting his shaky legs underneath him, he struggled to stand and collapsed on the wet sand a few feet away. Sharp shooting pain on both sides of his lower rib cage made taking deep breaths impossible.

The sun had set not too long ago, and the western sky was still painted in crimson and shades of pink. He thanked God for letting him find a way out and asked for the strength to do what he needed to do next. Taking stock of himself, he was momentarily bemused seeing himself in just his boxers. His forehead wound was still seeping some blood and there were nasty abrasions and scrapes on his left elbow, the left forearm and the knuckles of both his hands. There were abrasions and some missing skin over the lower rib cage on both sides where he had been caught in the tight opening between the rocks. He was glad to have escaped without any major injuries, and it was only when he started to run that he fell recoiling with pain. Looking at his feet he saw the deep bleeding gashes and cuts that he had sustained when making his way through the rocky tunnel and especially during the last frenzied effort before the final escape to the outside.

He had intended to climb the hill by walking up the gently rising grade on the farther side, finding the hidden vents in the roof of the subterranean cavern and letting Nyla know he had made it out. But now considering his present circumstance, he decided against that. He was cold and bleeding from deep cuts and abrasions in different parts of his body and as a result of this blood loss he was starting to feel faint. He was exhausted and going around the hill to climb it and then coming back down would easily add close to two hundred yards to the distance he must cover as soon as possible. He was also worried, and this thought really terrified him, that in this darkness he could possibly fall through one of the two holes in the roof of the cavern and then all this effort would have been for naught.

He therefore decided to take on what now felt to be at least as daunting a task as what he had just undertaken by finding a way out of the cavern. He had to walk, crawl, or otherwise go and get help before complete exhaustion and loss of blood made it impossible for him to stay conscious. Taking a step onto the rocky ground made him wince with pain, and he involuntarily sat down, his eyes closed as he tried desperately to ward off the darkness that besieged him. After a minute of sitting on the ground, he crawled back to the stream and lay on his belly drinking as much water as he could possibly drink without vomiting. Looking around he saw green wavy algae undulating in the clear water and he had an idea. He plucked out as much of the slimy strands in his fists as he could and wrapped these around his feet. He did this several times and when he stood up now he could tolerate the pain which was now merely excruciating and not utterly unbearable. He saw and grabbed a fist thick branch that the water and sun had bleached to a perfect white color and using it to brace himself he tentatively started his journey toward home.

The search teams had all returned with the setting sun, and Gulzar's parents were beyond grief when they could not find their son. His mother was crying inconsolably as she sat next to Mrs. Kafrooni and Mrs. Ibrahim whose son and daughter were the first to have left in search of her son that morning. Mrs. Kafrooni tried to reassure her saying that her son knew the woods well, and he was still out there searching. An hour after the sun had set, both the ladies left the distraught mother and went home to wait for their son and daughter respectively.

Around ten that night Mrs. Kafrooni finally could no longer contain herself and called Nyla's mother to see if she had returned. Learning that neither had returned caused both the mothers to become increasingly alarmed.

Every member of the search party had returned hours ago.

They should have been home by now.

Junaid had promised he would have Nyla back by sunset.

That he had not returned was cause for concern, and she spoke with her husband who was as anxious as she was. He told her that if Junaid and Nyla had not returned in the next hour, he would call the police and inform them of the missing teenagers.

He also planned on going into the woods himself soon.

Limping badly and using the stick to support most of his weight, Junaid covered ground as quickly as he could. The struggle had added to his exhaustion and while the algae around his feet provided some relief from pain, the bleeding increased with every additional step he took. He was over half a mile from the dirt path when a severe bout of dizziness caused him to fall unconscious. He lay insensible for over an hour until a nightmare he could not recall woke him up shivering. It took him a few moments to realize where he was and how he had come to be in these dark woods on this dark night. He found the stick next to him and using it he struggled with all his might to stand up. Regaining his whereabouts in these woods that he had known since he was a little boy, he started to limp in the direction of home.

He was still a thousand yards or more from the dirt path, that final few hundred yards to home when he had another severe episode of lightheadedness that caused him to sit down before he could pass out.

He knew now that in his present condition he could not make it all the way home. He realized he was losing too much blood and that if he lost enough blood he was not going to survive and then no one would know where Nyla was trapped. He could not, must not, allow that to happen. Junaid now reconsidered his options and made a decision based on how much time he felt he had remaining. With the dizziness abating somewhat he turned and made for his tree house, less than a hundred yards from his position. The relative proximity of his new objective gave his faltering body a jolt of energy and he moved with renewed determination, his eyes focused unblinking on the dark shadow of the giant tree that loomed ahead.

Mr. Kafrooni called the police and Mr. Ibrahim, informing the former that his son and Nyla had gone missing and the latter that he was going into the woods to search for their children. Mr. Ibrahim told his friend that he was on his way and that they would both go and look for their children together.

Around midnight, two narrow slivers of moonbeam made silvery pillars of heavenly light that gleamed down from the small openings in the ceiling to the water below and then continued almost unbroken to the bottom of the crystal clear lake. Nyla had dozed off with Gulzar's head on her lap as she sat with her back against the wall of the cavern. In her dream she saw Junaid struggling and in pain, in need of help and then he had called out her name. That is when she had awakened from her dream and saw the pillars of light, unworldly and ethereal. She remembered the  dream and her aching heart told her that her Junaid was no longer in pain; he was never going to be in pain again. The thought made her glad and unimaginably sad at the same time. She looked at the two pillars of light with bitterness and wished the moon would move off and her cavern would be dark again. She closed her eyes as a single tear escaped her will to keep it captive.

Junaid stood leaning against the peepul tree, warding off the bouts of shakiness that assailed him again and again. Letting go of the tree, he grabbed for and found the rope ladder that dangled from it. He now leaned on the ladder and almost panicked knowing what he had to do next. Taking it one step at a time, in the ultimate sense of the phrase, he now started to climb the ladder that he had climbed untold number of times. This time he was climbing it for a reason far more significant than merely getting to the tree house. This time the stakes were astronomical. This time the pain he felt in his feet at each and every step brought him one step, one rung closer to attaining his goal. This agonizing climb was merely a necessary step to negotiating what was for him the single most important thing he must accomplish irrespective of whether he lived or died thereafter.

Halfway up the ladder, the world started to spin around him, and it was a miracle that he grabbed and held on to the ladder until the episode passed. Without looking up to keep him from getting discouraged and without looking down to avoid becoming dizzy and fearful of a fall, he looked at and focused on each step of the ladder as he climbed steadily up.

Finally after what to him seemed like an eternity, Junaid pushed off the last rung and fell face-first on the wooden floor of his tree house. He lay there for several minutes and then turned over onto his back as his eyes searched for what he hoped he would find. On the bench below the window he saw two plastic bottles of water. He crawled over eagerly to find that one bottle that was lying on its side was nearly empty but the other was full of water. He drank the two bottles down to the last drop and then struggled over to the door of the tree house and lay down on his belly. Reaching down under the door he undid the two hooks that the ladder was hanging from and let it fall, hoping that the hooks would not catch on any branch on the way down. He heard the ladder fall with a rippling sound followed by the reassuring metallic thud of the hooks hitting ground seconds later.

Junaid rested for a minute or two allowing his eyes to refocus and his head to stop spinning and then throwing down the empty bottles of water, he started the climb down the tree, but this time he would have to do it without a ladder. Holding the branches and the stem of the tree in his hands and using his feet to find support he began the excruciatingly painful task of sliding and slipping downward. Every time he slid a few inches down, he had to keep his lacerated feet pressed against the rough bark of the tree to allow the traction to keep him from slipping and falling, and each time he did this he experienced flinching, nauseating pain. One such slide of necessity was a few feet long and the tearing insufferable pain made him scream out in abject agony. He then stood trembling and shivering against the rough bark, forcing his mind to ignore the stinging, scathing pain in his mutilated feet. With tears in his eyes he looked up at the full moon directly overhead and wondered if he was ever going to see the moon again with Nyla. For a moment his rambling imagination took him to the terraced roof of his home. For a moment he was there holding Nyla in his arms. For a moment this same moon was smiling down upon them as he kissed her lips. For a moment he allowed himself the luxury of this reprieve from reality. But only for a moment.

Well past midnight, and the pillars of light were gone. She was thirsty but dared not move as Gulzar looked to be dreaming a peaceful dream, and she did not want him to wake up and find himself in this dark and gloomy place. He deserved to be happy even if only in his dreams. The morrow was coming soon enough. She sighed and looked at the darkness that was all around. Darkness that permeated her mind and soul just as completely as it seemed to pervade this chamber.

Dreading every slide and desperate to repeat it as soon as his sanity would allow him to inflict more pain upon his shredded nerves, Junaid made his way down the tree. Finally he slid down the last few feet and fell on his back laughing deliriously. As he lay there he wondered which hurt more, his feet or his ribs, and he finally decided that his ribs hurt very much but only when he breathed and the feet caused him unbearable agony but only when he stood up or walked. Neither breathing nor walking could be avoided however, and getting on all fours he braced himself against the tree and ignoring the pain in his feet he stood up.

It took him a few minutes to roll up the rope ladder and as he attempted to pick it up onto his shoulder he realized that he had been a fool. The rope ladder was about sixty feet long, and it was heavy. It would have been heavy enough for Junaid to carry if he was unhurt and fresh, but now it was close to impossible. He had several hundred yards over rough and difficult terrain to the stream and the hill which he must then climb by going around it.

Anger took the place of despair as he thought of Nyla trapped in that dark place that he must return to. He felt anger at all that had happened to cause Nyla and Gulzar and himself to be in the predicament they were in but most of all he felt anger at himself for letting hopelessness come near him. Hopelessness when two lives were counting on him to be courageous and strong. He stuck one of the empty bottles in his boxers and without giving the matter any further thought and holding the two hooks in his hands he started to drag the ladder behind him.

The water he had been able to drink had given Junaid some respite from thirst born of a continuing loss of blood. As he now struggled and dragged the ladder behind him, he did so more with the power of his will than any substantial reserves of energy in his consumed body. His will to not fail was the only thing that was keeping him from falling down on every impossible step he now took. His brain was free of complicated thoughts. He had a mission and he was in the process of completing it. This mission was the directive from his mind and this body was his tool that was going to accomplish it. That is all there was to it.

In the deepest recesses of his foggy consciousness he thought he heard, far away and barely audible, someone call his name and that of Nyla, but he was unable to acknowledge the voices as real and therefore merely a figment of his battered imagination. Soon the faint voices drifted away and were gone like the summer wind that makes a willow tree moan just long enough for you to hear the things you want to hear.

He had lost track of time and was no longer interested in it.

Knowing the time or guessing an approximation of it was a complication he had no use for. It would make little difference to him in the carrying out of his mission.

Every now and then the ladder would get caught in some rock or a root, and he would tug to free it. A few times he had to walk back to untangle it, but he did so without annoyance or frustration. He no longer had the energy for either. The only anger he had was reserved for himself in case he showed any despondency in the carrying out of his objective.

After the passage of an interminable period of time, and altogether spent in mind and body, he eventually lurched and stumbled on to the foot of the hill that he had left several hours ago. As he bent down to drink the cold water he fell senseless as merciful darkness granted him temporary respite. He lay there long enough for his abused body to once again be able to respond to the dictates of his mind and then as if in a trance and afraid that he might never wake up if he did not get up now, he struggled to his feet. Dragging the ladder behind him, he compelled his legs to move him forward. The algae around his feet had long since shredded and fallen off. The pain in his alarmingly swollen feet was however numbed by his loss of perception to as much physical pain as was necessary to keep him from fainting. He rounded the hill and climbed it from the gently sloping ground behind it. Far in the distance, the eastern sky was turning a purplish blue and the remaining stars were beginning to fade one by one. Falling on all fours as much from utter fatigue as from his desire to not fall through a hole, he inched forward looking for the opening that was close to the wall where Nyla had found the half broken stone stairway.

They both thought they had heard it.

A single, distant, agony filled cry of "Nyla!" had drifted to their ears and was not repeated. Try as they might they could not locate the source of that very faint call and with the wind making sounds as it whistled through the branches of the scores of trees around them, they eventually began to doubt they had heard a human voice at all. It was not until the eastern sky had started to turn light that Mr. Kafrooni and Mr. Ibrahim, exhausted and dejected finally went home to their hopeful, waiting wives. The pain of having to tell their wives of their failure heavy in their hearts.

Many times had she awakened that night, each time from a nightmare and each time to a reality that made her wish she was living the nightmare instead. The gloomy night was about to give way to a dismal day. A day during which she would not have even the momentary escape of sleep from the life she was forced to endure all alone. How long she wondered, would it take for her to die of starvation with just water as her sustenance. Not long she hoped. Then she looked down at Gulzar and shuddered.

Junaid had given his life trying to find a way for them to live. She was not going to just give up. Never.

"Not…yet, not yet…," gibbered Junaid incoherently to himself, fighting the battle within his utterly depleted and feverish body to stay awake just a little longer, just a few moments more. His mind commanding his body that its services were required still and that unconsciousness was a luxury not yet to be enjoyed, not just yet. He crept forward on his belly, pushing his body forward with his bloodied elbows, his fingers searching for what his blurred vision could not, the void that he sought must be near, it must! And then it was, an emptiness that his right hand found by its very lack of substance. He leaned forward an inch or two and felt the smooth and polished, innocuous borders of the entrance to the cave, the jaws of the monster that had swallowed something precious, the gullet of the beast that he was now going to reach down into and pull out his Nyla! He had found it!

"Hold on…Nyla…," he murmured under his breath with a tongue too thick to pronounce anything comprehensible to anyone but himself. With energy he did not possess and with arms that did not know when to quit, he pulled and gathered the ladder in a circular heap next to him. Nearly pushing the pile into the hole, he barely caught himself and grabbed the two hooks that he must first anchor. Looking around, rubbing his eyes with his blistered hands, he searched for something he could trust to hold with complete confidence, a hold that must not be broken. He found none. Crawling a few inches on the south side of the hole, he felt a depression with a two-inch lip that he tried to anchor the hooks to but failed. In desperation, he looked at his hands and found what he sought. It would have to do, his body was exhausted and devoid of every last bit of reserve, there was no more time and nothing else to do. He wrapped a few turns of the length of rope beyond the metal hooks around his waist and holding the hooks in his hands he turned over on his back, kicking the ladder once and then again, he saw it disappear in the darkness of the gaping hole. Before he felt the weight of the ladder he threw himself backward into the little depression and jammed his swollen feet against the few inches of its rocky lip, straightening and locking his knees just as the ladder stopped falling.

At that very moment she heard a scraping sound from the ceiling and then heard something grate against the wall above and about twenty feet to her right. It was too dark to see and she could not make out what if anything had made the noise that was loud enough to have awakened Gulzar. He saw her staring above and tried to locate what she was looking at.

She wished she had the flashlight now, she said.

"I can get the flashlight, Nyla!" Gulzar said emphatically.

"No. It is too far away and the water is deep," she said without much emotion.

"I am a good swimmer! That is how I was able to swim after falling into the water, Nyla. Please?" he begged her.

He dug out two fresh batteries from the backpack and held those in front of her.

She looked at his eager face and could not disregard his enthusiasm.

"I want you to swim to that rock near us and come back so I can see how you swim," she told him.

Taking off his pants and shirt, Gulzar took a running start and dove head first with arms outstretched in front of him. He was at the rock in a few seconds and slicing through the water on his way back like an expert swimmer.

He splashed onto the sand smiling happily. "See?" he said.

"OK, but be careful, and if you cannot find it, I want you to come back right away. The batteries in the flashlight died sometime yesterday, so it may not be easy to spot it."

She cautioned him and reminded him again to come back as quickly as he could.

Gulzar was a skillful swimmer and was in the water swimming rapidly to the wall where the flashlight was last seen. He was there in less than two minutes and retrieved the flashlight from where it was gently bobbing up and down against the wall. Happily he grabbed it in his right hand and pushing off from the wall he made his way back to an anxiously waiting Nyla. He was back in less than five minutes from the time he had left and Nyla hugged him with relief. Gulzar used Nyla's scarf to dry himself and then put on his clothes while she put the new batteries in the flashlight and turned it on, pointing the beam in the general direction of where she thought she had heard the sound.

Nyla's jaw dropped with surprise when she saw a ladder dangling through the opening near the wall they were sitting against. The ladder came to a few feet beyond where the stone stairway had broken off, but it was close enough that an outstretched arm could easily reach it. She was astonished to see the ladder and was surprised at the same time that no one had shouted out to them or made any attempt to tell them they were found. Using the flashlight to show the way, Nyla grabbed

Gulzar's hand and walked through the knee-deep water to the base of the stone stairway. Looking back she saw Junaid's backpack with his clothes on the sandy strip and not wanting to leave it behind, she walked back and put it on her back.

Mixed and disordered thoughts troubled her weary mind. She was gratified at the chance to be able to see her parents again; God knows they must have suffered in her absence. She was truly happy that Gulzar would be reunited with his parents. She was at the same time heartbroken on leaving the place that Junaid would never leave. She was guilt ridden that while he died attempting to help her escape this trap, she was soon to be free while he was forever trapped. Or was it the other way around, she grimly reflected. She felt miserable at the prospect of living on knowing that she would never see him again. When she was imprisoned in the cavern and even though he was already gone, she still had a sense that they were suffering together and that she was unlikely to make it out alive.

The fact that she was about to be freed and was soon to be amongst other people was already making her feel his absence more. To be separated from all humanity was much more tolerable than to be kept from only him and no one else. To be lonely in a crowd of people is much more agonizing—the sign of a broken heart. She was beginning to learn of this pain. She would live amongst others and be constantly reminded of his absence. It was painful to be alive and living when the one you lived for was gone, forever.

While she could no longer be with him, the memory of their time together would now be her constant companion. Nyla looked at Junaid's watch and saw the seconds hand ticking tirelessly. A painful smile betrayed her thoughts as she recalled

Junaid telling her about him winding the watch every morning. She reflected upon how he would never and could never wind it again. The simple dignity of being able to wind his watch had been taken from him. She could not bring him back, she thought, but she could wind his watch for him. She felt connected to him through the movement of the hands of the watch, hands that he had himself set in motion just yesterday, hands that she could keep from stopping. She would wind it for him, for them, every morning without fail, happily she would wind it and make sure it never stopped running. Her throat tightening with emotion she unstrapped the watch from around her wrist and gently turned the crown and then looking at Gulzar, she smiled and put the watch back on her wrist.

She recalled the moments of tenderness and love, made the more precious by how fleeting and few she now felt those to be but were nevertheless theirs and could never be taken away. She was learning that love, truly and deeply felt and honestly shared was impervious to the shackles of distance and of the state of being alive or dead and instead lives on within the spirit of those who have had the courage to let it in and then the good fortune to have found another so inclined and equally dauntless. So while she had lost the person she loved, she would ever continue to love him.

She managed a faked smile and artificial excitement for the sake of Gulzar and guided him up the stone steps, wondering still about the lack of any communication from those who had sent down the ladder. Nyla explained to Gulzar what was to be done now that they were at the top of the broken steps and reaching out with her left hand while holding him with her right, she grabbed the ladder. Guiding him onto the ladder, she herself stepped on around him, covering him so that he could not fall even if he were to slip. They had to climb some fifty feet to the opening which was now a shade lighter with the faint glow of the early morning. Steadily they climbed, step after securely placed step, anxious to get out and careful not to fall back in. Still they could not see or hear their rescuers as they arrived at the opening at last. Nyla saw a few stars in the misty dark of the early morning sky and it perplexed her to find no one above as she helped Gulzar climb out first and then followed him to the roof of what had been their subterranean prison.

She pulled herself out and looked around and behind herself to see if she could find someone. In the milky light of the cold foggy morning her eyes followed the ladder and fixed on two swollen feet and a body lying in a shallow depression just beyond. Bewildered, she rushed forward and saw what was to trouble her dreams for a very long time. Pale as death, devoid of every stitch of clothing but for the tattered remains of his boxer shorts, his face, neck and chest matted with dry blood, his forehead with an ugly gaping gash, his hands a mass of cuts and blisters and his left elbow ripped open deep to a glistening white bone, his feet lacerated and slashed and swollen to the extent that they were barely recognizable as feet, so lay her Junaid, holding in his rigidly frozen hands the hooks that secured the ladder that she had climbed to get out of the chamber that had held her captive.

So deathly colorless was he, so stiff his body looked and so motionless did he lay that she was convinced he was dead.

Unable to fathom finding him when he was in her broken heart already gone, seeing him as he now was in front of her and trying to understand all that he must have been through, she fell upon his chest crying as she had not allowed herself to cry since seeing him last. She shook him by his shoulders, screaming for him to wake up, to look at her and to let her look at him look at her, one more time. She kissed his dry, cracked lips and told him she loved him, that she could not live without him and that she would be very angry with him and never forgive him if he did not come back to be with her. But he did not move, did not answer her, and did not open his eyes. The body had shut down, forced to endure and pushed beyond its limits, it had finally won its battle against the dictates of the mind that no longer controlled it, a mind that was still aware but unable to convey its awareness by any means physical.

Sobbing with tears streaming from her closed eyes, she laid her head on his chest to imagine for a moment that they were both together, together in their tree house, rolling around on the floor and cuddling, warm, and comfortable, alive with life and passion. She imagined more than she heard, she thought, a beat of his heart, faint and distant, she felt or heard it again, erratically now, struggling to beat, needing a reason to beat, again she heard it, no she did not imagine it, two beats in quick succession and then a pause before another beat. She sat up with a start, her eyes wide open and heart pounding wildly. He was alive, still. *He* now needed *her!* Leaning over him once again, she put her mouth close to his right ear and told him she was here next to him, that she was safe, that he had got her out of the cave she was trapped in and that she needed him to stay with her now more than ever. She told him she loved him more than she ever had. She told him she was proud of him and that Gulzar was safe because of him as well. She felt how cold his body was and removing the rope from around him, she started to carefully dress him in his pants and sweater that she had brought in his backpack when leaving the cavern.

Nyla grabbed the empty bottle of water lying next to Junaid and telling Gulzar to not move an inch from his side she ran as fast as she could down the hill to the stream below. Her mind racing and beginning to comprehend what Junaid must have done and endured in the almost fourteen hours since she had seen him last. She had assumed that he had become trapped in the tunnel and had drowned when the flashlight had come up, but now she knew that he had somehow found a way out in the darkness amongst the rocks. He must have sustained those cuts on his body while attempting the escape and then in that precarious state had somehow made his way to the tree house, climbed the ladder to the top and had unhooked and thrown it to the ground. The thought of him then making his perilous way down the tree in his battered condition and to then drag the heavy ladder all the way back and then to the top of the hill was a feat she could not fully fathom.

Out of breath, she ran back to his side and holding his head up in her lap she dripped a few drops of water in his parched mouth. She needed to get him help urgently. She needed to decide how to go about it. Carrying him in the state he was in was impossible for her to manage alone. To leave him there alone defenseless in these hills with jackals, snakes, and leopards was unthinkable for her. Even if there was no such danger from animals which might attack him, she could possibly be leaving him to die alone due simply to his current extremely delicate state. Leaving Gulzar with him did not alter these arguments or lessen the risks.

In desperation, she poured a little more water down Junaid's mouth and heard a gurgle and then felt him choking as the water trickled down his airway.

Junaid had finally passed out. He had finally allowed his body to stop and do nothing more than to maintain the position he had assumed with his legs locked straight and the hooks ensnared in his frozen hands, fingers tightly curled in an almost rigor mortis like tightness. He felt no pain and no hunger; no cold assaulted his near nakedness and no dreams disturbed his peaceful slumber. He was at peace, having done all that was humanly required of him. So as he lay lifeless but not without life, his mind filtered out every sensation that had brought him pain. His skin no longer felt the sting of cuts and abrasions; his muscles no longer cramped from fourteen hours of constant struggle; his bones no longer ached and his eyes no longer suffered the constant strain of guiding him. But his hearing, his hearing was the one connection with the painful world, the one channel that was still open, albeit just barely.

In the dreamless deathly quiet of his stuporous sleep, his mind, no longer aware of his physical body and floating as does effervescent foam on a gently breaking wave, was disturbed all at once. It was troubled by something that it was presented that required its attention. It was a perception, perhaps unreal, perhaps a figment of its own concoction, a barely perceived sound, a voice, a peculiar voice it was. Though it barely registered it had a power and a potency that was difficult to ignore. It required the participation of the higher centers of cognition and analysis and as it was repeated, it was now impossible to evade. The voice, once vaguely recognized, was not unpleasant but rather pleasing and a tonic that was then feverishly sought. Again it was heard and this time deciphered as the one sound he had longed to hear.

Though unable to move a muscle or even twitch his eyelids, Junaid became aware of the voice of his love, his Nyla, coming from very close. It seemed to be whispered into his ear, and it spoke to him of love and faith and trust and promises that it implored must be kept. It was a voice, an appeal that pleaded with him and reassured him; the voice begged him to stay and not leave, to be brave and strong, and to be patient and not give up.

He tried to move his lips and to answer her, to open his eyes and to see her and to move his hand and to touch her, but all that he could do was to listen to her gentle voice and the only thing his heart could do was to skip a beat, a beat that was heard by the ear pressed against his chest.

The voice was then gone all of a sudden. It was gone for what to Junaid's starving ears seemed like a very long time, and then it was back, soothing and calming him again as he now barely felt his head lifted and gently placed in the lap of what felt like love. His lips were kissed gently and then drops of cool water entered his dry mouth, wetting his tongue that was longing to call out her name. He felt more water in his mouth, and he tried to swallow but his parched throat would not cooperate and a drop or two of water seeped down to the opening of his airway, causing him to choke and sputter, giving the first signal that he was returning to the world where pleasure and pain went hand in hand.

She observed him cough and suppress a gag and then relax his head back in her lap. His breathing became steady as she spoke to him gently and she saw his eyelids flutter and open a little and then open a little more, the pupils constricting as he tried to focus on her face. She noticed him close his eyelids tightly and then open them again; she then saw him find her face and blink slowly with placid satisfaction.

She had nothing to give him but water. He needed nothing more, as long as it was offered by her hands. The cool water, moistened his mouth and throat and slowly as she continued to drip it into his mouth, it began to hydrate his desiccated body; cell by cell and tissue by tissue it brought him back to life.

He felt strength return slowly to his arms and legs just as the pain came creeping back. Moving his tongue to the top of his mouth and swallowing, he attempted to speak a few times before he could say a single word.

"Nyla…" was the first word he uttered, more a raspy whisper, barely recognizable but instantly understood by her. She smiled. "Yes, Junaid, I am here," she said softly as she kissed his forehead, making him wince with pain but smile with pleasure.

"You have been a busy boy, Junaid!" she said affectionately, gently caressing and holding his right hand, as she sat leaning toward him, her legs bent under her on the rocky ground.

"I cannot imagine what you must have gone through," she whispered softly with her face inches from his.

"I…needed my…" He swallowed. "My backpack back," he said haltingly but with a smile that cracked open a cut on his lip, making him flinch.

"Well, I am glad I brought it up with me then!" replied Nyla with a warm smile, encouraged and amused by the light-hearted joke given his precarious condition.

"I also…needed… my Nyla back," he whispered through dry, cracking lips.

"And you have her, forever," she said as she kissed his lips softly.

Minutes passed upon minutes and Junaid felt the warmth of life and love slowly creep into his broken body.

"We need to get you back home, Junaid, you and Gulzar. Women have to do everything for you guys these days!" she said with mock exasperation.

"Yeah…good thing you are so tough…just carry us both… on your back, superwoman!" he responded, trying to sit up.

"Easy, easy, let me help you. Do you have a part of your body that is not broken or cut up so I can grab it to help you up?" she asked, looking at his arms and legs with concern.

"My back hurts less than the rest of me," he replied, grimacing with the pain that was now beginning to assault him again.

"I would go down and get your hiking shoes, Junaid, but looks like it would not do you any good," she said, looking at his swollen and lacerated feet with distress, as though she could feel his pain.

"But I have something better for your feet than your stinky sneakers!" she added with enthusiasm, taking her soft and warm scarf from around her neck.

Making a small tear in the middle of the scarf with her teeth, she tore it into two long lengths and then after washing his feet gently, wrapped the soft cloth around his feet as snugly as he could tolerate.

Gulzar was sitting behind Junaid, helping prop him up. He had a worried look on his face and was very quiet. Sensing his distress, Junaid told him to come around and sit facing him.

"I heard you were great at keeping Nyla from getting all scared last night, big guy! And the way you swam out to get the flashlight, that was very brave!" said Junaid, trying to show no pain on his smiling face.

Gulzar looked over Junaid's wounds and gulped.

"Does it hurt much?" he asked with his eyes filled with concern.

"Only when I move," said Junaid truthfully, "so you are going to help me move. OK?"

"Sure! I am strong!" Gulzar showed him his biceps, making Junaid and Nyla smile.

The sun was peaking over the eastern horizon and starting to warm up the flat top of the hill. With his clothes now keeping him warm and the sun coming up, Junaid's spirits were rising and despite Nyla's attempts to have him stay where he was while she went to get help, he insisted on coming.

Nyla considered his weakened state and knew that it was not altogether safe to leave him completely alone and defenseless, so she finally relented.

With Gulzar holding his right arm and Nyla supporting him at the left armpit, Junaid was lifted from a sitting position to his feet. For a second or two, he felt dizzy as his body became accustomed to the upright position. As he took a step forward the pain in his feet made him stumble, and he would have fallen had Nyla not held him up, letting him lean on her. Quickly regaining his balance and grimacing with pain, he took another step and then another. While few parts of his body were truly pain free, it was his feet that troubled him most as he hobbled along the rocks and the loose stones and as he stepped over branches and perspired over the prospect of having to jump over a few obstacles on the way. Their progress was painfully slow, and they stopped frequently to let him catch his breath. Once when he sat on a tree stump to rest, Nyla cringed at the sight of the blood-soaked scarf around his feet. Giving him some water to drink, she adjusted her backpack and asked him if he wanted to go on or rest here while she got help. He still insisted on coming and they moved on again.

By the time the sun was directly overhead they were finally at the dirt path and Junaid was exhausted to the point that he could not go on another step.

Mrs. Ibrahim came over to Mrs. Kafrooni's home shortly after sunrise. Their husbands had both searched for the children most of the night and were now finally taking a nap. The two mothers were not satisfied with staying home waiting, and they decided to go into the woods on their own. They walked slowly, covering as much ground as they could and after three hours they arrived at the base of a large peepul tree. As they sat resting for a few minutes in its shade, Mrs Kafrooni found a smooth white stick with bloody finger and hand prints at one end. She held it now, not knowing that her son had gripped it just a few hours earlier during a life and death struggle to get to that very tree. Thinking that it was time for them to go back home now, they stood up and started the walk back, calling out for Nayla and Junaid at intervals.

It would have been easy for Junaid to pass out, to let his spent body fall to the ground and stop the pain he felt. But he knew with every step they came closer to home and to making sure that Nyla was no longer in danger. His heart would not allow him to rest until he felt that was the case. So it was only as they at last left the woods at the head of the narrow dirt path that led directly to home, that Junaid finally collapsed and fainted. Quickly and yet gently, she rolled him over on his back and telling Gulzar to stay with him, she had just started running toward Junaid's home when she heard her mother call out her name from behind her. She stopped and now heard Junaid's name being called. She was somewhat surprised that the voices calling were behind them in the woods and thought the search party was beginning their hunt for them again. Just then she saw her mother and Mrs. Kafrooni leave the woods and run toward them.

What happened in the next hour was a blur in Nyla's mind.

Crying while telling the ladies whatever she could, Nyla was able to convey the gist of what they had gone through. In quick short sentences and between sobs, she begged them to not let Junaid die. She had done all that was within her ability in bringing him to this place where he now lay unconscious, and she needed them to take over and keep him safe.

Her mother hugged and kissed her more than she had let her in a very long time. Mrs. Kafrooni was grief-stricken to see her son in the physical condition she found him in but felt blessed and was proud of what he had done. Minutes later Nyla ran as fast as she could to tell Mr. Kafrooni and not much later an ambulance surrounded by the entire neighborhood was at the scene. Gulzar's parents could not believe their eyes when they saw their son running to them happily and without as much as a scratch on his body.

Nyla was by Junaid's side when he had an IV put in his arm, when he was placed on a stretcher, and when he was put in the ambulance and taken to the hospital. She was by his side when they took him into the emergency room to work on his wounds and when he started to regain consciousness. It was her face he saw first as she stood by his feet with tears in her eyes but a brave smile on her face for his sake. He looked at her and she saw on his pale lips the slightest shadow of a smile as a nurse started to carefully take off what was now a bloody mess wrapped around his feet. As his feet came unwrapped, Nyla cried openly and was taken out of the room by her mother who herself grimaced when she saw the deep cuts and gashes on his feet.

Outside, in the waiting room, Nyla was questioned and she told the gathered crowd what she could before her father told them to leave his daughter alone for now.

After Junaid had been examined, x-rayed, bandaged, and started on the IV fluids and medications, his bed was wheeled to his room. His parents together with Nyla and her parents went with him to the room where he was now sleeping peacefully. Nyla went up to his bed and bent down to tell him in his ear that she loved him and that she was now leaving safely with her parents and would be back to see him soon.

That night, after a long hot shower and a hearty dinner, an utterly exhausted Nyla fell asleep peacefully. That night, for the first time in several years, she slept with a marble in her right hand, a marble with a pink flower within.

# Chapter 15

The news of the safe return of Gulzar spread all over the city and beyond rapidly.

Radio, television, and newspaper reporters had descended upon the city interviewing and questioning anyone who could give them the details of the child's disappearance while hiking in the hills and his unlikely and daring rescue at the hands of two young people, one of whom was still hospitalized and the other was a pretty and gifted student from the same school as the heretofore missing child.

The reporters were most interested in two aspects of the story. One was the human interest story about the emotional rollercoaster that the parents of the missing child had to endure. It was their reunion with the lost child that made this story special and the fact that Gulzar was physically unscathed during the entire ordeal gave it the storybook happy ending that readers around the country found so endearing.

Junaid and Nyla's efforts in bringing about the rescue and the extraordinary circumstances of it were the other part of the story that reporters could not get enough of, especially since the details of what had happened were not completely known to anyone other than the three children themselves.

Gulzar had been questioned in his parents' presence and had told all he had seen with his youthful eyes. Nyla and Junaid understood how they had suffered during those harrowing hours and had told the reporters what they felt comfortable relating but without going into the most painful details nor openly telling the world of their personal feelings. It was their remarkable self-sacrifice and perseverance in the face of extreme hardship and danger that was worthy of much praise but at the same time quite puzzling to the population at large. They were not privy to the strong emotional bonds between the two that had allowed or indeed in some ways guaranteed that they would act in this selfless manner during the trying test that they had endured.

In the days that followed, their proud parents and closest friends became increasingly aware of their mutual love and how it had ensured they would go on and not give up even in the face of very poor odds.

There was one person, one single individual that they both knew who was baffled by their self-sacrifice and held their self-less behavior in utter and complete contempt.

Junaid had been in the hospital about a week and was making good progress toward recovery. His feet were healing, and he was starting to take a few tentative steps on his own around the room and into the hallways. His forehead wound was going to take a little time to heal fully. The hand and the left elbow injuries were greatly improved and while he still felt pain when bending his arm at the left elbow, there were no functional impairments. It was found that he had fractured two of the ribs on each side of his lower chest during the vigorous attempt to squeeze through the narrow rocky passage.

Dr. Marwani had been a constant source of support and information for the family as he coordinated Junaid's treatment among the different specialists who cared for him. It was during this painful time of recovery that Junaid started to appreciate a profession that had as its primary mission the alleviation of pain and suffering.

Nyla had come to visit him for several hours every day of the week, and it appeared that he would be able to go back home in a few more days but that he would still need more time to fully recover at home before he could resume his normal activities. During one such visit Nyla was sitting on a chair by his bed after coming back from school when they were surprised and somewhat alarmed to see their parents walk into the room with Tahir and Mr. and Mrs. Ayoub.

Nyla stood up to greet them and Junaid attempted to sit up in the bed as his mother came forward to help him. Mrs. Ibrahim took the chair her daughter was sitting in as Nyla herself stood between her and Junaid. After a round of greetings and salams, Mr. Ayoub looked at Nyla and smiled warmly. He was a stocky man of average height with small black eyes set under bushy eyebrows, a full head of graying hair and a neatly trimmed extended mustache that was pointed at both ends and that gave him a rather distinguished appearance.

"You have grown up, Nyla!" He beamed.

"Thank you. You both look just as I remembered you."

There was a pause as Mr. Ayoub shifted his gaze to Junaid who sat propped against the pillow his mother had placed behind him. His feet and his left arm were bandaged. Another white two-inch wide dressing circled his head around his forehead.

"I have heard and read much about you, Junaid. Do you know who I am?"

"I understand you are Mr. Ayoub, Tahir's father. I have heard quite a lot about you as well, sir."

"Mr. Ayoub and I are very old friends. We have known each other since our high school days," intervened Mr. Ibrahim, as he came forward and stood by his wife.

Mr. Ayoub, standing between his son and wife at the foot of the bed smiled at his old friend then looked back at Junaid and continued, "If the reports in the newspaper are correct, you almost gave up your life to rescue Nyla and the little boy, Gulzar. What drove you to risk your own life for them?"

Junaid looked at Nyla and her parents on his right side and his own parents standing to his left and then finally he looked back at Mr. Ayoub. He seemed to be deliberating the response to this seemingly innocuous question and after a moment with a somewhat pleased look he looked into Mr. Ayoub's eyes and calmly responded, "I believe it would be disrespectful of me to think that there is anyone in this room who does not know the answer to that question."

Mr. Ayoub maintained a straight face as he locked his unblinking gaze at Junaid for a second or two and then he broke out in a wide smile as he looked around him and then back at Junaid, "Well said and very true!" He then walked around to Junaid's right side and took his right hand in his. "Get better quickly, son. You and Nyla belong together, and I am very happy for you both." Turning to his left, he put his left arm around Nyla and kissed her on the head. He then went back to stand next to his son and wife.

Tahir's parents had arrived just two days ago. They had held long conversations with their son and Nyla's parents and it was the clearly visible evidence of Nyla and Junaid's love and detailed account of their own son's passionate attachment with Gulbadan that had swayed their opinion. Knowing that pride and honor are not the same as pride and arrogance and far from wanting to take a position where his having his way would only inflict pain upon four people in love, Mr. Ayoub showed why he had earned the respect and admiration of his friend over the years. Nonetheless, he had wanted to see with his own eyes what he had been told before he was to make the announcement that his wife wished him to make as soon as possible. They had met with Miss Gulbadan earlier in the day and had found her to be very agreeable.

Nyla and Junaid smiled at each other and looked at Tahir who was clearly as relieved as they were. Mr. Ayoub stood between his wife and son and putting an arm around each of them and beaming with happiness and pride, he announced the impending engagement of his son to his soon to be daughter-in-law Gulbadan. This caused an uproar of congratulations from everyone and Tahir could not help blushing and smiling from ear to ear. Feeling as if he was the happiest man in the world, he excused himself after a few minutes so that he could go and tell Gul about this happy turn of events.

Feeling relieved and his fears allayed, along with the constant support and encouragement from his parents, well wishers, and especially with Nyla by his side, Junaid made rapid progress and was discharged from the hospital to recuperate at home by the end of the second week.

# Chapter 16

It was the first day back to school for Junaid, almost three weeks from the day Gulzar was reunited with his parents. Junaid was anxious to get back to normalcy, and Nyla had come over to his home to walk with him to school.

She had come to visit Junaid every day he was hospitalized and while he was recovering at home and today going to school together was very special for both of them.

Junaid, walking alongside Nyla with a barely perceptible limp, was eager to return to his normal routine. As they got closer to the school, he was glad to notice her wearing his watch.

"It looks good on your wrist Nyla," he complimented her.

"Thanks!" Nyla replied, glancing happily at the watch. "By the way you are not getting it back."

"Oh?"

"Yeah. I like it. Besides I need to make sure it is wound up every morning," she said, no longer smiling, as she gently covered the watch with her right hand and turned her head to look at him.

They walked on quietly for a moment.

"I am glad. I wouldn't dream of taking it back."

"Good," she smiled and gently bumped into his side making him grin and shake his head.

Everyone at school knew well the details of Gulzar's rescue and as Nyla and Junaid walked into the campus they were greeted by well wishers and friends who were happy to see him feeling better and back to school.

Walking to their morning class they were surprised to see Parveen a short distance away as she hurried off to the nearby restroom wiping tears from her eyes. Junaid glanced at Nyla with his eyebrows raised and she shrugged her shoulders.

They found and sat in their usual seats that Nyla had been saving. Mr. Bhutt started the day's lecture with a warm smile, saying, "Welcome back, Junaid. Hope you have fully recovered."

"I am glad to be back, sir, and I thank you." Junaid smiled back.

"Yeah welcome *back*, Junaid. We have all missed you, *especially* Nyla!" said a familiar voice from behind them.

Nyla and Junaid looked back following Mr. Bhatt's gaze and saw Jameela as she grinned smugly.

"Thank you, Jameela, I see you have not changed a bit," replied Junaid with an amused look on his face as he and Nyla both turned around to face forward.

"I really don't like that girl," whispered Nyla, sounding clearly annoyed.

"Ignore her, Nyla, she cannot help being what she is."

As they walked to the astronomy class later that morning, they were both looking forward to seeing Miss Gulbadan. His classmates were glad to see him return and looked at him with a bit of deference.

They were delighted to see Miss Gulbadan walk in looking energetic and with a happy glow on her face. She saw them sitting together and looked pleased.

"Junaid, I am happy to see that you are well enough to come back to school. I am somewhat jealous however of you sitting so close to the lovely Miss Ibrahim!" she teased aloud for her class to hear.

"I am *only* sitting next to him in case I need to rescue him, *again*!" said Nyla with mock exasperation on her face, "so no need for his pretty teacher to be jealous at all!"

Junaid did not say anything, content to let the ladies continue the lighthearted banter, but the grin on his face told everyone he was happy to be back and be the focus of the ribbing.

This was the jovial atmosphere that Junaid remembered and had missed and which was in fact absent from the class during the time he had been away.

The class over, they talked with Miss Gulbadan for a few minutes and became acquainted with the latest news of her engagement and impending wedding. Her parents were to be in town for the engagement in a week and then again for her wedding at the end of the school year in a few months. She was clearly feeling joyous, and they were gratified to see her so jubilant.

It had been three weeks since they had lunch together at school and today they sat eating on their favorite bench under the cool shade of the trees in the playground. They were not there long when they noticed Jahal and Jameela come together hand in hand and sit down on a bench on the far side of the playground. Jameela was very animated and talking loudly, almost as if she intended everyone to hear what she had to say to Jahal, who she was apparently thrilled to have as her new boyfriend. The cause of Parveen's anguish that they had witnessed earlier in the day was now quite clear and as much as they did not particularly care for Parveen they could not help but feel a little concern for her sorrow.

They remembered seeing Jahal take physical liberties with Parveen and that Jahal and Parveen had been very close to each other was known to the entire school and neighborhood. It was therefore quite understandable why she had looked so devastated that morning. This new liaison between the two sitting across the playground was therefore likely to be very recent.

Having finished their lunch and with still a little time before the history class, they got up and left the playground. Neither said anything but both were thinking about Jameela and how she had very aggressively pursued Junaid until it had become clear to her that her flattery and physical attraction was not going to sway him or take him away from the girl he loved. Jahal had likely been subjected to the same advances from her but lacked either the fortitude or more likely the desire to escape the temptation and allurement she offered. Nyla looked at Junaid with pride as she once again realized his love and devotion to her. She remembered the time a few years ago when Jahal had made overtures toward her, and she had thwarted his advances after hearing that he had physically attacked Junaid. Nyla felt thankful now for making the decision she had made then. She looked at Junaid who was walking next to her and smiled warmly; then squeezing his left hand in her right she leaned close to him and whispered, "I love you."

Junaid had similar thoughts and feelings as they walked together. He remembered Jameela's audacious behavior and the words she had used even in Nyla's presence.

He also remembered Parveen's behavior toward himself and Nyla and how she had allowed herself to be used and now abused by someone like Jahal. He could not help but compare Jameela and Parveen to Nyla and felt proud of her. He looked at her with joy just as she squeezed his hand and leaned close to him to whisper those three tender words. "I love you too," he replied.

The history class was now much more enjoyable for them. They were thrilled to see two of their favorite teachers in love with each other and happily noticed the joy in Tahir's voice and manner.

The day over, Junaid was beginning to feel his energy flagging as they started their walk back home.

They were almost across the tree cover beyond the playground when they heard some angry voices that they had no trouble identifying. The intensity of the words and emotions made them stop in their tracks.

"Jahal, how could you just leave me for that floozy! Don't you love me!"

"I don't think you know what you are talking about, Parveen! I never told you I loved you!"

"Liar! You did and you promised me we were going to be together always!"

"I promised you nothing! We were just having fun together and you knew it! All along you knew it! Calling me in the middle of the night to come see you!"

"I love you, Jahal! How can you do this to me! I could not do all that I did with you if I did not love you! Don't leave me. I will not know what to do if you did! I cannot think, I cannot eat or sleep! Please, Jahal, please don't do this!" She pleaded.

"Stop being so childish, Parveen! And I am done with this! I don't want you to talk to me again, ever, or else!" He threatened with a voice seething with anger and devoid of any concern for what Parveen was saying or feeling.

They could hear her crying.

"OK. OK, Jahal, I will not bother you again," she said sobbing with grief and then they saw her hurry out from behind the patch of trees and walk away briskly with her hands covering her face.

Moments later, Jahal emerged with an unnaturally angry, almost grotesque expression on his face and was startled to find Nyla and Junaid standing there. He looked at them for a moment, grunted something incomprehensible and walked off whistling happily as if he had not a care in the world.

"I need to sit down, Junaid," said Nyla, holding his hand and feeling a bit faint.

He led her back to the playground, and together they sat down on the nearest bench. Junaid put his right arm around Nyla and pulled her close to himself. Neither said anything and were both lost in their own thoughts. They had known Parveen and Jahal since the fourth grade. What they had just heard and seen bewildered and saddened them even though they were not close to either one of them.

It seemed incomprehensible to them how callous Jahal had been in discarding Parveen as if she was an object that had outgrown its usefulness and was no longer needed. They knew for a fact that Jahal and Parveen had been emotionally as well as physically intimate with each other and now it appeared quite clear that it was only Parveen who had invested her true feelings into their relationship.

Nyla could not forget the almost inhuman image of rage that she had seen on Jahal's face. And equally or perhaps even more frightening to her was the ease with which he had switched from that anger to a whistling in the wind content mood upon seeing her and Junaid. Was this even humanly possible? She asked herself as a cold sweat ran down her back. A chilling dis- quiet made her shudder and wonder.

Junaid had also seen Jahal's face of fury but he had seen that rage once before and it was only upon seeing it again that he recalled the first time he had seen it. The first time when he, Junaid, was himself the object of that hateful stare, several years ago, not more than a few feet from where they sat now, when Jahal had physically attacked him. Junaid remembered clearly, as if it had just happened yesterday, the furious manner and the blazing eyes full of hate and contempt.

Junaid also recalled the threat that Jahal had made against him and Nyla that dark night when walking with Parveen as the two had passed by his home, not knowing that he was watching and listening, just a little over six months ago. It had surprised Junaid to hear the threat as they hardly ever saw each other anymore.

As he thought about Jahal's behavior now, he recalled bits and pieces that he had seen over the years that had never really bothered him then but were causing him grave concern now. Perhaps it was the first time he was putting it all together consciously; perhaps he had repressed these unsettling and inexplicable observations in the deepest places in his mind, places where they were powerless to cause him confusion and pain.

One such memory now came to his awareness, fresh again and still able to make his heart race. He recalled once, seeing a young Jahal not more than twelve years old, when he had received Shaytan, a young puppy, as a birthday gift from his parents. Junaid remembered this well as he was then recovering from his first serious bout of malaria. Things that happen during a time of great physical or emotional pain have a way of becoming permanently etched in the substance that makes up our memories. The debilitating illness had confined him to his bedroom and robbed him of the great pleasure he derived from the walks and hikes in his beloved woods. Instead, weakened and unable to walk more than a few steps, he had taken to sitting at the window in his bedroom that overlooked the open grounds, the trees and the hills beyond.

On one such afternoon, as Junaid sat listlessly at the window, he saw Jahal walk into the woods with his new puppy on a leash. Hoping and wishing that he could do the same, Junaid watched closely as Jahal led his excited pet beyond a line of low bushes. He then looked around as if making sure no one was watching and then without any warning as to his intentions he kicked the little puppy viciously on the belly, lifting it off the ground as if it were a lifeless doll. The puppy gave a yelp of surprise and pain and tried to run away as Jahal yanked on the leash and kicked the dog even harder than he had the first time.

Junaid was not sure what he was seeing and wondered if indeed his illness had anything to do with what he thought he was imagining.

As the puppy yelped again, Jahal pulled on his leash brutally, timing it so that it throttled the yelp and this was followed by two quick and ruthless kicks. He seemed to be in a trance and the rhythmic movements of his arms and body were followed every now and then by a kick that was timed to be part of his malicious dance. The puppy lay on his side motionless as Jahal again yanked and pulled on its leash, urging it to get up and move. When the puppy stayed down, it seemed to infuriate its owner who moved forward once again and was about to land another kick when Junaid shouted "STOP!" at the top of his lungs with all the energy he could muster in his weakened state.

As if hit by a bolt of lightning or jerked back by a leash around his own neck, Jahal recoiled and with eyes wide open with fright and guilt, he looked about for an adult who had caught him in his brutal act red-handed. Instead, he looked up and finally located a pale, small boy, one of his classmates, Junaid, who was he knew to be quite sick with malaria. Breathing a sigh of relief and regaining his confidence he looked at Junaid with defiance.

"Yeah! What's it to you!""

"Stop kicking that dog, Jahal!"

"It's my dog! I can kick it if I want!"

Junaid was confused as to why Jahal would want to hurt his own dog.

It made no sense to him.

"What did it do? Why are you kicking it?"

Jahal gave the boy a mischievous look.

"It makes me feel good…that is why!" he said with a sinister grin and tugged at the leash harshly without looking at the inert little dog.

All this shouting had brought Junaid's mother upstairs to his room, and she now stood next to him looking out the window at the boy and his dog that lay motionless on the ground next to him. Mrs. Kafrooni was surprised to see her son look so agitated, and she asked him what had happened. Junaid did not respond and kept staring at Jahal, who now seeing Junaid's mother was a little worried as to what she had seen and was attempting to pick up his puppy and soon carried it off in his arms.

Junaid now remembered how Jahal's parents had taken Shaytan to a vet, and it had taken months for the little puppy to finally be able to walk again. He also remembered how the puppy always acted spooked and terrified around Jahal and how one look from its master would send it whimpering, its tail between its legs.

Junaid could never comprehend what Jahal had meant by saying that "It makes me feel good," and nor could he forget his empty, cold, hard eyes as he had said that. Now older and more mature, Junaid still had difficulty making sense of it. The only rationale for his actions in Junaid's mind was that this was simply a part of a pattern of the way Jahal behaved. It was more an observation than an explanation but that is all Junaid could grasp at that time. It was different from the way ordinary people behaved, but it was apparently normal for Jahal to act that way. And saying and doing what he said and did was something that made him "feel good," even if it nearly killed his dog or caused untold emotional pain to a girl who said she loved him. Apparently feeling good was more important to Jahal than anything else in the world and anybody that could provide that feeling was to be used without remorse. It hinted of something lacking in Jahal, something vital, something that ordinary people were born with and that he seemed to lack completely.

"I think Jahal is not normal, Nyla," he finally said in the only words he could use to describe him without sounding overly worried or paranoid.

"I do not understand him. He frightens me," she responded, looking troubled.

"I remember things that make me feel he has been like this for several years, and for as long as I can remember really. I just never thought about it seriously until now," he said looking at her eyes.

Seeing that she was worried, he smiled encouragingly and said, "He only hurts those who are somehow dependent on him or who he feels are weak. Neither one of us fits that picture, especially not you!"

She smiled back and said, "Yeah, I can kick his behind if he comes near you, Junaid! I remember the time years ago when he attacked you. He told me he did that to protect me from you! That snake!"

They sat quietly for a moment, both deep in their thoughts.

"You know what, Junaid! I just thought of something!" she said excitedly.

"What?" he asked with an expectant and pleased look on his face as he turned to face her.

"That you protected me from Jahal all those years ago!"

"Really? How so?" he asked, looking at her quizzically.

"Well, think about it. If you had never given me that apple and that thank you note, Jahal would have never attacked you in his jealous rage, and I would have never known about his craziness!"

"I guess that was worth my bruised hand and ego!" He smiled as she leaned forward and gave him a quick kiss on the lips.

"My hero!" she said.

"Nyla, do you realize that if you had never defended me from Parveen's hurtful remarks that I would never have thought to give you the apple or the thank you note in the first place! So by standing up for me and helping me you caused me to indirectly help you avoid getting close to Jahal! See karma really does work!"

"I never thought of it that way. You are right. We are good for each other. We were made for each other," she said, putting her arms around his neck and letting him kiss her lips.

They finally stood up to go home after promising to be extra careful when it came to anything to do with Jahal or anyone close to him. As they walked home together, Junaid knew he was never going to let Nyla walk home alone again. He would have to be constantly aware of the one simple fact he knew with certainty about Jahal, that the feelings and pain of others meant nothing to him. A conscious awareness of Jahal's malign and injurious disposition against those closest to him, made Junaid think of Jameela and how she was in danger of getting hurt, just as Parveen was already hurting, or worse.

As they arrived at Nyla's home, he decided to voice this concern to her.

"I feel sorry for Parveen, Nyla. But at the same time I feel she is better off without him. I think in the long run she will be grateful for him getting out of her life."

Nyla was quiet for a moment, looking down at her hands as she twirled her thumbs and then taking a deep breath and exhaling audibly, she looked back at Junaid. "I am no fan of Jameela after the way she was trying to win you away from me, but I cannot help but feel that she is a foolish girl who is in harm's way." She seemed to have read his mind and said what he was driving at.

"I was about to say the same thing, Nyla. I wish there was a way to warn her, but I have a feeling she is not one to take advice, especially not from you or me."

"Between the two of us, she is likely to listen to you more than me. I think she must hate me. If we do not warn her and something happens to her, we will never be able to forgive ourselves or live with the guilt, Junaid."

"I know you are right. Even foolish people or perhaps especially foolish people need to be given good advice. I will see if I can find her alone for a few minutes somewhere at school."

"But I do have a fear, Junaid! I fear that if Jahal finds out you tried to warn her about him that he might get ugly mad. If she tells him about your warning her and she listens to you and tries to get away from him, he might take it out on her or you!" she said looking concerned.

"True. Perhaps we should warn her by writing her an anonymous note?" he suggested.

"Great! I like that idea. Can you write the note tonight and we can go over it tomorrow and then type it up and somehow get it to her without Jahal finding out about it."

"Will do. See you tomorrow. I will miss you."

"I will miss you more," she said and looking at the two windows on each side of the door to make sure no one was watching, she kissed him goodbye and opening the door she went inside.

The next day after the two morning classes they decided to have lunch in the cafeteria and sitting at a secluded corner table they looked at the note Junaid had written.

> *Jameela, please be very careful.*
>
> *I have known Jahal for quite some time and have realized through personal experience that he is a selfish and in some ways a very dangerous person.*
>
> *Get away from him before you become more involved.*
>
> *But be careful to do it in a way that he does not become suspicious of someone warning you about him.*
>
> *Do not make him angry. Make it look like you are just not good enough for him.*

Nyla read the note a few times and felt that it was good as it was written.

She offered to type it up that evening and then tomorrow, Friday, they would find a way to get it to Jameela during or after the morning class.

They saw Parveen walking in the hallways between her classes. While she seemed quiet and her eyes were still a bit puffy from crying, she appeared to be managing as well as expected and some of her close girl friends seemed to be offering her moral support.

On the way to their astronomy class, they saw Jameela and Jahal coming out from behind the library after lunch. Her hair was messy, and she was reapplying the lipstick to her pouty lips. They needed to contact her as soon as possible, before it was too late, before she was no longer able to think rationally; perhaps it was already too late.

The next day, Nyla handed Junaid the note typed on a plain white paper and folded into a plain unmarked envelope with just the name "Jameela" typed on the front. They needed to get the note to her well before the lunch break so she would have ample time to read it before she saw Jahal. The two were in the same classes after lunch and then left the school together in the afternoon. It was for this reason that Junaid and Nyla had come to school a half hour before their first morning class. They had decided to leave the envelope at Jameela's seat before anyone was in class and then to leave and come back to class at the usual time. There was a risk that someone else might take the envelope, but they were quite certain that the presence of the envelope with Jameela's name on it would keep anyone else from sitting in her seat or taking the envelope for that matter. Nyla entered the empty classroom as Junaid kept a watch outside. She left the envelope on Jameela's seat, and they went to the library thereafter.

They returned to the class a few minutes before Jameela and entering from the back of the class, they passed her seat and saw the envelope untouched. Shortly after they had settled down in their seats, Nyla took out a small mirror from her purse and angling it to look behind, she saw Jameela take her seat and pick up the envelope. Nyla looked at Junaid and gave a little nod to let him know.

There was no way to predict when Jameela would read the note or what she would think of it and whether she would have the sense to keep it a secret from Jahal, the very person it was warning her about. All they knew was that she had the note and what she did with this information was not only up to her but would likely affect her in a manner she was not able to appreciate at this time.

Sleep did not come easily to Junaid that night. He tossed and turned uncomfortably and finally got up and sat down at his desk, looking out the window. It was a dark, cloudy night, starless, and without any moonlight. A few fireflies like tiny dots of incandescent light floated in the darkness.

He could not stop thinking about Jahal because he could not decide *what* to think about him. His behavior was "bad" but that was too vague and not very descriptive of how Jahal treated others. Calling him bad was like saying that the bite of a Cobra was rather painful—it was much more than that.

Junaid knew that something done wrong accidentally and that unintentionally hurt someone or their feelings was unfortunate, and it made the victim and the offender both feel bad. People, even good people occasionally made mistakes and felt sorry for it. He could not recall a single instance when Jahal had hurt someone and had ever said or acted in a way that gave even the slightest hint of remorse.

Junaid recalled the time when he had witnessed Jahal viciously attack his own puppy and how he had looked around first to make sure no one was watching. An awareness of this fact was troubling him greatly. It pointed to a malicious act without guilt; it was a wanton and premeditated attack on a defenseless animal. It indicated a total lack of any concern for another living, breathing, and feeling creature. That, in his own words, he did it because it made him feel good was an indication that not only was he pitiless but that there was much more to his wickedness.

In addition, the way Jahal had attacked him several years ago and the manner in which he had treated Parveen recently also pointed to what amounted to a sinister lack of conscience. A guiltlessness that was frightening and seemed to portend nothing but more of the same in the future.

As the clouds parted momentarily, a bright full moon bathed the woods in its unearthly radiance.

This was an insight into the pernicious character of Jahal that had taken years to come to the light of Junaid's consciousness. It was impossible to understand the true nature of his character for anyone meeting him casually or knowing him superficially if he had not shown his true colors to them. In outward appearance he was just another young man, tall, of average build and possessing better than average looks. He was quick with an obliging smile and his mannerism did not readily reveal the cold emptiness within. An emptiness that was only seen by those who were so unfortunate, for one reason or another, to be considered by him worthless enough to be held in scorn such that they were then introduced to the true malevolence of his poisonous disposition.

It was therefore understandable that Parveen then and now Jameela were both unable to detect anything suspicious in him, especially when looking at him through the rose-colored glasses of budding love. His victims in love would have to be the more trusting and careless women who ignored any warning signs early in the relationship. He would however be particularly careful during those early days and weeks to keep hidden behind his charming facade those attributes of his personality that may be a red flag to someone circumspect and wary.

Junaid felt that it was not only reasonable and appropriate but it could even be argued, obligatory, for him and Nyla to have cautioned a fellow human of the calamity she was unknowingly about to fall into.

These thoughts comforted him somewhat, and he finally lay back down on his bed and fell asleep just as the dark clouds covered the moon and engulfed the land in deep darkness.

Less than a mile away, and well past midnight, Jahal stood in front of Jameela's bedroom on the first floor of her home, looking at her through a window she had left open for him.

# *Chapter 17*

The day before, Jameela had brought Jahal home after school to meet with her mother, Mrs. Hasan, and her fifteen-year-old sister, Sakeena. Their father was usually gone for days on business trips and would not be back for another week.

Jahal had his best behavior on display for Jameela's mother and sister. He was courteous and polite and complemented Sakeena on being even more beautiful than her sister. Blushing elatedly, Sakeena told him that she was already nearly as tall as her sister even though she was almost four years younger. He said it was too bad he had not met her first, and they all laughed happily. They talked niceties over some homemade snacks and lemonade that he was keen on complementing. The ladies were taken by his charming manners, and Mrs. Hasan was happy to see her older daughter find such a friendly and nice-looking suitor. Mrs. Hasan then left the young people to talk and went into the kitchen.

While her mother prepared dinner, Jameela had taken Jahal to show him her bedroom and there alone with the door still ajar, he had brazenly led her hand to brush against him.

Seeing Jameela's big innocent eyes look frightened but excited at the same time, he had nonchalantly asked if she wanted him to come over to be with her tomorrow night. She had eagerly said yes, and he had then told her to leave her bedroom window open and that he would come to see her after midnight when her mother and sister were asleep. Her mother's room was on the far side of the house across the living room but her sister Sakeena slept in her bedroom on the other side of the bathroom that she shared with Jameela.

Jameela had asked him to stay longer, but seeing that she was excited about his visit tomorrow and had clearly fallen for him, he left her after giving her a quick peck on the cheek. Jameela's heart was pounding with excitement, and she could hardly wait for him to be with her tomorrow night.

Jameela arrived at the school and walked straight to her calculus class. She entered at the back and casually observed Junaid and Nyla sitting together near the front of the class. She looked at them and smiled, herself feeling the euphoria of young love. As she came to her seat, she found the envelope with her name.

For a moment she wondered who it was from and then smiled knowingly, assuming Jahal must have left her a love note early in the day. She excitedly opened the envelope and removed the single plain white sheet of paper with a typed message for her.

Jameela, please be very careful.

I have known Jahal for quite some time and have realized through personal experience that he is a selfish and in some ways a very dangerous person.

Get away from him before you become more involved.

But be careful to do it in a way that he does not become suspicious of someone warning you about him.

Do not make him angry. Make it look like you are just not good enough for him.

She read it once and again and then a third time. There was no indication of who it was from, but it had an air of concern and honesty about it that she could not shake off or dismiss easily.

The words and the message perturbed her, and she tried to imagine who could be trying to warn her. She thought about Nyla and Junaid but felt that they were happy to have her leave them alone and would not bother with whom she was dating. They did not seem to care enough about her to have gone through the trouble of typing and leaving the message for her to find in this manner. Besides, she had seen them walk into the class this morning just ahead of herself. She asked the students sitting around her if they had seen someone leave the envelope and all said it was already there when they had arrived.

Confounded, she had put it in her bag. She was not interested in Mr. Bhatt's lecture, and she took no notes that day.

She agonized over what she must do next. Should she ignore the ominous tip, throw the letter away, and go on with what her heart was telling her. The excitement and wonder of the past few days was new to the eighteen-year-old and nothing like what she had ever felt before.

She had the habit of standing in front of the full-length mirror in her bedroom and gaze admiringly at her newly found voluptuous figure. She had become aware of new feelings and desires and surely if anyone deserved a man, it was a beautiful and sensuous woman like herself! And what could a young woman want if not someone as lighthearted and adventuresome of spirit as the tall, dashing figure that she found Jahal to be. Yes, he was exciting and he would know how to satisfy her needs as a woman. She must not allow him to feel disappointed in her as he said he had been in Parveen, the girl he called dull and without any warmth that a young woman must possess to satisfy her man. It is no wonder he had left Parveen for her, she thought, because as he said, he could see in her, in Jameela, the pleasure-loving qualities that he so needed and desired in a girl.

What could be more natural and more thrilling!

The thought aroused her and provoked emotions that were appealing to her.

Or should she *not* ignore the little voice inside her head, that little nagging voice that was *always* playing the spoiler whenever she was trying to have some fun! The fleeting but ever intrusive voice that seemed to be with her constantly but which had been weakening of late, as if it was slowly being suffocated and soon would cease to trouble her at all.

That imperceptible thought in her head now told her the exact opposite of what she, the happy-go-lucky, go-with-the flow Jameela wanted to do. It told her to read the note again and see if it did not sound sincere. Whoever had sent the note had not written their name and did not want to be praised or even recognized for alerting her to danger. Surely such a person was not acting out of any self-interest!

And what if what the note implied was true?

She was new in this school and this city for that matter and did not really know Jahal, except that he was in some of her classes and he had an attractive smile and an engaging manner. He knew just what to say to make her feel like a woman, just what she wanted to hear and when she wanted to hear it. He constantly compared her with other girls and always found her to be more attractive and the only girl that was good enough for someone like him. What if she was letting the flattery get the better of her judgment? What if he really was as dangerous as the message stated he was? What if he truly was not what he seemed to be on the surface? She remembered once, when it had been raining earlier in the day and she was walking back home accompanied by Jahal for part of the way. They came across tiny frogs, barely bigger than the tadpoles that they were just a day ago as they hopped across the walkway going from a small pond on one side to a patch of grass on the other. Without any show of emotion, either anger or joy, Jahal had started stepping on the little frogs as they crossed the path, pouncing from one small flattened frog to the next as if he was playing a game. Jameela was shocked and had asked him why he was doing that and to stop. She remembered the blank stare he had given her as he told her he hated the little noisy things for making the racket that kept him from sleeping at night. He had stepped on a few more frogs and then suddenly as if bored with the macabre game, he had stopped and taking her hand in his had continued walking as if nothing had happened. She remembered this now and wondered why she had ignored what he had done and was surprised that she had actually forgotten it for some reason.

But her heart was always there to guide her back to the awaiting pleasures of love. What if anything had he done to confirm that he was as bad as the message suggested? Nothing really, nothing of substance that is. The frog incident had reminded her of a few other times his behavior had caused her to raise an eyebrow, but she had wittingly or unwittingly kept that from forming a negative opinion of him. She was quick to give him the benefit of the doubt. She saw him as stirring, polite, and very much a man in some ways. How he had excited her when he was in her bedroom alone just yesterday evening! What if the anonymous message was from someone jealous of her being with him? What if it was Parveen trying to create a rift between Jahal and his new and true love? That must be it! Who else would send her such a letter, such a mean and cruel letter! Calling Jahal dangerous and selfish! And telling her to be careful and not tell him that someone was warning her. Who else would try to break them apart without letting Jahal know about it? Only Parveen, that is who!

As the reason of her mind and the caution of her instincts gave way to the passion and confusion of the fever of love or what she fancied to be love, Jameela decided to not change her plans to have Jahal over to see her later that night. She, however, decided to not tell him about the message warning her about him either. She rationalized that as soon as she saw the slightest evidence that what the letter was cautioning her about may be true, she would tell Jahal to get out of her life.

She told herself that she was not a child and could handle herself and protect herself if need be. She convinced herself that she was making this decision because this was the smartest and most prudent thing to do and not because she was unable to fight off the disturbance and ferment that his making her touch him had created in her and the gratification of her senses that had promised to foretell.

Having thus assured herself and at the same time silenced the little voice of prudence and caution, she almost forgot about the letter in her bag and looked forward to meeting Jahal during the lunch break.

Nyla and Junaid were a little concerned when they saw Jameela leave the class looking calm and collected as though nothing had perturbed her thinking in any way. Had she read the message? Was she waiting until later to read it? Had she read it but thought it was a joke or a fabrication of someone's cruel imagination? Had she already fallen so far in love with Jahal that nothing, not even the possibility of grave harm to herself, would cause her to take the personal initiative to leave him? Was she even now waiting to share the letter with him?

What if she thought it was from Parveen? What if Jahal thought it was from Parveen? What would he do? What was he capable of doing to protect his interest in Jameela if he thought Parveen was trying to separate them? These concerns and doubts about whether they should have tried to caution Jameela were beginning to trouble them. The possibility that Parveen could be harmed by this was of the greatest concern to them.

Be that as it may, what was done could not be undone and they took comfort in knowing that what they had done was solely with the intention to help Jameela and that not trying to caution her when they knew the danger she was allowing herself into would not be something they could live with.

After the astronomy class, they were sitting having lunch on a bench under a tree when Jameela and Jahal came and sat down on the empty bench next to them. They could hear some of what they were talking about and sensed that she had not told him about the letter. She was holding his hands lovingly and talking as animatedly as ever, and there was no indication that she had taken anything in the message to heart or that she had indeed even read the message.

Nyla heard her say something to the effect that she could not wait to see him tonight, that she would leave the window open and that her mother was always asleep by midnight. Jahal told her to keep quiet and not talk too much, after which they got up and left without looking at them.

"At least she has not told him about the letter, if she has read it," said Nyla.

"I am sure she has read the letter. And from the way she was acting and from what she said about seeing him tonight, I feel she has disregarded the warning. But why she has not told him of the letter is confusing to me," reflected Junaid.

"Junaid, I hope she has not yet read the letter and will finally read it at home. I hope she will see the letter for what it is and do the right thing."

"We will have to just wait and see Nyla, nothing else we can do now."

They went to the history class, and then tired from waking up earlier than usual that morning, they went home to rest.

Jameela had dinner with her mother and Sakeena and then retired to her bedroom stating she was going to take a shower and then sleep after doing her homework. Mrs. Hasan was a bit under the weather and was ready to sleep earlier than usual.

By eleven at night, Jameela was done with all that she needed to do and began waiting impatiently for Jahal to arrive. It was a dark and cloudy night. The fog that hung low to the ground shrouded the pale yellow light of the street lamp in mystery and gloom. Her bedroom was on the side of the house adjacent to four vacant lots that were heavily wooded and covered with thick undergrowth. She opened her window and the thin white curtain with pink and yellow flowers blew gently in the night breeze.

She was wearing her new off-white satin sleeping gown that was tied across her slender waist. Standing in front of the mirror, she gazed upon herself with admiration and pride. Her wavy dark brown hair fell around her face and to just above her breasts that made soft round mounds in the silky fabric. Earlier that evening she had painted her finger and toenails a bright pink color that she knew was Jahal's favorite. She sprayed a bit more perfume around her neck and walked to the window, her arms across her chest as she shivered just a little in the cool air.

Well past midnight now as Jahal left his bedroom on the second floor of their home and walked down the stairs and out the back door, quiet as a thief, his parents sleeping in their bedroom downstairs. He had his own key for the back door and knew they would still be sleeping when he returned.

He liked this new girl, this Jameela, mainly because she was so pretty but also because she seemed so gullible. So easy had it been for him to have her fall for him that it was almost a bit disappointing. He had been bored of Parveen for some time by the time Jameela had shown up. She was from out of town and seemed eager to want to be with him. As soon as he had felt that Jameela was his for the taking, he had ditched Parveen as calmly and casually as he was used to throwing half-eaten food in the trash.

He was surprised and frustrated that Parveen had made such a big fuss about it all. Why did she think he was going to be with her forever? What was all that emotional outburst about? So childish and so inconvenient for him it was! He was sure that Junaid and Nyla had seen him that day, and he spat on the ground with disgust. He was quite certain they had heard the crying and the whimpering and the carrying on by Parveen. They had surprised him that day and must have seen his angry face, the face he only showed to some worthless people when they really deserved it! "Good if they saw it, I hate the very sight of them!" he said aloud as he paddled his bike toward the waiting Jameela's home.

*That wimp Junaid, always acting like a Boy Scout and trying to get on the good side of all these pathetic people. That little weasel has been tormenting me for as long as I can remember*, he told himself. *From the day he saw me teaching my own puppy a lesson in who is the boss, to this day, I hate him!* he said to himself. *I would love to kick him the way I kicked Shaytan that day.* He smiled as the thought pleased him.

And worse than him was his girlfriend, that overanalyzing Nyla who took Junaid's side even though he had roughed him up for her own stupid sake! It was because of her that he had to settle for Parveen, he thought. He needed someone, anyone, to fulfill his needs, his desires, the way only a girl could. He liked girls. As long as they were being good. Good to him that is, in the way he liked them to be, the way he wanted them to be, to serve him in the right way, like a woman should. He disliked and was secretly afraid of girls who were too smart for their own good, he thought, such girls were hard to understand and it was harder to get them to understand him. He had learned to ignore them and not waste his time with them. He felt that Nyla was one of those and that was her loss. She would have to spend her time with little wimps and obedient boys like Junaid. She couldn't handle a man like him anyway.

He thought about his parents as they slept unaware of where he was and he scoffed with loathing; he sure had them where they belonged. Over the years they had become painfully aware that their son was different in some vital and deeply unsettling way, ever since he was just a boy. He had repeated the third and then the fourth grade as well, which is why he was two years older than his classmates now. It was not because he was not intelligent enough but rather that he could not apply himself to what he felt was a mundane and useless way to spend his energy. School was a forced vocation that he had little interest in beyond being a place where he could be around others that were ripe to be taken advantage of and where he could feel superior to and better than the many stupid people around him. It made him feel good. Over the years his parents had tried to talk to him, to make him understand, to try to get through to him in an effort to somehow make him see how average and normal people think and behave toward each other, but it had all been in vain. Over the last two years his insolence had taken on a different brazenness, and it seemed to only worsen when they attempted to communicate with him seriously. They had learned that the easiest way to maintain even a modicum of peace and harmony with him was to simply leave him to himself, a solution that was to Jahal's great liking. He was free to come and go as he pleased, and they were counting days until he would finish school and be off to college somewhere. His plans were quite different from what they were hoping but he had not made them aware of that, not yet.

As he drew closer to Jameela's home, his thoughts took on a more pleasant turn. He thought of the young woman who had fallen for his outward charm, who had failed to see through his brilliantly performed act. He was now going to reap the reward of this victory, this win.

He imagined with relish and anticipation, her soft and warm body as she offered it to him to take as he pleased. It had been several days, over a week now since he had become aware of his need for her, tonight he wanted to satisfy his hunger.

He recalled with malicious glee how he had taken Parveen to the woods on the pretext of hiking. He had felt that she liked him but could not be certain. He had felt bouts of jealousy whenever she had mentioned Junaid even in passing. Once she had said how surprised she was to see Junaid do so well in school; the malignant look he had given her then made sure she would never mention Junaid again except in a negative way. He felt he had lost Nyla to Junaid and now the slightest hint that Parveen may like Junaid and may leave him too made him utterly furious. Under this guise of fury was a fear of being left for another man, yet again. A man he loathed and had hated for as long as he could recall. He did not want to lose Parveen.

He had taken her deep into the woods, deep enough that no one would hear her screams and there under a giant peepul tree he had forced himself upon her, ignoring her pleas to stop, until bleeding and weak he had finally taken her back to her home late at night and left her at the door to figure out a way to explain her late night return to her parents. He was surprised then how she had treated him with affection despite that and had found ways to accommodate his desire and need to see her at her home at night, to do homework and study together, she had told her parents. She was good in those early months he thought but then it had changed for him. She was no longer fun. She was no longer a challenge or exciting. He liked change.

He did not want to get bored of Jameela too soon. No, she was to be savored and enjoyed; she was good enough for that. Yes, Jameela will please him, for as long as he wanted, until he found someone better, until he became bored with her, which he eventually would. But for now, he wanted to be with her.

He remembered the frightened yet thrilled look on her face, and he sneered with contempt. He will make her feel the thrill of being with him. He quickened his pace, his cold eyes empty.

Nyla woke up with a start, perspiring from a nightmare she could barely recall. A nightmare with a cry for help from a voice in the fog.

# Chapter 18

His heart racing with anticipation, Jahal arrived in front of Jameela's home. Getting off the bike, he picked it up and entered the vacant lot. He then leaned it against a tree and silently walked toward the faint light coming through her bedroom window.

Nyla could not go back to sleep.

She could not stop thinking that Jameela had read the letter and ignoring it she was still going to see Jahal tonight. She also knew from the way he had been behaving around Jameela that she had not told him about the message warning her against him, at least not yet.

What if she decides to show it to him tonight?

How would he react?

Could he lash out at her?

Could he feel threatened by the prospect of losing her, fearful that she might believe in the truth of the message?

How would he react then?

Could he force himself upon her?

Could he assume that Parveen was trying to warn Jameela?

How would he react then in desperation and anger?

These thoughts troubled her, and she finally got out of bed. She did not care much for the way Jameela had acted toward her and Junaid, but she also felt that she was gullible and child-like in some ways and that she was in harm's way.

There was not enough time and she was likely already too late, but Nyla could no longer just sit and do nothing. It was 11:00 p.m.

Parveen had been one of the brightest and most able students since elementary school all the way to high school; she had made her parents and her teachers proud of her. But there was a change in her performance and her behavior during her tenth year such that her grades started to drop, her desire to compete and excel was gone and she seemed content to be merely passing her classes. There was a general lack of direction in her that was noted by her teachers and her parents.

Her mother, Mrs. Zakaria, could pinpoint the exact day when her daughter stopped caring for her future. The day she had come home after midnight, her clothes disheveled and dirty. Her daughter had been in physical and mental discomfort that night and had missed the next three days of school, something she had never done her entire life. She had also refused to be seen by her doctor and had simply stayed by herself in her room for the duration of her recovery.

Then when Jahal had started coming over to the house at odd hours and sometimes not leaving Parveen's room until well after midnight, her mother put two and two together but refused to ask Parveen any questions that her daughter was not going to feel comfortable answering and that she herself was certain to feel uncomfortable hearing the answers to. Mrs. Zakaria knew that if it was possible for her daughter to explain to her the cause of her newly found attachment to Jahal, she would have done so without being asked. She also knew that Jahal was not the type of man she had in mind for her daughter but that if he was in Parveen's life for some reason that Parveen herself could not deny or disallow, then she would have to accept him and simply hope and pray for Parveen's safety and happiness.

Mrs. Zakaria knew that it was Jahal and his influence that had caused her daughter to have lost her way. She had lost the desire and will to perform to her potential and ability at school, and worse, she seemed to have changed her disposition and her very temperament in the way she related to her other friends, her teachers, and her own family. Mrs. Zakaria would have had extreme aversion toward anyone who caused these changes to occur in her daughter, and Jahal was no exception. She held her tongue and allowed him access to her daughter only because she trusted that Parveen had no other recourse and that her taking a stance for Parveen was likely to worsen rather than improve the predicament her daughter was in. Reluctantly, Mrs. Zakaria swallowed bile and hoped for a miracle and the day when her daughter would find a solution to her misery.

That day had come, some two weeks ago, when her daughter had returned home crying and distraught and without being questioned had volunteered the information that Jahal had left her for another girl. While Mrs. Zakaria was distressed to see Parveen so heartbroken, she was secretly thankful to see Jahal break his association with her daughter. In time, she knew her daughter would come to realize this truth and will be thankful for her good fortune.

It was a half hour before midnight, and Parveen was in bed trying to fall asleep when her mother came into her room telling her someone needed to speak with her urgently.

She was getting out of bed when Nyla was led in by her mother who then left the room, closing the door behind her.

"What are you doing here, Nyla? At this time!"

"I need your help, Parveen. Jameela needs your help. Only you can save her," said Nyla quickly, her hands clasped and voice quivering with urgency.

"What are you talking about?" said Parveen, not understanding.

Nyla explained to her what she and Junaid were concerned about, what they thought of Jahal's behavior over the years, how they felt she had been used and abused by him, and how another girl was now in danger of the same at his hands. Nyla told Parveen how all the pain she had endured could either be just that, meaningless suffering without reason, or it could become the motivation for keeping someone else from experiencing the same.

Parveen, reminded of the pain that was still raw, cried with tears. Nyla moved forward, sat down on the bed and put her arm around Parveen's shoulder.

"You did nothing wrong. Loving someone is never wrong. If the person you loved does not love you back, it is their loss. If that person hurts you as Jahal did, then that person was not worth loving and you will come to terms with your loss and be stronger for it," said Nyla softly.

"I am sorry for treating you and Junaid as I have. When you are close to someone with hate in their heart, you overlook so much that is wrong and act in ways you never would otherwise," sobbed Parveen.

"I know and we both feel sorry for you, Parveen."

"What do you want me to do, Nyla?" asked Parveen, wiping her tears away and sitting up straight, looking at Nyla with searching eyes.

Nyla explained to Parveen the anonymous warning they had given to Jameela and how she had seemingly ignored it and that she was to meet Jahal tonight.

"We have to talk to Jameela, both of us and especially you, before it is too late. We can warn her in person, what she does then is entirely up to her."

Parveen thought for a moment, looking at the concern on Nyla's face. She realized that Nyla had nothing to gain from this and was going through all this for the sake of someone only because it was the right thing to do.

"Give me a minute to get ready," she said with a glint in her eyes.

It was quarter past midnight when Jameela heard sounds outside her window. Excited that Jahal had arrived, she rushed to the window and to her amazement she found Nyla and Parveen standing there instead.

"What are you two doing here!" she blurted out with astonishment.

"We need to speak with you, Jameela. We want to help you," replied Nyla as calmly as possible. She was relieved to see that Jahal had not arrived yet.

"Go away, both of you! I don't need your help!" Jameela said as she began to lower the window shut.

"Listen! Do you think we came all this way at this time of the night for our amusement? We came here to tell you some facts, what you do with that is up to you. But we will leave if you don't care about what happens to you," said Nyla with exasperation.

Jameela hesitated.

"Jahal should be here any minute," she said, looking beyond them toward the street lamp.

"Then there is no time to lose," Parveen said with an urgency and earnestness that made Jameela take notice.

"OK, come in but be quick. I don't way him to see you two here!"

They easily climbed into Jameela's bedroom over the low window sill and then as Jameela, clad in her silky gown, sat on the side of her bed the two girls stood in front of her.

Quickly and as concisely as possible, first Nyla told Jameela what she and Junaid had known, felt and discussed about Jahal's actions and conduct over the past several years, and then Parveen with as much control of her emotions as she could muster and yet still unable to keep from shedding her genuine tears, told all she could about her personal experience with the initially charming Jahal who had turned into her worst nightmare.

Jameela sat on her bed stunned, quietly looking at these two girls who had decided to help her despite receiving less than civil treatment from her. There was no doubt in her heart about their honest desire to keep her from harm. She reprimanded herself for ignoring what her own conscience, her own inner voice had been trying to tell her. Nyla and Parveen had just confirmed the worst possible scenario she could have envisioned for herself by associating with Jahal. She had willfully ignored the very red flags that should have cautioned her, and it was when she had neglected to heed the advice given her in writing that these girls had then taken the next step and had actually come to speak with her in person, on her own behalf.

Tears came into her sorrowful eyes as she recalled how she had treated them.

Her blood boiled with anger when she remembered how her mother and sister had entertained him, trusted him, and how he had fooled them just as easily and heartlessly as he had fooled her. She felt guilt and remorse eat at her for letting him get to her family through her.

Penitent, she stood up and hugged Nyla and Parveen together, thankful for the concern they had shown for her. Then she pulled away and stood facing her two new friends, the tears drying on her rosy cheeks and a fire blazing in her lovely eyes. How dare he!

Junaid decided to wait outside, behind some bushes, within easy sight of Jameela's bedroom window. He could see the girls inside, Jameela sitting and Nyla and Parveen standing in front of her. He saw all three hug and talk for a few more minutes. The light then went out and a small table lamp was turned on, the curtain partly drawn and the window lowered almost completely shut.

He waited patiently. It was almost 1:00 a.m. as he yawned and looked at the streetlight twenty yards away, its yellow lamp shrouded in thick mist. He should have been here by now, and then he was, walking quietly and intently toward the window. He wanted to warn the girls inside but trusted in their ability. After all, Nyla was with them too. He smiled with confidence.

Jahal stood in the darkness outside the window, looking in. Only a small lamp was on inside, the window was almost closed, and the curtain partly drawn. He could see Jameela standing in front of her mirror, with a gown around her that she had slipped off her shoulders as she looked approvingly at herself.

He stood there for a few moments taking pleasure in the anticipation of gratifying his desire. He smirked now, thinking of the way Jameela would respond. Would she scream out like Parveen, or would she bite her lip and stay quiet, afraid to attract her mother and sister to her room, afraid to have them discover her in bed with a man. He smiled wickedly, the thought of forcing himself upon her in her own home, with her mother and sister sleeping just a few feet away aroused him.

He looked around himself carefully and then softly called out her name through the narrow opening below the window pane.

"Jameela," he whispered again, but when she did not look back, he put both his hands under the window to lift it up and just then the heavy window slammed down on his fingers with bone-crushing force.

Squealing with pain, but biting his lip to stay as quiet as possible, he attempted to pull his hands free from under the window but the metal guide on the sill held him tightly under the immovable window.

Now, with his face twisted with agony and both his hands trapped under the window, the light inside the room was turned on and the curtain fully opened to let him see within.

Parveen stood next to the window, staring at him. She had an amused expression on her face and both her hands pressed on and kept the windowpane where it was.

"What the hell are you doing here, Parveen!?" he cried out in pain, her presence adding to his misery, as his mind frantically tried to make sense of it.

"Interesting question, given the circumstances! You can see what I am doing, Jahal. I am pushing down on this window so you cannot pull back your broken fingers!" she said with a bitter smile on her lips.

"You crazy bitch! Let me go! It really, really hurts!" he hissed, saliva foaming at his mouth as the pain become unbearable.

"Really? It hurts so I should stop? You mean I should stop even if you ignored my pleading and begging that day you defiled me?" she said with a calm voice that added to his torment.

"That was different! This is… Aaaaaah," he wailed as she pushed down on the windowpane.

"That was different! You are right, that was much worse! What you did hurt me much more than how I am hurting you. You hurt me physically but also took advantage of me in a way that changed me forever." There was fire in her eyes, her face livid with anger and repugnance.

"OK, OK! I am sorry. Now let me go!"

"Nope, I don't feel like it. I am having fun just like you were having fun that day. I think another three hours of this might perhaps satisfy me somewhat."

Junaid, standing behind the bushes a few yards away could see and hear everything and was amazed at how the girls had trapped Jahal. He also remembered how just a few days ago Parveen had been begging him to not discard her for Jameela and how he had ignored her pleas without any show of the slightest care in the world. It was good to see Parveen recognize him for what he really was.

Presently he saw Jameela appear wearing her nightgown. She came up to the window and sat down next to where Parveen was standing.

"I know what you did to Parveen, Jahal. I also know what you are really like under your mask."

"You don't know anything, Jameela. She is lying to you. She is trying to break us apart! Don't you see!" said Jahal with a face that seemed permanently contorted in agony.

"I could not see what you are, Jahal, the same way Parveen could not. It was too bad no one could warn her. But I was far more fortunate."

"Now I want you to beg her to forgive you. I want you to tell her you will never ever take advantage of another girl this way."

"Never! You can both go to hell!" he whimpered.

"It is your choice. Either you beg her forgiveness and maybe we let you go or we call the police, and they catch you with your hand in the cookie jar, literally," Jameela said and looked at Parveen who shook her head in approval at the comment.

"You cannot call the police. Everyone will know you wanted to have me come over to see you!"

"Seriously? They will come and see you standing here with your hands under the windowpane at this time of the night, trying to get in, and they will believe what you tell them?" said Parveen with a quizzical expression on her face.

"Now, beg for forgiveness or else!" And she pushed down on the window again.

"OK, OK. I am sorry and I will not do this again!"

"What was that?" said Jameela.

"Say, 'I beg Parveen's forgiveness and I will never do anything like this to any other girl as long as I live!'"

As he hesitated, Parveen increased the pressure on the window just a little more and he promptly repeated what Jameela had said.

"No, say it with feeling, with conviction, like you mean it!" came Nyla's voice as she came into view and stood next to Jameela.

"What! You are all in this together?" squawked Jahal, now jumping up and down from one foot to the other in intolerable pain.

"Yep, we sure are, and we have all seen what you were trying to do and how you got caught and how you begged for forgiveness and promised to change your ways," said a smiling and pleased-looking Nyla.

Unable to tolerate the excruciating pain any longer and in fear of being seen by Jameela's mother in what was evidently and clearly an attempt to get into her daughter's bedroom at this ungodly hour, he finally, with as much emotion as he could muster, rasped, screeched, squealed, and bleated a most sincere sounding apology and a promise to mend his ways.

The girls looked at each other, and Jahal was mightily gratified when they decided to lift up the window. But before they did that, Jameela brought out her Polaroid camera and said, "Now say cheese, Jahal, and know that if you break your promise in any way, you will become very famous with these pictures, very quickly!"

She then took four pictures, gave one to each of the girls and kept two for herself.

Jahal was watching all this and wondered aloud, "Who's the fourth picture for?"

Nyla smiled at his observation. "That is for the person who is watching all this, except you do not know who that fourth person is."

"That is to keep things a bit interesting and keep you even more motivated to honor your word!" said Parveen, looking at the whimpering Jahal. Over the past hour since Nyla had come to visit her, she had felt her mental anguish diminish and lose some of its sting. She felt that he was too pitiable a creature to have the power to cause her any such suffering. Seeing Jahal as he really was removed from her heart any affection she had ever felt for him.

Love hurts when it is real and is taken away. But it also hurts when it is felt to be real and when its cloaked fallacy and its very absence cruelly and suddenly comes to the victim's awareness. In some ways this is worse. It makes one feel cheated coldheartedly and one's most sacred emotions remorselessly and callously trifled with. It can take some time to come to terms with such evil and such outright malice suffered at the hands of someone trusted and even loved.

The painful emotional bonds that his companionship had created would take time to heal, but she was well on her way to eventual freedom when she would be able to look back without suffering excessive guilt or shame for her forced association with a deviously abusive and manipulative individual, at a time when she was too naive and trusting to have known better.

Without knowing, having helped Jameela she had helped herself. And when she now smiled it was a genuine and heartfelt smile, something she had not done in quite some time, something that felt very good. She had not only rid herself of her attachment to someone loathsome but had at the same time gained two friends for life.

Parveen looked at her two friends, and as they nodded, she lifted the window a little. Jahal gingerly removed his hands and hobbled away in agony, muttering some incomprehensible gibberish to himself.

# Chapter 19

Jahal was shocked by what had just happened. He had gone to Jameela fully expecting to find her desperately waiting for him; he had seen it in her eyes and in her attitude the previous day and more so even earlier during the day on Friday when she was obviously excited about the prospect of him paying her a visit late at night.

He was perplexed, frustrated, and in pain. Suffering both physically and emotionally, he picked up his bike with the palms of his hands and quickly walked to the street, mounting and paddling away as quickly as he could, away from the scene of his abject humiliation. He needed to get to a place he could feel less threatened and where he could think, regroup, and plan. Revenge he must take, that was his nature, just like a snake must bite, but first he needed to collect himself.

By the time he got home, he was relieved to finally be able to move his fingers again and felt that he had not broken any bones. The deep indentations the window had left on the four fingers of both of his hands were beginning to fade, and he felt some comfort in knowing that he would not have to go to the hospital after all and would not need to explain the cause of his unusual injury.

It was close to 3:00 a.m. on Saturday morning as he sat on his bed thinking about the events of the past twelve hours, trying to make sense of what had transpired.

As his thoughts became less chaotic and his thinking less deranged, he recalled again how Jameela had been attached to him all Friday afternoon, talking with excitement and anticipation about their plan to have him come over to be with her later at night when her mother and sister were asleep. The only reason she would have changed her opinion of him and her plans so drastically would be persuasion by Parveen and Nyla. They must have approached her some time during the evening or even earlier that night and somehow managed to convince her to change her mind about him completely.

He felt certain that it was only Parveen who could have told Jameela anything that would have scared her enough to alter her perception of him in a very unfavorable way. It was, he reflected, only Parveen who could have told Jameela the details of her personal experience with him. He reasoned that Nyla's general dislike for him could not have convinced Jameela to resist the temptation she had felt for him.

His frustration mounted as he realized that not only was he no longer able to use Parveen but that she had also taken away Jameela from him, leaving him now utterly alone.

It would have to be done. The revenge will have to be taken. But how? How could he fulfill his need to see her suffer as he felt that she had made him suffer, without anyone blaming him? If any of the three felt in any way that he had hurt them, they were likely to expose him as the most likely culprit. Further, he did not know who the fourth person was, who evidently had witnessed the entire shameful scene. It could be Junaid, he reasoned, but he could not be certain of that. It may very well be Jameela's sister or her mother or even a teacher for that matter.

He vowed to find a way, carefully planned and executed that would single him out as the one person who could not have been responsible. He looked at his fingers, throbbing with diminishing pain, but it was his injured psyche, his chagrined ego that was still raw with grievance.

Angrily he smashed his right fist against his pillow, "That *bitch*!"

He hissed, "That bitch *will pay* for this!"

Junaid joined the girls soon after Jahal had left. Whereas before these three had ill feelings toward each other, now he found them together, happily talking as if they were old friends.

Nyla came to stand by Junaid as Jameela and Parveen thanked him for his help.

"I must confess I was just providing moral support. Nyla did this by herself with your help. Full credit goes to the three of you girls," he said, smiling at the beaming Nyla.

"Thanks for writing the note warning me, Junaid, it was very sweet of you," said Jameela. "I wish I had taken it seriously."

"True, but then we wouldn't have had all this fun!" quipped Parveen lightheartedly and everyone laughed.

"And we would not have become friends!" added Nyla.

"I guess this was meant to happen the way it did," said a sober Jameela.

"Taking the pictures was a great idea, Jameela, excellent thought," Junaid said, looking at Jameela, who seemed to relish his compliment and handed him the picture.

"Thanks, and this is for you."

"Priceless expression on that face!" declared Junaid upon seeing Jahal's picture with his hands caught under the window.

"The pictures and not knowing who the fourth person is should help him mend his ways," Parveen said sounding optimistic.

"I hope so, but I have a feeling he is beyond mending his ways. I don't know if he is even *capable* of changing who he is," Junaid said pensively. "So, ladies, don't let your guard down. There is no knowing what devious plan he might come up with," he added.

"Parveen, you and Jameela have to be especially careful, he might be in a particularly vengeful mood, at least for the near future," Nyla warned them.

It was close to 4:00 a.m. when Junaid and Nyla walked Parveen to her home just a few blocks from Jameela's home. They had left their bikes in front of her home earlier and now they rode to Nyla's place together. Before Junaid left, they stood talking for a few minutes.

"I am proud of what you did Nyla. You made a big difference by deciding there was more that could be done than just writing an anonymous note to Jameela."

"And I am glad you understood what I felt when I called you and that you came and were with me. I felt more confident and secure knowing you were there," she replied with a warm smile as she held his hands in hers.

They kissed goodbye and Junaid rode his bike home. Exhausted and relived of the burden that had been upon their shoulders, they were both soon sleeping a restful dreamless sleep.

Jameela lay in her bed wide awake with a thousand thoughts swirling in her head. Knowing now what she knew, she considered what could have happened had Nyla and Parveen not decided to take the trouble to come and see her last night, or if she in her stubbornness had decided to not hear what they had come to say. She shuddered as if cold under her warm blanket.

Jameela knew that her passion and desire had made her oblivious to what that little inner voice had been telling her all along. That little voice, which was weak in her and which was apparently much stronger in Nyla. Strong enough to have kept Nyla safe from Jahal years ago and strong enough to have now forced her to do something to protect someone who had treated her poorly.

It made Jameela uncomfortable to think that she had been unsure of what was right or wrong and even what was good for her or very detrimental to her and her family. It made her feel like an immature child.

Worse however than this was the shame that afflicted her; the remorse she felt for having been, what she felt was the cause of Parveen being treated in a most infamous way by Jahal. Whether Jahal leaving Parveen was in Parveen's best interest did not help her feel any less guilty. Jameela felt dejected and perturbed; she tossed and turned, unable to find relief.

She remembered too the manner in which she had treated Nyla and Junaid, and she covered her face with shame under her pillow. "What is wrong with me!" Her scream was muffled by the pillow; her eyes wet with tears.

*Am I just as bad as Jahal? Am I just a female version of the same despicable nature? Just as corrupt, just as disgraceful and just as foul! Is that why I am not good enough for someone decent like Junaid and am only able to attract someone as base as Jahal? Or would someone like Junaid take a liking to me if he was not already in love with another?* Had Junaid ignored her obvious attempts to seduce him because he was in love with someone else or had he found her transparent flirting offensive? Would he have responded positively to her if there was no one who already owned his heart? She wondered.

Or was she just not good enough? Not attractive enough? The thought troubled her and she got out of the bed, and stood looking at herself in the mirror. She did not see anything she thought would not make any man eager to be with her. Was it then her very nature that was not good enough? Yes, it must be. It must be her conduct and her attitude that was to blame.

She did not want to appeal to those who merely saw her physical attractions and who would only see her superficially and not her inner self, who would be inclined to use her and enjoy her physically and not love her as she felt she deserved to be loved, longed to be loved. She would now entertain a romantic relationship only with someone who would appreciate and respect her; who would not flatter her like a gullible child nor use her as a mere object.

This was a precondition she would not negotiate away. This was an argument that the little voice inside her was adamant she not ignore and she felt peace in not resisting it. She had learned that ignoring her conscience was likely to put her in harm's way and there may not be the miraculous intercession by people like Nyla and Parveen to help her in the future.

She had to try and become someone who need not live in shame and fear. She must allow her mind to catch up with the maturity her body had achieved in the past few years. Her intuition and judgment must rule the dictates and appetites of her body.

Gradually, the agitation of her thoughts calmed into peaceful quiescence. And before her consciousness was immersed in deep sleep and as the layers of concern and worry were peeled off, she became aware of one single and simple truth, that in order for her to be treated as a lady she would first have to act as one.

Outside, a stiff, cold wind, the first of the winter season had blown in from the north and the dense fog had lifted.

Parveen arrived home, washed up, and made herself an early morning breakfast of omelette, toast, jam, milk, and orange juice, something she had not done in a very long time.

Sitting at the breakfast table and looking out the picture framed window, she saw the blustery wind thrash the slender young Jamun tree in the backyard.

The relentless agony that had troubled her for the past two weeks was gone. But there was more to the relief she felt deep within. The last two weeks she had felt the pain of rejection and betrayal from an association that had been forced upon her over two years ago; an affiliation that in time and due mostly to initially a lack of a realistic understanding of her plight and later to the loss of any hope of finding an honorable resolution, had turned into an attachment of her injured psyche to the very cause of that injury.

It had become easier to live as a partner to the very monster that had ensnared her than to find the courage needed to run away and thus show the world that she had indeed been an unwilling captive. She had come to know that often it is easier to live with hidden shame than it is to let others see the shame one has been forced to endure.

One may lose one's very identity and self-respect in this manner, but for some reason that seems preferable, at the time, to letting others learn of this loss, while at the same time continuing to bear it with patience.

Behaving in a way that was alien to her true self was preferable to fighting to regain her true identity as that would indicate her having lost herself to someone as contemptible as Jahal. She had, in other words, given up hope.

She had initially hated Jameela for taking Jahal away from her but now as the fog and confusion lifted, she saw that Jameela in reality had been the cause of her rescue from her hopeless entrapment.

She shook her head and smiled, reflecting upon how Jameela had appeared to be the devil one minute and an angel the next. She was happy that while Jameela had rescued her from Jahal without intending to do so, that she, Parveen, had helped save Jameela from him fully cognizant of what she was doing and why. It made her feel good about herself.

At the same time, she did not fail to appreciate that none of this would have been possible had Junaid and especially Nyla not taken it upon themselves to help Jameela. She had known those two from an early age and was beginning to realize that they had always supported each other and now together they had stood up for her and Jameela. She felt grateful to have them on her side as her friends.

The sun was about to rise in the eastern horizon when her mother, awake for the morning prayers, walked into the kitchen and was surprised to find her daughter fast asleep sitting at the breakfast table after eating what appeared to have been a substantial breakfast. She helped Parveen to her feet and gently led her upstairs, laying her down and tucking her in her bed. She noticed the serenity on her daughter's face, a peace that she had not seen since that dreadful night some two years ago. The night when Parveen had knocked on the door just after midnight and her mother had then helped her to her bed just as she had done now.

What had happened in the past few hours since Nyla had come to call on Parveen was unknown to her mother, nor was she going to inquire just as she had not questioned Parveen about the events of that terrible night. It was sufficient for her to see that she had the desire and energy to prepare herself breakfast and now to be sleeping in blissful tranquility.

Tenderly she kissed her daughter's forehead and then left, closing the door softly behind her.

# Chapter 20

Jameela was intent on changing her ways for the better. She felt the responsibility for setting a good example for her younger sister Sakeena who had always looked up to her for guidance.

"What type of a role model would I be if I cannot have my own life in order?" she asked herself.

What kind of a person did she want to bring into the life of her sister and her family if she was so careless and self-absorbed as to have fallen for someone so selfish and egotistical as Jahal?

No, she must not let her poor and childish decision making destroy her future and threaten the people she loved most.

The events of Friday night had changed her and made her reflect on her life and future in a way that she had never done before. She felt grateful that her newly found friends had not judged her based on her atrocious behavior toward them and had in fact acted in a way that had taught her much about kindness and thoughtfulness toward others.

Had these same people sat down with her and lectured her on the proper way to live one's life and the need to treat others with respect and dignity, it would have made little impression on her. They instead had exemplified graciousness, forgiveness, and consideration for others by their actions and she being the recipient of their goodwill had the good sense to receive it with appreciation for her own benefit.

Jameela genuinely wished to become the person who would then deserve someone better, someone worthy.

She arrived at her morning class quite early and saw Junaid sitting alone near the front of the class. Nyla had not arrived yet, and Jameela decided to sit with him until then. There were only two other students in the classroom this early.

She walked over to Junaid and stood next to him.

"Hi! You came early!" she said.

"Hello. Yes, woke up a bit earlier than usual today. How are you feeling, Jameela?" he asked, as he motioned for her to sit.

Jameela took the seat next to him, looked at him, and then down at her hands nervously, as if she wanted to say something but was having difficulty finding the right words.

"Jameela? What is it?" asked a concerned Junaid.

"Oh, nothing I guess," she lied.

"I have not known you to be someone at a loss for words." He smiled.

She looked at the door at the back of the class, as if expecting to see Nyla. Then she turned to face him.

"Junaid, I need to ask you something and you need to answer it honestly. Can you do that?" she said softly but with hesitant urgency in her voice.

"OK. Ask," he replied with earnestness, as he turned to face her.

She hesitated, looked around to make sure no one was listening.

"If, and only *if*...just asking, only *if* you did not love Nyla, if she was not in your life, would someone like you...do you think you could like someone else...I mean do you think you could like *me*?" she stammered, without looking at him, her eyes focused on her hands that she kept wringing nervously.

Junaid, asking her to look at him, said, "I like you, Jameela. You could be, in fact you *are* my friend!"

"No. Not just a friend! I am asking could you like me, as someone you love," she replied quickly, now looking into his eyes intently as if she could find the answer there.

Junaid considered her question for a moment. He looked at her face, eagerly awaiting his response, asking him if he could love her, if and only if there was no one else that he already loved. He recalled her behavior when they had first met in this very class. He had also seen how she had been the cause of Jahal leaving Parveen and how if not for Nyla's intervention, she could be with Jahal and in the same dire circumstance as Parveen had been. He knew that the Jameela he had met initially was someone he could never fall in love with, but he had also seen how when nearly at the brink of disaster and almost blind with what she imagined was love, she had listened to reason and had shown a rare gift, the humility to accept good advice. She had also shown appreciation and gratitude instead of anger and obstinacy. She was clearly regretful of her behavior and was asking him a most heartfelt question, asking if she was good enough, not then, but now.

"As you are now, Jameela, if I did not already love someone as deeply as I love Nyla, I would surely be in great danger of falling in love with someone as wonderful as you," said Junaid, looking at her eyes with sincere affection.

Jameela stared at his face for a moment, felt she saw honesty in his brown eyes, and smiling she looked away. "Thank you, Junaid, that is all I needed to know. I am sorry for the way I behaved when we first met." Just then Nyla came and sat down next to Jameela who tried to get up and give Nyla her seat. Nyla smiling warmly placed her left hand on Jameela's shoulder, asking her to stay where she was until the class started. The two girls talked amicably for a few minutes and then as Mr. Bhatt entered the classroom, Jameela stood up and left, thanking Junaid with her eyes as she walked back to her seat.

"She seems like a completely different person to me!" Nyla observed, as Junaid took her hand in his and squeezed it lovingly.

"She is! You are a miracle worker, Nyla," he teased her.

"What was she talking to you about?" Nyla asked.

"Just asking if someone could like her the way she is now."

"Someone? Or you specifically?" It was her turn to tease him now.

"I think she was asking if someone like me could like her, *if* there was no one like you in that *horrible* scenario, Nyla." Junaid smiled.

Nyla thought for a second and then said, "I assume you told her that *if* there was no one else you were *already* in love with, that you could possibly fall in love with her?"

"As I said, that is a most horrible scenario, to say the least," whispered a smiling Junaid, as Mr. Bhatt began writing the day's assignment on the board.

"It must be so inconvenient for you that you cannot have Miss Gulbadan because she is taken and that Jameela cannot have you because you are taken!"

"Very well put, Nyla, my love, very insightful!" he teased her again.

She elbowed his ribs playfully and shushed him trying to start working on the day's problems.

Jameela, sitting a few rows behind and above them, saw the teasing and giggling and elbowing from her vantage point and could not help but feel a bit lonely. She took a deep breath and told herself that anything worth having requires patience; she recalled everything she had told herself to try and become the person she could be proud of, someone deserving of what she longed for. With a collected and composed expression on her face, Jameela focused on what Mr. Bhatt was saying and nothing else.

With happiness on her beaming face and her head held high, Parveen walked from class to class and mingled with her friends. She felt free and light of heart as if a lingering illness that had sapped her of all energy and joy had suddenly left her.

Her friends and classmates saw the change in her expression and her demeanor but what really stole the show was when Parveen, Jameela, and Nyla all stood together in the hallway, talking animatedly, joking and laughing as good friends who had been reunited after a long separation.

Jahal's quiet sulking and his inability to look anyone in the eye was seen as a marked contrast to their jovial mood.

Something had changed drastically over the weekend to cause Parveen, Jameela, and Nyla to have become friends to everyone's surprise and against all expectations and to have caused Jahal to be left to his own sullen self. Both his hands were heavily bandaged and he had let it be known, to whoever asked, that he had broken several of the fingers of both hands in an accidental fall while he was walking his dog Shaytan in the woods over the weekend.

Sunday evening while Nyla was upstairs in her bedroom, she had happened to glance out the window and had seen Jahal outside his home that was just a few houses away. He had no bandages on his hands and looked comfortable. She remembered thinking that despite what they thought of him, it was good he had not broken any of his fingers. She had said this to the girls earlier today, and they all felt as she had.

Now, the bogus news of his accidental fall in the woods was cause for much hilarity and many mirthful comments from the three girls. They were surprised however as to why he would put on bandages on his hands and lie to people as he had. The three were sitting together having lunch in the cafeteria.

"Shocking! To think that while our wild imaginations had him squealing with his hands trapped under Jameela's window at two in the morning, he was actually out enjoying himself in the woods!" Parveen said with mock astonishment.

"And what a wonderful time to be walking one's dog in the dark woods!" quipped Jameela.

"No wonder the poor man fell and broke his fingers in the dark! Hopefully he did not injure his ego much," added Nyla and they all erupted in laughter.

The anger and frustration building inside Jahal was in need of relief, urgently. He had imagined the three girls together, but actually seeing them gleefully jesting and joking and laughing out loud was much worse than his imagination. Each time he heard their laughter it felt like a dagger to his tortured ego. He had wanted to hear what they were saying, but it pained him to see them so amiable and chummy with each other and he had to get away from them quickly.

He had sneaked a quick look at them however and seeing Parveen look so bright and cheerful had infuriated him. How dare she feel such happiness and exhibit such obvious joy when he had left her? How could she not feel the pain of losing him? Had he not prepared her adequately for the fall that she had suffered? Had she not been blindsided? The past two weeks she had been weak, crying, and displaying the sadness that was appropriate after losing someone like him, but now her cheerful manner was causing him great distress. It would have been easier for him to deal with his own misery if he could see her suffering as well, if she could show that losing him was a great loss indeed. That would make him feel worthy and worthwhile. That would have made him feel worth loving and therefore his life worth living.

Could she be actually happy that he had left her? Was she as indifferent toward him as he had been toward her? Had she used him just as he had been using her? He decided not to attend the afternoon classes and went home, to sulk alone but more importantly to devise a stratagem.

Did she never really love him? he asked himself. He did not love himself, he could *not* love himself. Unable to love, he was also unable to feel love in return, but he survived knowing that there were people he could fool into liking or even loving him. That was the game he played, the only game he knew how to play and he played it masterfully. He played it to keep himself from falling into depression and from keeping himself from thoughts of hurting himself.

He was convinced that people existed simply for his personal use and satisfaction. He had a grandiose sense of self and felt entitled to using people as he wished without remorse. Deep inside he felt worthless and the only way he could feel better about himself was by seeing someone else in a position that he considered inferior to his own. To this end, he would use his charm to get close to anyone not on their guard, which was most people most of the time, and once he had their confidence and felt that they needed him in some way, he would remove the mask that hid his real self and was free to proceed with callous exploitation unburdened by the restrictions of a conscience.

Once he found that he had achieved his goal of subjugating the person, he lost interest, the challenge was gone and the game was over. A new challenge was then needed. A new challenge had to be worthy however. It had to be someone who appeared to be better, superior in some ways to himself. It was the process of bringing such an individual under his complete control, of making him or her subservient to him, of serving his needs with disregard for their own, that was the only goal of his life, the only thing that gave him any satisfaction, and this was a game that he played over and over again. He was to play this game for the remainder of his life because there were always enough gullible people who blindly believed in the goodness of others, of people like him; they were always willing to give him the benefit of the doubt, until it was too late.

However, his most extraordinary quality, the most egregious thing about him was not just that he harmed or aimed to harm those around him but rather the total disregard for the suffering he intentionally inflicted upon those who knew and trusted him most. It was his utter disregard for the way they were left to feel and endure in the wake of his abuse which perplexed his victims most. As if he had no empathy for any living creature. As if he did not have the ability to feel another's pain, the ability that is present in most people and which must be present for a man or a woman to be categorized as a human being in the first place.

If one definition of evil is to do intentional harm to someone who has done you no harm, then he was indeed abominable and yes evil.

Being so isolated after being caught red-handed and discovered for being selfish and cruel if not for the entirety of his malign nature, he felt no remorse, only anger and a desire for revenge. He was made to feel inadequate and that enraged him; he must regain the upper hand, he must put them in their place, he must control their feelings and make them uncomfortable, he must make them stop amusing themselves at his expense. That was the only way to soothe his outrage.

Shaytan lay quietly on the small rug next to Jahal's bed. He had been brought to this home some seven years ago as a little puppy. Jahal's parents had picked him out of a litter of energetic, bouncing two-month-old puppies at the local pet shop. Shaytan, a name given him by Jahal, was picked because he was the most spirited of the lot, tireless in the exhibition of his boundless energy. Jahal's parents knew that their son was either not willing to or not able to make and keep friends for long and the dog would keep him good company and perhaps teach him about taking care of another living creature. Jahal had immediately and inherently liked the idea of owning a dog, a living creature that was on a leash and could be made to go wherever his master chose to go.

Soon Jahal had became somewhat annoyed by the puppy's vitality and vigor, it's sprightly and cheerful nature made its young owner feel an unexplained resentment. Jahal wanted to show the dog that it could feel joy only if he, its master, would allow it, that the dog's spirit was under the sway of its master at all times. To this end he had given the little puppy severe and repeated beatings when no one was watching. Initially he had done so at home in his room when his parents were away or were not able to hear the dog's whimpers but as the beatings became more severe, he knew he had to continue the lessons elsewhere. On the very first occasion when he had taken the little puppy to the woods, he had attacked the helpless creature viciously, almost killing it. The robust and energetic puppy had eventually recovered from the multiple injuries he had sustained at the hands of its owner, but it had lost forever the passion and zeal that its master so despised in him. The puppy had lost its spirit and the domination of its master over it was complete.

That is how his master liked him. And that is how Jahal would like every living creature to be, under his control and domination, if he could help it.

Jahal's assault on the puppy had been witnessed by the young Junaid who was at that time recuperating from his first bout of malaria. From that time to this day Jahal had developed and never lost his severe dislike for Junaid.

Sitting alone in his room Jahal's thoughts drifted to the times when Junaid had seen him when he was being himself, without the cloak of civility that he always had on when interacting with people. Junaid had seen the real Jahal more than once, and he could begin to put two and two together and start to arrive at a realization about his true, hidden, and malignant nature. He could even share his thoughts with others around him. He could already have done so! These thoughts troubled Jahal.

He began to recognize that Jameela's abandoning him must have something to do with not only Parveen but more importantly with Nyla. Parveen was too passive and was feeling too sad and likely was extremely angry with Jameela to have cared to warn her. It must have been Nyla and ultimately Junaid who had intervened to recruit Parveen and together they must have caused Jameela's feelings to turn against him. Nyla's presence at Jameela's a few nights ago started to make sense to him. The fourth person must be and could be no other than Junaid. His hatred for Junaid was a constant and had never decreased in intensity over the years but now it acquired a new ferocity that was frightening.

But hidden behind the anger he felt for Junaid was a deep-seated fear and dread. Over the years Jahal had seen in Junaid what he knew he did not have and could not have, the ability to love genuinely and to be loved in return. He had felt the frustration of Nyla rejecting him in favor of Junaid many years ago. Now he felt that Parveen and Jameela had cast him aside as well, dismissing him and making him appear to be the loser in a game that he played to win. They had pushed him away almost certainly due to one reason, Junaid's awareness of Jahal's true nature and him having warned them of it either directly or more likely through Nyla. Unable to love and unable to form an emotional attachment, Jahal's only goal in life was to make people around him look bad and inferior to himself, inadequate in comparison. The events of the last few days had him feeling rather less than adequate in his own eyes, a situation that he must remedy.

Awakening to the realization of his real foe, his real adversary, the one he had dreaded and hated all these years brought him a morose satisfaction, his eyes narrowing fiercely, a bitter smile on his strangely placid face.

Things were starting to make sense to Jahal. Confusion about what had happened was replaced by an understanding of the cause of his great distress, which was therefore now the singular focus of his vengeance. He felt handcuffed by the knowledge that they had material evidence to point the finger at him if he did anything rash. He looked around him, exasperated at his impotence to hurt them as he wanted to. He spotted Shaytan, his big black dog lying at his feet. Shaytan's head rested on his outstretched front paws, his big sad eyes looked at the troubled face of his master.

Ever since Shaytan was a little puppy, he had been brutally taught the lesson to do the bidding of his owner. Without hesitation and without having to be asked twice must he do what he was commanded. If his master told him to go after a jackal or a rabbit or another dog, Shaytan would do that instantly. If he was commanded to attack a person, Shaytan would attack forthwith, without hesitation and not stop until ordered by his master to stop. Jahal had taught the dog to do exactly that. In the woods, he had trained Shaytan in this manner, tearing smaller animals to pieces in the process. A sinister thought now came into his scheming mind, a baleful glint in the emptiness of his black pitiless eyes.

He knew Junaid loved Nyla. Nothing would hurt him more than taking Nyla away from him. It would be justice, he thought, taking away Nyla from Junaid as he had taken Nyla and Jameela away from him. He felt guiltless rage in his desire to do harm to Nyla to hurt Junaid. He felt that the end result of causing extreme and cruel pain to Junaid justified the necessary means which must be employed. Besides he cared nothing for Nyla, she was only useful to him as a source of emotional torment that he must inflict on Junaid. Sooner or later Parveen must also feel his wrath, he contemplated, sooner rather than later, he mused.

Shaytan missed Parveen. She was kind to him. She used to give him treats. His favorite was the ones that were in the shape of little animals. She used to rub his head and tickle his tummy. She used to talk to him with a sweet voice. The girl was suddenly gone. He missed the girl.

For two years she had been together with his master. She made the master tolerable for him. He feared the master less when she was present. His master knew it because he would wag his tale and lick her face whenever he saw her. He never licked the face of his master and never wagged his tale. He never did anything to upset his master by looking or acting happy in front of him. When told to do something, he did it instantly. He used to look to his master for a smile or a pat once he had done what he was commanded, but he had learned that neither would be forthcoming and so he had stopped looking for any such display of affection and reassurance.

He did not understand why he could not resist doing what he was told to do. He did not have the capacity to understand the psychological trauma he had sustained as a puppy and how he was now programmed to do the bidding of his master. He had attacked small animals when commanded by his master. Once he had attacked a rabbit and after scaring the rabbit but not hurting it badly, he had let it flee. The beating he received from his master was never to be forgotten. The next rabbit he caught he had killed and still his master had not given him the signal to stop. It was only when he had torn the little carcass to pieces that he had been given the *stop* order. Later he had walked back behind his still unappreciative master, with his head hung low and his tale drooping.

On one occasion when they had walked for hours in the woods far from home, they had come across an old man who was carrying a load of dry sticks on his back; his master for no reason he could understand had given him the *attack* order and pointed to the man. He had hesitated for a moment but seeing the fire in his master's eyes, he had attacked the man, biting his legs and arms but not his face or neck. The master had stood by grinning as the man screamed for help and tried to fend him off. After a while when the old man could no longer flail around or scream, the master had given the *stop* order and walked off as if nothing had happened. He had looked at the barely breathing man, whimpered with confusion, and trotted after the master, looking back at the man as he lay bleeding.

He missed the girl. She used to call him angel.

# Chapter 21

Jahal told his classmates and friends at school that Shaytan, his beloved dog, had died after being bitten by a poisonous snake while they were out in the woods together. Apparently, Shaytan had chased after a rabbit that had found a hiding place in a hole under the roots of a peepul tree, and while he was digging to get to the rabbit, a snake had bit him several times, killing him within minutes.

Jahal seemed greatly saddened by the loss of his pet that he said he had loved very much. Junaid was surprised to see Jahal so distraught as he had seen the dog treated cruelly by its owner on several occasions.

It had been over two weeks since the late night adventure at Jameela's place and things had settled down somewhat. Junaid had wanted to spend the next day, Saturday, with Nyla at the tree house, but she had just informed him that Parveen and Jameela had invited her to have a picnic with them and that they had told her they would have to cancel the whole thing if she refused. Nyla enjoyed the company of her new friends, and she had asked Junaid if they could spend time together the next weekend instead. Disappointed though he was, he knew how the girls loved each other's company and had acquiesced, telling her at the same time that he had put the rope ladder back on the tree house if they wanted to have their picnic there.

"No, Junaid, I want the tree house to be our special place, for just you and me!" she had told him coyly, adding that she was going to come see him later that night since they would not see each other on Saturday.

Later that day Junaid saw Parveen and Jameela as he was leaving the library before going home. They said hello and Jameela asked him if he was coming to the picnic that Nyla had invited them on.

Remembering that Nyla had told him earlier that *they* had invited her for the picnic, he was surprised but decided not to voice his confusion in front of them.

"No, I know you girls like spending time with each other. I have a few things to do around the house anyway."

"Oh come on, Junaid, it would be fun being out with someone who knows the woods so well!" pressured Parveen.

"Another time, Parveen," said a smiling Junaid. "You girls have fun tomorrow!"

"I am not sure I can go tomorrow either, but I think you should go," Jameela said as they walked off.

*Why would Nyla tell me they invited her when they just told him that she had invited* them *to the picnic?* he thought.

It did not make sense to him. And while the girls wanted him to go with them, Nyla had not asked him to join her and the girls. He felt a little hurt but told himself everyone needs a little time to themselves and perhaps he had been spending too much time with Nyla who needed a little space to relax and have fun with her girlfriends. It was only healthy, he told himself. Plus, she was coming to see him tonight, was she not? That made him feel better and he felt guilty for feeling so grieved at a perceived wrong when clearly there was none.

By the time Nyla finished her homework and put together some things for the picnic, it was already well past eleven at night. She called up Junaid who was starting to worry about her.

"I am so sorry I cannot make it tonight, Junaid!" she said, sounding truly sorry for not being able to keep her word.

"It's OK, Nyla, it is late and you have a full day ahead of you. Sleep well and have fun tomorrow," said an obviously discouraged sounding Junaid.

"I love you, Junaid."

"Love you too."

And they hung up.

Nyla felt dismayed for not finishing her chores and homework in time to be able to see Junaid, and she looked again at the handwritten note from Parveen and wished the girls had not specifically asked her to come without him, so they could spend time alone.

Junaid felt dejected for Nyla not coming to see him and for not asking him to come with her on the picnic.

He walked outside and climbed the stairs up to the terrace. Walking to the edge of the terrace, he leaned on the metal railing and stared at the moonlit woods. A cool wind was blowing down from the hills beyond. For a moment he thought he heard a faint bark in the distance, rising in the wind and then fading as the wind died down. For a moment he thought he recognized the bark, but it was too vague and then it was gone.

He looked at the half moon with melancholy. An unexplained uneasiness came over him and a cold chill made him shiver even as beads of perspiration appeared on his brow.

Nyla woke up early, well before the sun was up. She missed Junaid, not because she was not going to see him today, but for some other reason that she could not explain. She got ready after a light breakfast, still unable to account for the misgiving she continued to have.

They were to meet in front of her home at ten in the morning, and she heard the knock on the door shortly thereafter. Parveen had come alone as Jameela had been unable to change her plans on short notice.

Seeing Parveen picked up Nyla's spirits as her thoughts were diverted away from her unaccountable apprehension. They both had picnic baskets and after saying goodbye to Mrs. Ibrahim, they set out on their outing.

They were headed for a place Nyla had seen while hiking with Junaid, it was a hill with a flat top, which was covered with thick, green grass. Mulberry, mango, pine trees and wild rose bushes surrounded this small plateau and provided a welcome shade from the warm sun during the midday hours. This hill was about an hour's walk from the dirt path that led from near Junaid's house and about half an hour north of the tree house.

Nyla knew Parveen had gotten over Jahal when she asked Parveen if she wanted to avoid passing by the tree house and she had declined with a smile.

"I am fine, Nyla. I know what he is and how he used me. I am free of him and free from the constant pain of being with him."

"Good for you! I am happy to hear that!" Nyla said, smiling happily.

"You are a good person and deserve someone equally good, who can make you happy."

As they arrived at the tree house, they stopped under its shade and sat down to rest.

"You know, Parveen, when Junaid and I first saw you and Jahal under this tree that day, I was sorry for having seen what I saw. But now I am glad."

"Why is that, Nyla?"

"Well, I am not sure, but I think it is because what we saw made Junaid and I both take a closer look at our personal relationship. We both had been really good friends for a long time, but we seemed to be avoiding taking the next step even though we each felt more for each other than just friendship."

"I never thought my rolling around with Jahal under this tree would have helped force you and Junaid to get serious about each other!" Parveen laughed, looking at Nyla mischievously.

"Tell me, Nyla, how close *have* you become with Junaid?"

Nyla reddened with embarrassment.

"He is very loving and caring."

"Everyone knows that! Tell me something I don't already know, Miss Junaid's girlfriend!"

"Well, if you must ask, he is a very good kisser."

"And?"

"And, it is time for us to get up and get going, we are still half an hour's hike from the picnic spot!" said Nyla, getting up and dragging Parveen up by her arm.

"OK, OK! Keep all the good stuff to yourself! I will ask him myself!"

"Don't you dare, Parveen!" said Nyla, feigning anger.

They walked a few steps and then Nyla held Parveen's arm and stopped her.

"How does it feel, Parveen?" she asked with an inquisitive and yet shy look on her face.

"How does what feel?"

"You know, what you and Jahal were doing when, well that day, under the tree?"

"We were not doing *it*, Nyla!"

"I know, I know. I mean when he was touching you and playing with you, that?" said a big-eyed Nyla, suddenly looking like a little girl, wanting to know a big secret.

"Oh, so you don't know how even *that* feels!" said Parveen with a grin. "I guess I don't have to ask Junaid anything after all!" she added, rolling her eyes playfully.

"Well?" implored Nyla.

"Let me think, since you are my friend and I like you and since you are asking with such desire to learn and—"

"Spit it out already, Parveen!" said Nyla with vexation. "I wish I knew someone else I could ask!" she added with a pout.

"All right, you know when you start growing up a little, and your body starts changing little by little and pretty soon you feel all grown up, at least the way you look? And you start feeling and desiring a certain way that you think is bad and you feel guilty for feeling that way? And you start wearing a bra and become all aware of the way your clothes fit you and the way the boys look at you, and how your mom keeps telling you to be modest and cover yourself and all that?"

"Yes, it's a pain, so?"

"So, when you ask me how it feels, well it feels like all that hassle is worth it. It feels like the time you had your first ice cream cone and the first time you had buttered popcorn and pizza and how you felt when you realized that boys thought you were pretty, if you could put all of those feelings together, well that is what it feels like!"

"I get it. Don't say a word more!" said Nyla, biting her lower lip. "You didn't have to go into such detail, Parveen. You have got me actually wanting all those things now and all I have is peanut butter sandwiches and a couple of apples!"

"You wanted to know, and I obliged!" said her smiling friend.

"Just make sure you get this feeling from someone you love and who loves you back, that's all. Otherwise it can cause some serious pain. I should know! OK?"

"OK, Parveen, thanks."

"And, from what I can tell, Junaid would do just fi—"

"Get going, Parveen, stop wasting time!" said a laughing Nyla as she playfully shoved Parveen to move along.

They arrived at the hilltop just before noon, a little tired and very hungry. The sun was at its zenith when they found a spot to spread their picnic blanket under the cool shade of a thickly leafed Mulberry tree. Parveen had brought some roti and baked chicken that smelled wonderful. They devoured the chicken with the roti and then had some mangoes, washing all this down with some cool and delicious Rooh Afza, a sweet, flavorful drink made from the essence and juices of several types of fruit. Nyla's sandwiches and apples they decided to keep as a snack for later.

They lay on their backs together, looking up at the blue sky and the birds that were feasting on the sweet mulberries above them. They talked about everything and anything and wished Jameela had been able to come.

"I wish Jameela had come and I wish Junaid had come too," said Parveen with a sigh.

"I know, I wanted to bring Junaid but you said in your message not to bring him," Nyla said sounding surprised.

"A message? What message?"

"The note you left at my locker, Parveen! What else?"

"What note, Nyla? I did not leave you any note on your locker or anywhere else!" said Parveen, sitting up with confusion on her face.

"You mean you did not tape a note to my locker asking me to go to a picnic with you and Jameela this Saturday?" asked Nyla, looking just as confused as Parveen.

"No, I did not! I thought you wanted to go picnicking with me and Jameela. That is what your note said that I found sticking out of the bottom of my locker!"

Nyla was quiet, as she stood up and started pacing, with a worried expression on her face.

"I did not write a note either, Parveen. It looks like someone wanted us to be here together. Someone who did not want Junaid to come with us." Then remembering something, she searched in the back pocket of her denim jeans, pulled out a piece of folded paper, and gave it to Parveen.

"That is not my writing, Nyla. Wait! That is Jahal's hand-writing, I would know it anywhere!"

"What!"

"Yes! I am positive!"

Just then they heard a dog barking at the foot of the hill, less than a hundred yards away, a hollow, honking bark, closing quickly.

"That sounds like Shaytan, Nyla! But he is supposed to be dead!"

"RUN! Parveen, RUN!"

He smiled as he thought of his brilliant scheme. No one would suspect him. His dog, poor Shaytan was known to be dead, and it would be dead soon enough, as soon as it had done one last thing for its master. He was proud of his own ability to outsmart others. He was, he knew for a fact, much more intelligent than the feebleminded people around him.

He had spread the news that his dog had died of a snake bite, and no one had seen or heard the dog for an entire week. He had also made it known that his fingers were broken in a freak fall and the heavy bandages were proof enough of that! Even those who he was preparing to soon teach a lesson must think his fingers were broken and they may even feel a little sorry for him, a little sympathy perhaps! He smirked.

Jahal had one concern, that they may not see the note or one of the party, either Nyla or Parveen may not be able to make it to the picnic. He did not care if Jameela came or not but preferred that she did not. He felt it would be easier to deal with just two at a time and besides with them out of the way, he had hopes of trying his luck and charm with Jameela once again. She was a tempting dish and not too smart, easily swayed, he thought. But mainly his ego had been injured by her decision to end their relationship now rather than give him the chance to discard her at a later time at his convenience. He felt insulted by her taking the initiative to do away with him. He felt cheated of what he felt was his right to use, abuse, and discard people. He was therefore hopeful of rekindling her interest in him so that he could then have the opportunity to use her the way he had used Parveen.

He was also hoping that Nyla would not bring Junaid along as that would make his plan much more difficult to carry out.

Early on Saturday morning he had hidden himself in some thick underbrush not far from where the dirt path entered the woods and had waited patiently for his quarry.

An hour before noon and just when he was beginning to fear that perhaps they were not coming he saw Nyla and Parveen walking toward him on the path carrying picnic baskets. Gleefully he also noticed that Junaid and Jameela were not with them. His plan was working perfectly, just as he had wanted.

Jahal saw the girls walk to within ten yards of where he was hiding and then they had turned left, going west, away from him. When he could no longer hear them, he came out of hiding and hurriedly made his way north, toward a collection of large rocks, each the size of a small house, some hundred yards away. He was wearing a long black shirt that came down to his thighs and loose camouflage print pants. The soft rubber-soled sneakers allowed him to walk almost silently over the rocky ground. He made his way through the maze made by the scattered large rocks and at last arrived at a stunted pine tree to which tied with a heavy chain with an empty bowl next to him was his big black dog Shaytan, very much alive albeit hungry and quite thirsty.

He had come to feed the dog once every night for the past six nights. A leather muzzle was around the dog's jaws to keep it from barking and drawing attention to itself. The muzzle was only removed at night for a few minutes when Shaytan was eating and drinking and then replaced until Jahal returned with food the next night, some twenty four hours later. It was just barely loose enough to allow the dog to pant but too tight to allow any loud barking.

He undid the muzzle after putting Shaytan on a leash and then walked him to the deep pond behind the rocks to let him satisfy his thirst. The dog had been with him for nearly seven years, since it was just a few-month-old puppy, but he felt no affection for it. The tying up of the dog to a tree and leaving it completely alone for seven days was a necessity in the execution of his plan and he felt no remorse; for him the end always justified the means to achieve it. Jahal's baleful gaze was upon the thirsty dog as it lapped up the cool water, loathing it for not knowing what was in store for it once it had done what it was to be commanded to do, soon. The dog could not be seen alive by anyone again, except for the two who were to see it before long, and they did not really matter, they would become irrelevant shortly. The dog was dead to the world and must remain that way for Jahal to get away with his foul deed. The evil feat must not be connected to him, in any way. The dog must never leave these woods alive, just as his next two victims must never walk out of these same woods. Jahal clutched the muzzle in his left hand, it would be put back on later, much more tightly, when the dog had done its job. It would be put back on never to be removed again; it must be on when the dog was drowned in the same deep pond from which even now it drank life-sustaining water. Once, in the malevolent scheme of its master, the purpose of its life was over, the same water that had kept it alive for the past seven days would take that life from it.

Enough! He jerked at the leash harshly, pulling the dog back abruptly. The girls must not get too far away.

Each night Jahal had come and each night when the muzzle had been removed, Shaytan had hoped that it would not be put back on again but each time his master had replaced it and tied him up to the tree in the middle of the woods and left him, alone in the dark of the night. Initially he had struggled and whimpered and tried to break the chain, but it had only made his neck sore and made him even thirstier. It was also attracting the jackals who had come sniffing and added to his fear and misery. The muzzle had made things twice as bad. Without it he could have barked and raved and voiced his discontent and rage but as it was he felt smothered and could do nothing but suffer quietly. He had learned to calm himself to be able to breathe normally and to keep from feeling as though he was going to suffocate. How could master leave him in this dreadful position?

Shaytan had always feared his master, but the last several days and nights had added an element of loathing to this dread.

Today, however, the master had come early, during the day instead of the middle of the night, had removed the muzzle and led him to drink the cool water and then instead of tying him up again was taking him for a walk in the woods. Perhaps the master was not as bad to him as he had started to think. He turned his cheerless eyes hopefully at his master who as usual completely ignored him.

A jackrabbit hopped into plain view, standing on its hind legs, twitching its wet nose in the warm breeze. Shaytan stopped in his tracks, waiting for the master to give the *kill* command, but the master ignored the rabbit and pulled at the leash, urging him on, walking purposefully and looking ahead, as if searching for bigger game.

Before long the master stopped and stood looking in all directions, seemingly uncertain as to which way to go. Presently he took out a small piece of cloth from a pocket of his pants and had him sniff it, giving the *seek* command. Shaytan became suddenly and visibly animated. Delighted, his sad eyes sparkled with anticipation as he smelled the girl's scent on the cloth and eagerly sought it in the air and on the ground. Quickly finding it, he pushed onwards almost dragging his master behind him. He had not seen the kind girl in a long time, three weeks if he knew how to count, and was desperate to seek her out and let her rub his head and neck and tickle his belly and give him tasty treats. Yes, the master was being good to him by letting him seek out the girl. He must never distrust the master. He must always continue to do as the master says; he must always obey the commands. He hustled along, moving rapidly and as they approached the bottom of a hill he could tell the girl was close by. In excitement he began to bark his hollow honking bark, pulling the master behind him as he bulldozed up the hill.

Jameela finished her chores by a quarter to noon, sooner than she had anticipated and with nothing else to do she decided to surprise her friends by joining them at the picnic in the woods. She put on her walking shoes and rode her bike to Junaid's home, hoping that he could tell her the best way into the woods and where she was likely to find the girls.

Junaid came down upon hearing the knocks on the door and was surprised to find Jameela standing there all alone.

"Hi, Jameela! I thought you would be picnicking with the girls?"

"I had a few things to do first, but I am now free to go join them! Can you tell me how to get into the woods and where I can find them?"

"Getting into the woods is the easy part, just right down that dirt path you see there. But finding them is a little trickier. Nyla knows the woods very well and could have taken Parveen to any of several very good picnic spots. You are likely to get lost if you go in there alone, Jameela."

"Well why don't you come with me then? You can keep me from getting lost, and we can surprise both of them together!

"I wish I could, but I think they had wanted to go without me."

"Without you?"

"Yes. Nyla said Parveen's note to her asked not to bring me along so you girls could spend some fun time together."

"Parveen's note? Parveen never wrote a note to Nyla! It was Nyla who wrote to Parveen and me asking us to go hiking alone with her!" said Jameela as she searched for and pulled out a piece of paper from her pocket. "See! This is from Nyla."

Junaid took a look at the note and his eyes opened wide with fear, impending danger written on his face.

"That is not Nyla's handwriting, Jameela! I hope we are not already too late! It is Jahal!"

Junaid ran upstairs to put on his clothes and hiking shoes and was back downstairs within minutes. He then raced toward the woods telling Jameela to let his mother know where he was going. Then he was gone, leaving Jameela confused and frightened by his words.

So Jahal was up to no good, up to taking revenge, hurting those who he felt had hurt him, had caused him pain.

She felt responsible for the danger that Nyla and Parveen were in. She remembered how the two had helped her escape from Jahal's clutches.

It was now her friends who were in need of help. They had saved her and now she must do all in her power to come to their aid.

She told Mrs. Kafrooni what Junaid had asked her and then without telling her where she was going, Jameela ran to the dirt path and into the woods. Her friends were in peril, and she was not going to sit and do nothing.

She had warned Parveen and Jameela to be careful as Jahal could be expected to take his revenge and now as she ran with

Parveen at her heels, she blamed herself for letting down her own guard and exposing Parveen and herself to jeopardy by coming to the woods alone without Junaid.

The barking was drawing nearer now as they heard Jahal shout, "SEEK, BOY, SEEK!"

Parveen screamed with horror, her eyes bulging with terror.

Jahal had played his hand well and if he was truly as deranged as they thought he was, and there was now no reason to believe otherwise, they were in grave peril indeed. If he had gone to the trouble of making people believe that Shaytan was dead, and if he had faked notes to Nyla and Parveen, plotting to have them come to the woods alone, then he must have planned something truly evil, something more depraved than what would be the norm even for him.

How she wished that Junaid was with her now! How she wished she had disregarded the note and brought him along just as he had wanted to.

They had heard Shaytan and Jahal coming up the hill from the east, the same way they had climbed it. Grabbing Parveen's left hand in her right, Nyla ran as fast as Parveen would allow to the opposite side of the hill to try and put some distance between themselves and their hunters.

Thinking faster than Parveen was letting her run, Nyla considered their options. There was no time to climb a tree, especially with Parveen with her. They could run down the other side of the hill and go in the direction of the secluded pond where Junaid had taught her to swim or they could go down and go around the hill and back to where they had come from, hoping to reach the tree house. Neither option seemed very attractive to Nyla. The tree house was at least half a mile away, and Shaytan was sure to catch them long before they got to it. She knew Shaytan was on their scent and she decided to try to throw him off by getting to the swimming hole and then wading down the shallow stream that went winding through a dense thicket. She felt it was their only hope and therefore worth a try.

As they came to the crest of the hill, they looked back and saw Jahal and Shaytan no more than seventy yards away. Telling Parveen to run down the hill and keep going straight, Nyla lingered waiting just long enough to see Jahal unleash Shaytan and shout, "KILL, BOY, KILL!"

Junaid was troubled by a confounding realization. Jahal was taking his revenge, and Nyla was the price he wanted to extract. Junaid knew now that Jahal had finally understood that the reason he had lost Jameela could not be anything other than Junaid warning her through Nyla. That is why Nyla had been present that night in Jameela's bedroom.

But Nyla had simply been the messenger. The intimation clearly warning Jameela as to who Jahal really was had to have come from Junaid, the only person who could have known his real identity. The only reason Jahal wanted to hurt Nyla was to hurt Junaid the same way Junaid had hurt him by taking Jameela from him now and by having taken Nyla away from him years earlier. Parveen would have to pay the price for warning Jameela too, but the real enemy for Jahal, the real threat was and had always been Junaid.

Junaid and Nyla had both felt that Jahal would be focused on Jameela who had rejected him and Parveen who had warned her of his abusive character. They had thought it unlikely that he would realize the motivation behind Parveen warning Jameela would have to have come from Junaid. They had in effect underestimated Jahal's ability and his cunning in determining his true adversary and therefore the real threat to himself. This understanding of their underestimation of Jahal's shrewdness had come to Junaid and Nyla too late, and they were now paying the price for this oversight.

Banishing these concerns for the moment and thinking only that he must not let any harm come to Nyla, Junaid ran at breakneck speed over ground that he had known since childhood.

He recalled that Nyla had not wanted to go picnicking at the tree house with Parveen and coming to the end of the dirt path, Junaid, without slowing his pace down had turned west, going quickly through dense shrubs and tangled wines. Over fallen trees and boulders and through thorny brush he ran, as fast as his legs could pump and as he had never run before. The sleeves of his shirt were torn and thorns had cut into his arms and chest but he went headlong toward the flat top hill that Nyla had once said she wanted to go for a picnic one day.

The fastest way to the hill was over the deep rapids of a mountain stream that lay in his path but fording it was not possible. Over the years he had tried unsuccessfully to swing across it on the rope that he had hung from a high branch of a tree that was leaning over the water on this side of the stream but try as he might he had taken a dip in the cold water at each and every attempt.

He was still a hundred yards from this stream, which was just fifty yards from the hill, but still a full four hundred yards from the hill were he to go around the bend of the stream, when he heard the honking bark of Shaytan for the first time in over a week followed immediately by the screams of a girl. With no time to lose and the decision therefore now made for him as to which path he must take, Junaid ran full tilt toward the rapids and with reckless abandon he launched himself into the air while still a few feet from the edge and caught the rope in midair as he flew forward carrying the momentum of his flat out run. Never before had he tried crossing the rapids with such fierce determination, never before was the reason for the crossing so absolutely critical. In two blinks of an eye, he was over the deep water and across to the other side as he let go of the rope and landed on his hands, did a somersault that got his feet under him and was running to the hill again in one smooth motion.

As he dashed up the hill, panting and out of breath yet determined to reach Nyla before any harm could come to her and feeling frantic that he might already be too late, he heard the hollow honking bark of a dog that could only be Shaytan followed by Jahal's shout of "KILL, BOY, KILL!"

Almost berserk with righteous anger and fraught with anguish, he rushed to the top of the hill and barely caught a glimpse of Jahal as he went down the opposite side over seventy-five yards away; Shaytan barking somewhere below the hill on the other side.

"Good girl, Nyla!" he muttered.

She was making a run for it and giving him the few more minutes he needed to get between her and whatever threatened her.

"I am coming, Nyla!" he shouted as he charged after Jahal.

The girl's smell was strong in his nostrils now; she could not be very far. There was the smell of another with her, but he did not know who. Up the hill he ran, still the leash kept him from moving at his fastest, the master behind him holding on to the restricting leash, urging him on still.

Breathing hard, his chest heaving and with his tongue hanging out the side of his jaws, he made it to the edge of the flat top and saw, not far, the girl and another running away. He barked loud, again and again, telling the kind girl he was here, so she could come back and play with him. He wanted to feel her rubbing his head and to hear her giggle again. But she kept on running away, farther, with the other girl holding her hand.

Now the master stopped and removed the leash from the collar around his neck. He looked again and saw only the other girl standing at the edge of the other side of the hill. The kind girl was gone. The master now pointed at the other, the girl he did not know, and shouted the words, "KILL, BOY, KILL!" He looked at the master for an instant, he must obey the master, always he must obey. But he was unsure, it was only a girl, master liked girls, he rolled around with them on the ground and in the bed. Did he hear the master say the *kill* word?

"KILL!" shouted the master again, with blazing eyes glaring at him; he shouted the word again.

There was no doubt the word was *kill*, he looked and the girl was running; she moved fast and then she was gone. He now heard the *seek* command and felt the leash hit his side and without any hesitation he dashed after the girl leaving Jahal well behind.

Within a few seconds he was at the edge where the girl had disappeared and looking down he saw her running like a deer and making for the tree line some distance away. The kind girl was running a few yards ahead of her. He barked, and they both looked back with dread on their faces. By the time Jahal came and they both started to run downhill, the girls had disappeared beyond the tree line.

Nyla saw Jahal and his big black dog appear on the other side of the hill and then heard Jahal scream KILL as he unleashed the dog. For a moment she waited as if frozen and hearing Jahal scream again she raced down the hill; fear making her move at a pace she did not think she was capable of. She caught up with Parveen and they ran to the trees that stood less than fifty yards away as they heard Shaytan barking from the hill behind them. By the time Jahal and Shaytan started running down the hill, she had pulled Parveen into the cover of the trees and taking a turn to the left made for the swimming hole no more than two hundred yards away.

Just when Nyla was starting to feel that perhaps they were going to make it, Parveen stepped into a groundhog hole and fell to the ground with a scream. Nyla stopped and looked back to see Parveen wincing with pain and grabbing her left ankle.

"Nyla, don't stop! Keep running!" screamed a grimacing Parveen.

Nyla looked at Parveen's left foot and saw the ankle already swelling up. She grabbed Parveen's arm and pulled her to stand, then putting her right arm around Parveen's waist she tried to help her run on one leg. Parveen tried her best but the pain was severe and she was too exhausted to hop and run on just one leg. She told Nyla to leave her and try to save herself, but that was not something Nyla was willing to do.

"We came together and will leave together, Parveen."

Shaytan's bark was loud in their ears as he turned and entered the trees. Jahal's shouts were not far behind.

Nyla knew they could not outrun Jahal and Shaytan now. She led Parveen to a nearby tree, helping her to sit with her back against it. She then looked around and found a three-foot long, two-inch thick dry branch that she quickly grabbed and took her position in front of Parveen. Holding the club in both her hands, she got ready for Jahal and his big black dog.

The girl was sitting against a tree, and he could tell she was hurt. She was holding her foot and there was pain on her face. He could smell her fear. The other girl holding a stick in her hands was standing in front of the kind girl. He stopped running and walked up to them. He was not growling or showing his fangs, he was whimpering and moving slowly, his head held sideways, in a nonthreatening way. He came closer and the other girl raised the club in her hand, she shouted at him to stay away from the injured girl. He wanted to get close to the kind girl and lick her face, but the new girl was keeping him from getting close to her. He growled at the new girl and instead of making her fear him and back off it made her angry, and she swung at him missing his head by inches. He backed away, confused at her reaction. Any animal and any person he had ever attacked had screamed fearfully and tried to run away. This girl was different.

His master was running toward them. He was screaming and angry. He came closer and saw the impasse. He became infuriated with him for not attacking and biting and tearing. "KILL!" the master screamed over and over again. "KILL, BOY, KILL!" he shouted, pointing at the new girl. Yes, the new girl was keeping him from getting to the kind girl, the girl who played with him, who rolled around with master. The master only wanted him to attack the new girl, not his girl but the girl with the stick. The other girl, yes, she had made his girl run from him, he had seen her hold her hand and run away from him. Now she had hurt the kind girl, hurt her leg and made her fearful, he could smell her fear, see the fear on her face. He had to attack the new girl and save the kind girl, his and his master's girl.

Fangs bared, eyes narrowed with focus and hate, a menacing growl emanating from his deep chest, the big dog lowered himself on his haunches, ready to launch the attack his master had ordered, the most vicious attack that "KILL" demanded.

"No, Shaytan!" screamed Parveen, who had seen animals torn to bits by Shaytan when given the "KILL" order.

He kept his eyes focused laser like on his quarry, inching closer, getting close enough to suddenly explode past the stick and onto the throat of the other girl that had hurt the kind girl.

"Come on! Come on you devil dog!" yelled Nyla, her eyes locked on those of the big black dog, the stick held in her hands as one would hold a baseball bat.

There was a swishing sound of something or someone flashing toward them from the left, and for a split second Nyla took her eyes off those of the threatening dog and looked to her left and in that split second the hind legs that were coiled underneath it launched the beast at her throat.

Parveen screamed and Nyla, as if in slow motion, looked back toward Shaytan and saw his open jaws and long fangs dripping strings of saliva, airborne and mere inches from her face.

He saw Shaytan followed by Jahal running for the tree line below the hill. Knowing these woods like his own backyard, he knew Nyla was headed for the swimming hole and taking a sharp turn to the right, he hoped to intercept Shaytan a few yards sooner than if he had followed him as had Jahal. Junaid hurtled down the hill and taking a flying leap he cleared a large bush and not ten yards ahead he saw Jahal with Shaytan crouching on the ground ten feet from a determined club wielding Nyla as Parveen sat against a tree behind her. He knew immediately that Shaytan was ready for his attack and was waiting for the slightest wavering or break in Nyla's focus to launch himself at her.

As Junaid broke the cover to their left in full flight as if winged, he had the big dog as his first objective. Junaid was less than ten feet from Nyla when he saw her break her eye contact with the dog to look to her left and in that very instant just as Junaid catapulted forward the dog hurled himself into the air.

Junaid collided with the big dog's midsection just inches before its fangs got to Nyla, and they both landed on the ground a few feet to the right of where she was standing. Shaytan, in full attack mode and growling savagely, instantly went after his assailant, fangs bared, fur ruffling and rippling. Nyla got the split second she needed and stepping forward landed a painful blow to Shaytan's flank, making him lose focus and look back at her in confusion as Junaid, panting and breathless, scrambled to his feet and jumped over the dog to stand between it and Nyla.

"Stop, Shaytan!" screamed Parveen again, with her face now level with the dog, mere feet from her.

"Stop, angel!" she shouted again and as if by magic, the savage growling and angry snapping of the jaws turned to meek whimpering. Before they could move an inch, the big dog rushed between Nyla and Junaid to Parveen's side and began licking her face between her flailing arms like a big sloppy puppy.

Shocked and relieved at the same time, Junaid and Nyla looked toward an infuriated Jahal who had finally stopped shouting, "KILL, KILL!" and was moving toward them with the leather muzzle in his left hand and the leash in his right.

"I see you let these girls do all the work for you, Junaid," he scoffed.

"Only because they don't need my help dealing with the likes of you, Jahal."

"I don't know what they see in a wimp like you!" he spat on the ground with contempt.

"They see it, that is all that matters." He said indignantly, having caught his breath and now staring at the agitated face of a clearly ruffled Jahal.

"You and your friend had no business interfering with me and Jameela! She loved me until you told her lies about me, Nyla! You and Parveen!"

"When will you stop lying and stop trying to hurt everyone around you, Jahal?" said Nyla angrily, her fists tightly clenched on her hips.

"I do not lie! If you would just stop trying to hurt me!" Junaid whimpered, sounding like a hurt and offended victim.

"Your dog has miraculously returned from the dead, and look, the broken bones of your fingers have healed in just a week!" said Parveen sarcastically, rubbing the fur between Shaytan's ears as he lay next to her with his big head in her lap.

"It's my dog, and I can say anything I want about him," said a belligerent Jahal, not making any sense to anyone but himself. That is how he had lived his life, telling himself things that suited him and his way of thinking.

He had owned Shaytan for over seven years and had not formed any attachment with the dog; his goal for the past week and until a few minutes previously had been to use Shaytan for his nefarious plan against Nyla and Parveen and then to drown it without any compunction in the least.

Shaytan, on the other hand, albeit nothing more than a dog, was capable of forming a meaningful attachment with another living being who had treated him with affection. He also now understood that the other girl was not trying to hurt the kind girl. Now as Jahal moved forward to put the leash on his collar, Shaytan felt the fear he always had for his master evaporate under the kind touch of the girl and in its place was a deep enmity and loathing born of years of abuse and neglect. He did not want to go with the master who had been cruel to him. He wanted to stay with the girl who was kind and caring. He also began to understand that his master had been wanting him to harm the girl all along, first to SEEK and then to KILL and the other girl had been trying to protect her and not harm her. That is why she had thrown down the club now that he was next to the kind girl. He knew this to be true with prehistoric certainty, the same ability that had allowed his kind to understand human nature enough to live with their kind since thousands of years ago.

As Jahal reached down to put the leash on its collar, Shaytan growled and snapped his powerful jaws inches from his hand. Startled, he instinctively jumped back several steps, fearful that Shaytan may come after him.

"COME, BOY!" he ordered.

Shaytan did not move.

"COME!!" he commanded again with anger.

Shaytan whimpered and looked at Parveen, who continued to talk to him softly and kept gently stroking his fur.

"Look what you have done! You have even taken my own dog away from me! The dog that I love so much!"

"No one is stopping him from going with you. But it appears he has a new owner and a new friend!" Nyla said, looking at Parveen and her new dog.

"I hate you all!" Jahal said furiously, quivering with anger and impotence.

"We know that, Jahal. We have known that for some time now," Parveen replied with a bitter smile on her upturned face, her chin thrust out defiantly.

"We warned you Jahal! We will talk with Jameela now that you have broken your promise!" called out Nyla as Jahal turned and walked away, looking back every few steps to glare at them and to make sure Shaytan was not coming after him.

The tables had turned and once again he found himself at the losing end. He had planned well and had every expectation of pulling it off, but for the unexpected and unforeseen behavior of that dumb dog.

He had no affection for the dog and having lost it meant little to him. His only annoyance was that the dog had rebelled against him at a most inappropriate time.

He was somewhat pleased that he would not have to bother feeding and walking it anymore. The dog had become quite useless to him especially since it no longer followed his commands. That his own dog had growled and snapped at him did not hurt this feelings in the least, for he had none. In that regard he felt he had a decided edge over those who were liable to feel upset and sad in various ways while dealing with others. He had always felt baffled by excessive display of emotion. His own show of dismay at times was solely for the sake of others around him, it made them look at him kindly and kept them in the dark about his true nature which was devoid of love and empathy for any and all living creatures. He felt such emotions to be unattainable, unnecessary, and unproductive. He felt such emotions and attachment to another person or animal to be a sign of weakness.

Junaid too had interfered once again at a most inconvenient time and he had definitely become a thorn in his side. And why did they want to discuss with Jameela whether or not to expose him with the pictures in their possession? Perhaps, he reasoned, because it was the window of her bedroom that he was trying to get into in those pictures and she would have to give her permission for that to become public knowledge.

If he could only get his hands on Jameela he could make sure she never gave anyone any such permission. He had these thoughts in his head as he was walking back when he heard someone call out for Nyla and Parveen. The call was repeated at intervals and seemed to be moving away, farther into the woods. The call came once again and he now clearly recognized it to be Jameela's voice. Perhaps his luck would change for the better after all. Perhaps he will have his sweet revenge before too long. Jameela in the woods all alone, exactly what he would have hoped for. And shouting as she was for her friends, she was instead drawing him closer to her every time she called out to them.

Jahal was certain she did not know her way around the woods; she was lost and was calling for her friends. They were likely to hear her if she moved a few hundred yards toward them, just as he had heard her. He must reach her before they heard her. Running toward the sound that was repeated at intervals and which continued to move away from her friends, he quickly narrowed the gap to less than a hundred yards and then he saw her just as she saw him.

As a deer caught in the glare of an oncoming vehicle's head-lights at night, she froze, unable to move.

She had been walking for over an hour and had heard Shaytan's barking, which had led her to this general area but once the barking stopped she was lost and had wandered without direction, calling out the names of her friends. She was afraid of the woods and had been frightened when she had heard the deep honking bark of Jahal's big black dog but had courageously walked toward the sound of the barking in hopes of finding her friends who she thought she may be able to help in some way.

Now, seeing Jahal on the other side of a clearing she could not help but entertain the worst possible scenario. That perhaps he had overpowered her friends with the help of his dog, which was not dead after all and that he was going to do to her what he in his hatred and vengeance had likely already done to her friends.

It was only when Jahal started to run toward her that she came out of her trance and with a loud scream ran in the opposite direction. While she was not familiar with the woods, one thing she could do was run and run she did, like the wind. By the time Jahal made it across the clearing to where he had spotted her, she was a hundred yards north of his position and heading, without her knowledge, straight to where Nyla had learned to swim. She spotted a gigantic sheesham tree between some bushes near the top of a small hill and made straight for it. Going around the tree she abruptly came to the tranquil clear water pond with the flat granite and limestone rocks around it. She scampered down toward the narrow channel where the water exited the pond and ran into a troupe of rhesus monkeys that were almost the same color as the smaller rocks scattered about. Having never seen a wild animal in its natural surroundings, much less a large group in close proximity, she began screaming hysterically. The monkeys were as startled as she was and were about to run up the nearest tree, when realizing that she was alone and clearly afraid of them, they bared their long fangs at her and then ignoring her screams satisfied their thirst and casually ambled off into the woods along the other side of the stream.

Seeing the primates leave, she composed her wits somewhat and was trying to decide which way to go when she heard and turned around to see Jahal hurriedly coming down the small hill behind her less than twenty yards away. In panic, she hastily jumped over the narrow channel and darted up the other side, hearing Jahal's heavy breathing as he cursed and told her to stop. She heard him shout what he was going to do once he caught her if she did not stop running and it made her want to get away from him even faster.

Jahal had been gone for over ten minutes, and they were deciding how best to take the injured Parveen home when they heard a girl scream a few hundred yards away to the west. It was a single chilling scream and was not repeated. Clearly someone was in need of help, someone not too far away. Not wanting to leave Parveen alone, they decided to have Nyla and Parveen's new dog that she had named Angel stay with her while Junaid tried to locate the source of the scream.

He ran in the general direction of where he thought he had heard the scream come from and hoped that it would be repeated for him to be able to promptly get to the person in need of assistance. He had just arrived at a clearing two hundred yards to the west when he heard not one but a series of bloodcurdling screams coming clearly from the direction of their favorite spot in the woods. The voice sounded somewhat familiar and he thought it was Jameela but could not be sure.

He recalled that he had told Jameela to let his mother know where he was going, and it was possible she had followed him into the woods afterwards and become lost.

The short period of time between the first scream, the location of which he felt quite certain he was at now, and this series of screams coming from the direction of the swimming hole a few hundred yards away, told him that she had run quite fast in between the screams. If it was Jameela the first scream could be explained by her having run into Jahal as he was making his way back home. She must have seen him but she must also know that he had seen her as well or she would not have screamed to alert him of her presence. She must have fled upon seeing him and the second series of screams could mean that she had either been cornered or caught by Jahal. All this was in Junaid's mind as he sprinted to where he thought she must be.

"That is Jameela screaming!" said Nyla, sounding alarmed.

"What is she doing in the woods? Alone!" said a surprised Parveen.

"Her screams could mean one of two things; that she has seen some animal close to her and the animal is not running away despite her screams or that Jahal has caught her. And, Parveen, I hope it is the former."

"Junaid is sure to hear the screams and get to her soon. I am safe here with Angel, you should go Nyla, maybe they can use your help."

"Are you sure you will be all right all alone?"

"I am not alone," she said, looking at the big dog sitting by her.

"OK, but don't move, stay where you are, Parveen!" said Nyla as she started to run, grabbing her trusty club in her right hand.

She arrived at the clear pond a few minutes after Junaid, and they found no sign of Jameela or Jahal. Splitting up, they walked on either side of the stream calling her name but after another half an hour of searching they decided to look for her deeper into the woods.

Jahal had seen Jameela stand motionless and then when he dashed toward her across the clearing he saw her take off in the opposite direction with a speed that he had not expected. He was not too worried however as she was running deeper into the woods and away from any help. He would eventually catch her and when he did he was going to teach her a lesson.

He remembered well the day he had teased her in her room with a promise for more the next night when he had kissed her and left her wanting. Little had he known then that the one left craving for more would be himself. The next night he had arrived thirsting and needing her to satisfy him but she, or perhaps her friends, had been sly enough to have tempted him by letting him see her through the window to make sure he had attempted to enter her room and then he had been caught and trapped in a most humiliating manner. His desire for her had only increased in the subsequent days, which is why he had hoped that Parveen would come to the picnic alone with Nyla but without Jameela who he had hoped to attempt to seduce once Parveen and Nyla, her protective friends, had met with an unfortunate end of his arranging. Whether he wanted her for the sexual attraction he felt for her or whether he wanted to show his power and dominance over another human, he did not know or care to know.

He was about a hundred yards behind her when he saw her disappear behind a large tree trunk and shortly thereafter he heard her scream repeatedly. Arriving at the tree trunk just as the primates were moving off, he scrambled down the hill after her. She looked behind over her shoulder and barely managed to jump across the narrow water channel and made off in the opposite direction. He threatened her to stop now or suffer the consequences when he did catch her. When he saw her pull away from him as though he was standing still, he started to plead and remind her of the happy times they had together and how Parveen and Nyla being jealous of them had plotted to separate them. Seeing that she was not having any of it, he started to shout obscenities and began threatening her even as he started after her again.

After running for over five minutes during which he caught glimpses of her between trees and rocks as she made her way up the hill, he finally saw her standing looking up at the vertical side of a hill that had water gushing out from near its base. Jameela looked back and seeing that he was still coming after her, ran along the side of the hill to the right. He stayed after her and saw her climb up the hill from the other end where the ground sloped up. She had then raced along the top of the hill to the front where the water was gushing out from about two hundred feet below. He climbed the hill from the same slope she had and as he came up he saw her coming toward him, panting with exhaustion, as there was nowhere else for her to go.

He waited for her with his hands on his hips, a leer on his face, feeling that he had her now, finally. No one around to hear her screams, no one around to see what he would do to her.

She walked to within ten feet of him and stopped with a patch of dense oat grass between them.

"Sooner or later, I was going to get my hands on you, Jameela." He said, looking at her lasciviously.

"You disgust me, and to think I was actually falling for you makes me want to puke." Replied Jameela, abhorrence painted on her flushed face.

"You wanted me then and you want me now. Just admit it. I know it and you know it, Jameela. We were so happy when we were together, before these girls got to you and told you lies about me."

"They had nothing to gain by telling me lies about you. If anything they were caring and thoughtful about someone who had been thoughtless and insensitive toward them. They are my friends."

"Where are your friends now?"

"Right here, right now." She touched her chest.

Jahal took a few steps toward her, his eyes now narrow slits. "You stupid, girl! You think you can tease me like that and get away with it?" he said, moving closer.

"I *was* stupid to let you get so close to me, but I know better now! Get away from me!"

He came nearer, reaching for her, his angry face full of contempt; the first time Jameela had seen his real face, the face that showed his disdain for her, the first time she had seen him without the mask. It frightened her to see the rage within him displayed openly.

"Don't you touch me!"

"I will do much more than just touch you, bitch!"

"Over my dead body!"

"Sure, if that is what it takes! Your being dead or alive means nothing to me!"

He grabbed her by her right arm and she wrenched it away forcefully, brimming with anger.

"You wanna play tough!" he hissed, teeth bared, eyes like glowing coal.

She thought if there was a face of evil, this had to be it.

It scared her but it also made her hate him more.

He grabbed her arm again.

"Let me go!"

He now grabbed both her arms and they struggled as she tried to pull away from him again.

He twisted her left arm behind her making Jameela wince with pain. As he now tried to twist her right arm behind her as well, she leaned forward and bit him hard on his left hand, drawing blood and causing him to swear and let go of her.

She pushed him away and he swung out at her, punching her on the face.

She fell backward, hitting her head on the rocky ground.

Dazed and close to fainting, she saw him undo his belt and drop his pants. Fighting to remain conscious, and unable to get up, she saw him move forward toward her and as he bent down over her, she raised her upper body by planting both her elbows on the ground and then bending both her knees against her chest she kicked him on his face with all her might.

Jahal toppled backward on a patch of grass a few feet behind him and as she watched him fall he suddenly disappeared. Thinking that she must be imagining things after hitting her head on the ground, she sat up and heard a distant scream as if coming through a tunnel. Rubbing her eyes to clear the cobwebs she staggered up and saw his pants on the ground next to her and moving a few feet she saw the long grass slowly straightening up, hiding the hole in the ground that Jahal had fallen into.

She recalled how Nyla and Junaid had fallen through such an opening into an underground cavern where they had found the missing boy and from which they had made a miraculous escape.

She pulled out some of the grass and carefully leaned forward to look into the darkness of the cavern. She could hear Jahal splashing in the water far away and after a few moments she saw him attempting to stay afloat. It was hard for her to believe that the same man who minutes ago was a picture of hate, spouting the most vile filth from his mouth and intent on assaulting her, was now crying and whimpering like a helpless child, begging for someone to help him.

"Help! Someone help me! Please someone!"

"Get a hold of yourself, Jahal, you are crying like a little baby!"

"Help me. I am going to drown!"

He looked around and then looking up he spotted her in the opening through which he had fallen. The thick grass still blocked most of the opening but some light was coming through. Now with his eyes getting used to the dark, he was able to spot the sandbar on the side and swam to it doggy style, choking, gagging and swallowing water. As he stood up, he noticed he was not wearing anything on his legs. The realization scared him for some reason. It made him feel vulnerable. It made him feel like he was caught with his pants down.

"Jameela, please help me!" he cried.

"Help you! How can I help you? Why *should* I help you?"

"You cannot let me die in here, Jameela."

"Why not, Jahal? Why can't I just walk away and leave you where you are, where you cannot trouble me or anyone else. I think we would all be better off without you!"

"No you cannot! People like you just *have* to help others!"

"Watch me walk away, Jahal!" She moved her head away but sat next to the hole, listening to his odious bawling and blubbering. She knew she was not going to be able to just walk away, but she did want him to suffer the agony of thinking that she was gone. After a few minutes of hearing his keening and whimpering when she could not tolerate it any longer, she moved forward and looked in, finding him standing half-naked, with a most sniveling and woeful expression on his upturned face. His entire demeanor and pitiful manner was in direct contrast to the arrogance and selfish disdain he had displayed when attacking her minutes earlier.

He was playing the pity game to the best of his ability; it was his only and best recourse at the moment. Even now he knew it was only a ploy to help him get out of his predicament. But he knew the foolish girl did not know that; other people always took pity when they saw someone crying and begging, no matter what that person had done. That is why he was glad to be bereft of the feelings that made people willingly do things that were not in their best interest. It always surprised him to see people act this way, but it made his life a whole lot easier.

He also knew that the people around him could not tell if he was different, different in a most fundamental way, so different in fact that his dog Shaytan was actually more like them than he was. His dog could form emotional attachments to those around him and act in a way that showed the affection that such attachment brings. He looked down upon these feelings and consequently held those harboring such feelings in utter contempt. Winning at all cost was his main preoccupation in life. All emotions that hindered getting his way were useless and meaningless to him.

He was devoid of that basic sense that makes one belong to a group of people where one's desires and interests are not always in accord with the well being of the group but where the individual foregoes his or her own wants of personal gratification for the benefit of the group at large. For him there was no affiliation that obliged him to do anything other than what he himself wanted or needed.

Unburdened by the demands of any such true friendship or companionship with any other human being, he was like a wolf in sheep's clothing. A ruthless animal among unsuspecting sheep who could not possibly know that he was completely different from them in a most essential way. He, in short, lacked what makes a person a human being.

He had learned to fake manners and superficial civilities that people around him mistook for genuine feelings and the expression of those truly felt emotions. He was a master of depiction of these artificial affections and sentiments and it was this performance that fooled the people, it was precisely this ability which was his sheep's clothing, his mask, his camouflage and his license to go about his life undetected and unsuspected.

So even though he saw her move away from the opening in the ceiling of the cavern, even though she was no longer visible and he could not hear her, he knew she could not just go away. She was too normal for that. She was not like him. She was too predictable. He knew this with certainty, but he had to play his part in making sure he tugged on the right strings to make her act as she was genetically and socially programmed to act. One did not just leave another living creature to die when one could help them as long as there was no perceived immediate threat to oneself and especially if the other was seen as miserable and pathetic.

Sure enough and soon enough, the girl was back at the opening, looking down at his crying face; even now she was beginning to forget and overlook what he had been bent on doing just minutes earlier. She did not know that he was fully and remorselessly prepared to kill her after sexually assaulting her. But had she known this to be a fact, she would still be unlikely to just leave him to die in that cave; such was the pull of the conscience that the girl possessed, that most human beings live by and that society expects.

She despised what he was and how he had treated Parveen and herself, but try as she might she could not bring herself to just leaving him in the cave to die of starvation.

She would simply feel too guilty to let another person, no matter how loathsome, die even as he begged for her help. A call for pity it turns out is a useful ploy of those without a moral code and they find it almost always works on those who are burdened with their scruples about right and wrong. But she would have her revenge, she was not handcuffed to that extent by her principles.

"Stop your crying and carrying on, I cannot let you just die in this cave anymore than I can let a rat die of starvation in front of my eyes."

"Thank you, Jameela, you are an angel. I knew you were not like the others. You are special and—"

"One more word out of your lying mouth and I will really just walk away and no one would be the wiser as to whatever happened to you! You understand?"

"Yes!" he said, hiding the defiance and bitterness in his voice. He would have to patiently wait for the chance he hoped would come soon enough when he would get his revenge on this half-witted girl and her friends. He would throttle her in her sleep as easily as he would swat a fly if he had the chance and if he could get away with it.

"Now I am going to find and tell my friends what happened here and see if they feel compelled to send someone to get you out or let you rot where you are."

"Thank you, Jameela, thank you!" he said with exaggerated and phony gratitude. "Now please throw my briefs and pants down to me before you leave," he begged.

"No! You are going to have to explain to whoever comes to rescue you, *if* they come to rescue you how your pants ended up on top of those bushes over there and how you ended up in the cave without them on." She chuckled at his disgruntlement upon hearing her plan.

"No! You wouldn't dare do something that outrageous! You cannot!"

"Oh yes! I am fully capable of and very intent on doing that! That is the least I can do! In fact, I don't think I could go to sleep tonight knowing that you got away with it without doing some explaining about the dropping and loss of your pants. And keep away from me and my friends if you know what is good for you!"

Just before she left, she thought she saw, for only a fleeting moment, something malicious and vile on his strangely vacant face, something that quickly disappeared as her gaze lingered a second longer, replaced again in an instant with a wretched and pitiable expression. For a split second, she had seen the true expression of the corrupt soul within him.

They were a hundred yards from the underground cavern when they saw Jameela walking toward them with no sign of Jahal anywhere. They ran to her as she came toward them eagerly. Nyla hugged her and now looking at her closely they found that she had some minor scrapes and cuts on her arms and a nasty bruise on the left corner of her mouth.

As they walked back toward Parveen, Jameela related all that had happened to her since the time Junaid had rushed off to the woods to find Nyla and Parveen. She described to them how she had followed him into the woods but had become lost and how the barking of Shaytan had guided her close to them and when her own calling out their names had instead led Jahal to her.

They came to find Parveen safely sitting with her dog against the tree as they had left her and as they all sat together Jameela continued telling her story from the time she ran after seeing Jahal to finding Junaid and Nyla in the woods. Her friends were horrified by the account of her adventure and immensely proud of the way she had handled the quandary she had found herself in. They were particularly impressed by the way she had handled Jahal and thankful for the lucky chance that had seen him fall through the same opening and into the cavern that had trapped Nyla and Junaid not long ago.

There was a big difference however between who the cave held captive then and now.

Then, it was an innocent young child who had accidentally fallen in through the hole after becoming separated from his friends and so had Nyla who was out looking for him. Junaid had jumped in through the opening after Nyla, upon seeing her fall in. He had then risked life and limb in escaping the cave so that he could rescue the love of his life from the jaws of the monster that had swallowed her and she in turn had subsequently brought him to safety when he was himself close to death. In the end, they had risked everything to successfully reunite Gulzar with his grief-stricken parents.

Now, it was a cold-blooded and heartless man who had mercifully fallen into the same subterranean cavern just as he was about to soil and then murder a human being. His return to society, were he to be rescued, would inflict untold pain and suffering upon many.

Was it solely due to her charmed fortune that she had once again found herself in a most favorable situation when dealing with the fiend that had been stalking her? It was as if a Higher Power had taken it upon Himself to look after her, to protect her.

Even now she was beginning to realize that each time it had appeared as though good fortune was once again smiling upon her, it would seem to smile on her only when she herself had chosen the path that would empower her and facilitate the outcome that she desperately needed.

When her new friends had come to her rescue the night that Jahal was hell-bent on defiling her, she was saved only after she had shown humility and listened to the voice of reason that had allowed them to tell her what she needed to hear. Having heard what they had to say, she then had the courage to admit that she was wrong and decided to change herself in a fundamental way.

Today, she had ventured into the unknown woods all alone and had purposefully gone in the direction of the barking dog she was afraid of so that she may come to the assistance of her friends in case they needed her. She had then done her utmost in trying to escape from the demonic pursuit of Jahal and when it seemed that he would finally have his way, she had in a final and last gasp effort thrown him off of herself and as if guided by a supernatural hand straight into the concealed mouth of the underground cavern.

She was learning that in some ways we make our own fate. She was also beginning to feel that her inner voice was becoming stronger and it was becoming easier for her to listen to it.

When she left this time, he knew she was gone. He looked about him and felt no fear and no panic. He felt at home in the dark, quiet place that was as empty as his soul. He had heard how Junaid had found an escape from this watery dungeon and had almost died in the struggle. Only a daft idiot would risk his own dear life to save others, he thought. Unlike everyone else he knew, he had felt wretched and miserable upon learning of Junaid and Nyla's escape. How convenient would it have been if they had both died in this dark chamber, he mused. However, there was no need for him to follow the treacherous path Junaid had taken to get out. His rescuers would soon be on their way, and he would be brought out easily and comfortably. He would tell them a sad little sob story about the unusual and peculiar manner of his entrapment sans his pants, and the dim-witted gullible people would be too eager to believe it. They may even make him a bit of a hero in the process, caught as he was in the same famous cave as Junaid and Nyla.

His rescuers might wonder about the anonymous tip that would lead them to him, but that was preferable to Jameela telling them what had actually happened. She would not tell them the particulars because it would raise other questions and too many other people would become involved including Parveen, Nyla, and Junaid. She would be especially concerned about Parveen and would like to spare her any further embarrassment with regard to her previous association with him. Instead Jameela would hope that he had finally learned his lesson and would mend his ways for good. These naive people never learned that he could not help doing what he did simply because he could not help being what he was. If you want a snake to stop being a snake you have to crush its head, not reprimand it for being a snake nor admonish it and offer it advice while letting it out of a trap it could not get out of without your help. He could not help but laugh at the senselessness of these witless people. He loved to think of them as stupid, there was no better word to describe their foolish thinking.

Taking off his shirt, he tied it around his waist and sat down on the sand bar with his arms around his drawn up knees, waiting impassively for some idiots to walk all this way with a heavy rope ladder and unleash him on the world.

# *About the Author*

Fouad Azim is a Pakistan-born American novelist and Physician. He grew up hiking the woods and learned to swim in the mountain streams at the foothills of the Margalla Hills that are a branch of the picturesque lesser Himalayas in northern Pakistan. He moved to the Philippines with his parents during his teenage years where he was exposed to a multitude of different cultures and influences while at the International School and then at the University of the Philippines. He began his medical education in the Philippines and completed it in the United States.

He enjoys photography, astronomy, reading, and visiting museums. He has traveled extensively around the world and within the United States. He is a practicing physician and lives in Texas.

CPSIA information can be obtained
at www.ICGtesting.com
Printed in the USA
FFOW02n1156261117
43693032-42543FF